Really
WEIRD
Removals.com

Really
WEIRD
Removals.com

DANIELA SACERDOTI

Kelpies

Kelpies is an imprint of Floris Books

First published in 2012 by Floris Books
© 2012 Daniela Sacerdoti

 This book is also
available as an eBook

Daniela Sacerdoti has asserted her right under the
Copyright, Designs and Patents Act 1988 to be
identified as the Author of this work

This publisher acknowledges subsidy from
Creative Scotland towards the publication
of this volume

British Library CIP data available
ISBN 978-086315-902-2

Printed in Poland

To my dad, Franco Sacerdoti

*Many thanks to my clan: Ross, Sorley and Luca Walker;
to Euan Duff, for Luca's playlist and his enthusiasm;
to Lindsey Fraser, my wonderful agent; to Sally Polson and
Eleanor Collins, who made this story better; to everyone at
Floris for all their hard work; and to Nicola Robinson,
for her beautiful cover illustration.*

SPRING

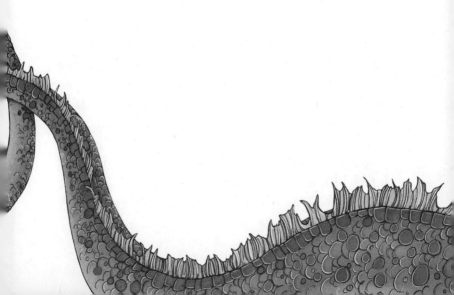

1. WEIRD THINGS HAPPEN WHEN IT'S WINDY

> **Alistair Grant's** *Scottish Paranormal Database*
>
> **Entry Number 411:** Vanishing lighthouse keepers
> **Type:** Supernatural wind
> **Location:** Muckle Flugga Lighthouse
> **Date:** December 1910
> **Details:** The three keepers of a lighthouse vanished suddenly, leaving no trace. Their log reported heavy storms in the few days before their disappearance; however, there was no sign of bad weather anywhere else on the coast.

My dad has hundreds of books. The walls of his study are covered in bookshelves, all the way up to the ceiling. He keeps books in unsteady towers all around his computer, under his desk, on the window sills. Big books and small ones, ancient ones and brightly coloured ones, fresh from the Eilean Bookshop down the road. If there's anything you need to know, just have a rummage in my dad's bookshelves, and sooner or later you'll find what you're looking for. I do that all the time. When it's pouring outside, when I'm bored or just because I feel like it. I go into my dad's study while he's writing, quiet as a mouse, and I read. My dad doesn't even notice I'm there.

That happens a lot. I mean, my dad not noticing I'm there.

I found a book in my dad's study once; it said that windy weather makes people go a bit crazy, that it makes strange things happen and, if it's blowing strong, you're better off staying inside.

Well, I live on Eilean, an island off the west coast of Scotland: I'm pretty used to the wind blowing all year long. But today, it's blowing us off our feet. The sun is shining, the sky is cornflower blue, but this gale is whirling and hurling around the windows, howling as if it was trying to get in. The sea looks choppy and frayed, all foamy on top.

I can't follow the book's advice and stay inside. I need to be at shinty practice by half past four, and I'm running late.

"There you are darling, don't forget your hat." My mum hands me my kit – the changing bag and the caman. I can smell a cloud of essential oils all around her. It's a good smell. It's my mum's smell.

Her name is Isabella. She has wavy brown hair all around her face like a halo, and blue-grey eyes with little brown speckles in them. She wears flowing skirts and dangly earrings, and lives in a world of her own, occasionally stepping into ours to look after my sister and me.

Mum and Aunt Shuna have spent the whole morning burning lavender oil and meditating in my mum's room, with my little sister Valentina sitting cross-legged between them. Like my dad, my mum has a room of her own, but it's not called a study, she calls it a "sanctuary".

The yellow sign outside says:

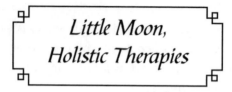

Little Moon,
Holistic Therapies

Even though she's in a world of her own, helping people with her massages and healing and all those weird things she does, Mum always knows what we're doing, and what we need. She remembers all the important but small details, our classes and birthday parties and parents' nights, and, if we need her, she always seems to materialise at our shoulder.

My dad was born and grew up on the island, but my mum comes from down south. Here on Eilean, "down south" usually means England. But my mum comes from a lot more *south* than that. She used to speak Italian, but now she speaks English, though a bit differently than the rest of us.

Time to go to shinty. I *love* playing shinty. I wouldn't miss practice for the world, not even on a windy day like this.

I open the door, and it hits me. The salty wind is in my mouth, my hair, it gets inside my clothes. It feels... exciting. As if something is about to happen.

"Adiiiiiiiiiiiiiil!" I wave to my friend across the road. The wind is so loud, I have to shout. I run to him and we walk down past the brightly coloured houses, a red one, a yellow one, a blue one. My hometown is amazing that way: it's like a rainbow. There are always a lot of tourists taking pictures of the houses and boats and seals.

Adil and I put our heads down and walk on against the wind, squinting, our hands in our pockets. When we finally make it to the sports centre, we run in quickly and stop for a second to catch our breath again.

"Phew!" says Adil. His black hair is standing on end, and he's trying to flatten it.

"What a day. To think the forecast said mild and sunny," says Lorna, from the counter. "I'll be surprised if anyone else turns up for shinty practice today."

I think she might be right. Shinty is played outside, on the grass. We'll be blown away. We are well used to windy, but this is something else.

I'm getting changed into our blue-and-yellow strip, pulling up my stripy socks, my caman leaning against the bench beside me, when Adil says just about the last words I want to hear.

"Gary must be here too. Great." He points to a Nike sports bag under the bench just beside us. "I was hoping he'd stay home, with this wind... But no chance."

For some reason, Gary McAllister has decided to make my life hell. I'm not sure why. He's so good at it, and he's been doing it so long that nobody besides Adil seems to notice. The thing is, Gary and I grew up together, we live in the same town, we go to school together, we play shinty together and we go to Scouts together. There's no way to escape him.

I once tried to talk about it with my dad, and it looked like he was listening, but after a long silence he just said, "Ok then," and resumed his writing. I don't think he heard a word. He was thinking about his book, I expect. My dad's books are read all over the world.

He writes about a little boy who travels in time. His name is Reilly. He's a hero. He's incredibly strong and he's got magical powers.

I'm nothing like him. I'm just Luca, the invisible son.

I don't want to worry my mum, so I try to manage the whole Gary thing on my own. Adil, my best friend, is on my side, but Gary is a lot bigger than him. He's a lot bigger than any of us.

My legs are like lead as I walk towards the door. I'm dreading it.

I open it carefully, expecting another salty blast of wind. But... nothing. The air is still. The little corner of sea I can see in the distance is as smooth as oil. The wind has gone all of a sudden. It must have been an Atlantic storm passing over us and moving on towards the mainland. But there were no grey clouds, none of the other signs that come with storms. It's strange.

Mr MacDonald waves at us from the far end of the pitch. There are only a few boys around him, but probably more will come when they work out the wind has subsided.

Gary has a smirk on his face. He's clearly delighted to see me.

"Pull up your socks, Luca," he says, waiting for me to look down, so he can slap me under the chin.

I ignore him. He'll have to do better than that.

"Right, settle down boys. Not enough of us to play a match, so we'll just practise. Each of you, get a ball. To the hail and back. And... Go!"

The rest of the team turn up after about twenty

minutes, so we play a game, five boys in each mini-team, and one sitting out.

The caman is heavy, which means players have to be careful with it. In spite of all precautions, though, accidents can happen. A lot of accidents seem to happen to *me* when Gary is playing. He's so good at it, so quick, only he and I notice. I often go home bruised, and nobody has been aware of any foul play.

Half an hour later, I've been stamped on, tripped and hacked, and I'm furious. I grit my teeth. I won't give up. I love this game and I won't stop playing because of him.

"Your mum is a nutcase," he whispers, brushing against me.

Last straw.

Before I know it I'm rolling on the ground with him, with Mr MacDonald shouting things I can't hear. It's as if the wind is roaring in my ears again, though all around me the air is still and calm. I can see nothing but Gary's face.

Ten minutes later, we're standing in the changing rooms in front of a very disappointed Mr MacDonald.

"What happened? What brought this on? You two are good friends..."

Yeah, right. Just because we grew up together, everybody assumes we're the best of friends. Nobody seems to detect Gary's cruel streak.

As we stand there I catch a glimpse of our reflections in the mirror on the wall opposite. Gary is tall, sturdy, with brown hair, a freckled face and little piggy eyes. He's about a foot taller than me. I'm slim, with fine blond hair and blue eyes. I look like a feather could knock me down.

On the other hand, I'm a very fast runner, the fastest in my school. I'm good at shinty because I slip between people and I get to the hail before they can get a hold of me. But when it comes to strength...

"I want to speak to your parents. I'll phone Duncan..." (that's my dad) "...and Alan tonight. We need to put an end to this."

"I don't think that's necessary," says Gary in his oily fake-reasonable voice. "It was just a silly argument. It's all sorted now." He offers me his hand. His eyes glint with malice.

"Is that true, Luca?" asks Mr MacDonald.

"Yes. Yes, of course." I take Gary's hand and shake it. It feels clammy and horrible. As long as my parents don't know I've been fighting. It's too humiliating.

"Sorry, Luca," says Gary. His voice is dripping with dishonesty. He doesn't mean it for a minute. Mr MacDonald is no fool, he's been teaching for many years and I know he's suspicious of Gary, but I don't think he can quite pinpoint why. "By the way, my mum is coming to see your mum today. She says your mum is great at what she does, even if you don't always understand what she says!" He gives me a big smile, and then turns to Mr MacDonald with a wide-eyed innocent look.

"I've never had a problem understanding her," says Mr McDonald coldly. "Now go, Gary, we're finished here,.

As Gary goes to get ready for his shower, Mr MacDonald puts a hand on my shoulder.

"Are you ok?"

"Of course. Yes," I lie.

"Don't mind him. He talks a lot of nonsense." His dark eyes are full of warmth. He probably knows what it's like for my mum, because part of his family is from Jamaica. People who don't know him still ask where he's from when they see his black skin. But Mr MacDonald was born on Eilean and is an islander through and through.

Maybe I should tell him about Gary... Would he understand?

But I hesitate, and the moment passes. He walks away, and I gather my stuff quickly. I don't want to be left alone with Gary. I'm not afraid, it's not that. I just don't want another fight.

Adil is waiting for me at the entrance of the sports centre.

"Hey..."

"Hey."

"You in trouble?"

I shake my head.

"That... halfwit!" Adil is the only boy I know who never, ever uses bad language. This is because if his father hears he's been swearing, he'll skin him alive. Adil's parents are very strict. So he comes out with old people's expressions, like "good heavens" and "holy mackerel". It cracks me up.

"He'll get tired of it." I try to sound unconcerned, but the whole thing is really getting me down.

We walk along the main street, past the coffee shop, past the tiny grocery shop, past the Eilean Bookshop with my dad's books displayed in the window – *Reilly's Egyptian Adventure, Reilly in Transylvania, Reilly and the Stone Age Hunters* – with blown up cut-outs of Reilly in his various incarnations. My dad's virtual son. Reilly would know how to tackle Gary, for sure. No, Gary would never have picked on him in the first place.

The bookshop door is open and a lanky tall man in a tweed suit is standing at the counter talking to Kim, one of the shop assistants.

"...Duncan Grant?" she's saying. That's my dad's name. I prick up my ears. "Sorry, I can't say. A lot of people come to look for him... you know, fans... He asked me not to tell folk where he lives."

"OF COURSE, OF COURSE," replies the man. He's incredibly loud, though his tone is friendly. "But I'm not a fan, I'm his *brother*," he booms.

Brother? Wait a minute. My dad has no brothers. He has a sister, Aunt Shuna, who lives with us. That's it.

Remember that book I told you about? The one that says weird things happen on windy days – it looks like it could be right.

16

2. I HAVE AN UNCLE?

Alistair Grant's *Scottish Paranormal Database*

Entry Number 167: A spell of exile
Type: Fairy
Location: Outer and Inner Hebrides
Date: First recorded April 1761
Details: Local fairies can cast a spell over
islanders, compelling them to leave the island by
any means possible. The first such incident recorded
was in April 1761, when a crofter named Alexander
Fraser left Harris on a boat and disappeared at
sea. The latest recorded incident occurred in
December 1995, when an unfortunate woman known only
as "Sharon" left Benbecula on a boat and was never
seen again. Many more such incidents are recorded in
Skye, Barra, Lewis and Seil.

"Duncan's brother? Well, that changes everything. Come and I'll show you the Grants' house."

Kim and the man step out of the shop, and I crouch behind the postcard stand, dragging Adil with me. I peer between the cards. He *does* look like my father. Blond, a reddish beard, blue eyes, the same spaced-out look, like he's short-sighted.

"Goodness, now I see you, you're his *twin!*" Kim echoes my thoughts. She points along the road. "You want the blue house, just five doors down. If nobody answers, go round the back – there's a narrow alleyway beside the house, with a sign that says "Little Moon".

Walk down the alley, you'll see a wee door, that's where Isabella works."

"It's still the old Grant house – where William and Beth Grant lived," the man booms.

"I wouldn't know; I'm a newcomer. I think so, though..."

Kim has hardly finished talking before he has walked on.

I blink once, twice. There's something perched on his shoulder, a bit like a parrot on a pirate's shoulder... Something black and transparent at the same time. Like a little stormy cloud.

I wait a few seconds for him to walk on a bit.

"Wait a minute. If he's Duncan's brother, how come he doesn't know where he lives?" I hear Kim muttering to herself. And then, "Adil? What are you doing behind the postcards?"

"Apologies!" I turn to see Adil standing up, his cheeks on fire. "I was doing my laces up."

The worst liar in the universe.

Luckily Kim shrugs her shoulders and walks back into the shop before she can see me. I don't want to talk about this uncle of mine until I've met him.

I wonder if my mum knows of his existence...

We slip into the alleyway beside my house and hide around the corner as the tall man strides ahead into our courtyard. I can still see the shadow on his shoulder. It must be some weird light effect. Maybe there's something wrong with my sight, or maybe it's a speck of dust. I blink repeatedly, squint, rub my eyes. Nothing changes. It's still there.

He finds the door and the sign on top.

"Isabella!" He calls, with his booming voice. "ISABELLA!"

Well, he's not shy, that's for sure.

Mum comes out. She stops in her tracks.

"Alistair? Is it really you?"

"It is indeed me. Sorry to land on you like this, but my house is infested and I have nowhere else to go."

Infested? Rats, mice, cockroaches? Where on earth does this man live?

I notice my mum's face. She looks flustered and happy to see him and worried, all at the same time.

"Oh Alistair. I don't know..."

"Where's Duncan? Don't tell me. He's in his study. Writing. Luca, come out."

He says it just like that, loudly, all in one breath. Adil and I freeze.

"Luca?" says Mum. "Come out from where?" she asks.

"He's round the corner. Look."

My mum comes and sticks her head out the gate.

"What are you doing? And why are you still in your shinty strip?"

"Well..." I begin, walking into the courtyard.

"Apologies, Mrs Grant," interrupts Adil, and runs away in a panic. It's all too much for him.

"Sorry, Mum. I heard *him* telling Kim he was my uncle."

"He is. This is your Uncle Alistair."

He looks a bit like Doctor Who, tweed suit, bow tie and all, except he's blond. And *very* loud.

"You've got something on your shoulder," I say, and his eyes widen. He looks at me like he can truly see me now. My mum looks at me too, then him, then me again.

"Luca, go get yourself something to eat. We'll come in a minute."

"*What* is he seeing?" I hear her saying as I step inside.

Their voices fade as I walk into my mum's treatment room. It's such a nice place. It makes you feel all relaxed and peaceful, just being in it. Every day there's a different oil burning and a different scent in the air: today, it's vanilla. There's a soft glow from the candles and the oil burners, and a table lamp with an orange cloth on it to give the room a sunshiny sort of light. On the wall opposite the entrance there's a painting of an American Indian woman and a wolf above a waterfall, topped with a little rainbow. For some reason my Aunt Shuna calls it "Morag and her poodle". Shuna teaches art at Eilean High School, so she knows a thing or two about painting.

I breathe in the vanilla for a bit, deeply. Then I open the door into our house and... I trip over something and nearly fall flat on my face. The something says, "Hey!"

My sister Valentina is sitting cross-legged in front of the door, with her rabbit, Petsnake, in her arms. Yes, you read right, Petsnake. You see, she really, *really* wants a pet snake, but my mum and dad keep saying no. She hasn't stopped trying, though. She even asked her teacher to tell my parents that a pet snake would greatly help her emotional development, but for some reason, the teacher refused.

"Ouch! What are you DOING?"

"I was just hanging out with Petsnake and then I heard shouting. What's going on?"

"Our uncle is here."

"We don't have an uncle!"

"We do *now*."

"What do you mean?"

"Shhhhhh!!!!" I can hear voices rising again. "I better go see what's going on. Who's looking after you?"

"I'm looking after *myself*!" she says, indignantly.

I know I should say my sister's annoying and she's a pest and all the things boys usually say about their little sisters, but the truth is, Valentina's a laugh. She's a bit spacey and eccentric. She loves walking barefoot; she has long blonde hair, which she refuses to tie back; and big brown eyes. She's also very, very sharp.

She has a passion for animals. But not ponies and kittens and puppies like most little girls. No, Valentina's into weird and scary creatures. My dad got her a subscription to *Reptiles of the Americas* (I suspect it has three subscribers: Valentina, the editor and the editor's mum), which she reads avidly and cuts up to make scrapbooks. She's into cryptozoology. You probably don't know what it is – I didn't either. It's about animals nobody knows about, like the Loch Ness monster, the Yeti, unicorns and stuff like that. She has a magazine for that too. I flicked through an issue of it once; it was all about strange armadillo-things that live in the lava of a Peruvian volcano...

"Your sister's looking after herself *and* me!" My Aunt Shuna comes into the hallway, her sunny smile bringing out her dimples, her green eyes full of fun. She doesn't look like my dad at all, though she's his sister – apart from the blonde straight hair, which I've inherited.

"Come and have a snack. You're still in your shinty gear? Go and get changed then..." She stops suddenly. She's heard his voice. My uncle's.

"Alistair?"

He comes through the door. Aunt Shuna looks like she's just seen Medusa – you know, that creature from Greek mythology with snakes on her head – the one who petrifies you if you look into her eyes.

She stands still for a second. And then they hug really tight, for ages.

My mum is smiling, and Valentina is staring at this stranger who looks a lot like her dad.

"You must be Valentina."

"Yes."

"I'm your Uncle Alistair."

"Ok." She looks at him for a wee while, then she tips her head to one side and says, "You've got something on your shoulder."

Uncle Alistair gives her the same look he gave me. Like he's truly *seen* her.

"They can both See..." he says. His eyes are shining.

"What. Do. You. Think. You. Are. DOING!"

A Dad-shaped iceberg has walked down the stairs. His voice has frozen everyone.

"Duncan, I was going to tell you..." Mum begins.

"I want you out."

"He's got nowhere else to go..."

"What? He's got a perfectly good house in London! He knows I don't want him near my children, ever!"

My dad can be scary. He's very tall, unlike me (I take after my mum where height is concerned) and he has a nose like a Roman statue – you know, big and straight. He hardly ever speaks to us, so when he does, we listen: we've either done something really, really amazing or we are in big trouble.

"Not in front of the children!" says Mum. I'm not sure why she says that, because Valentina is a tough cookie and I'm not really a child, I'm twelve.

"No. You're right, Isabella. Let's go up to the study," says Alistair, unfazed. I can see where Valentina inherits her cool. Mum and I get all emotional about things, while Valentina is unflappable. My dad is something else entirely – he normally doesn't notice what's going on or, if he does, he ignores it in case it interferes with his writing.

"We're not going anywhere. I want you on your way back to London as soon as you can find a boat."

"Duncan!" and "Dad!" shout four indignant voices.

"I'm not listening. I want..."

"I don't care what *you* want!" says a voice that is so used to being sweet that when it's not it sounds all funny. Like a bird barking. It's my sunny mellow Aunt Shuna. We all stare at her. "We haven't spoken to our brother for twelve years, Duncan. He hasn't had it easy since... you know what." She looks away.

"How do you know?" asks Dad. His voice is icy. Visions of penguins, igloos, polar bears come into my head.

"What do you mean?"

"How do you know he hasn't had it easy, if you haven't spoken for twelve years?"

Icicles, Eskimos, sleighs. Not the cheery Christmas ones.

"We have spoken, sometimes," says Alistair. He and Shuna look at each other, an incredible warmth in their eyes. The ice in my head melts away.

"I want you to stay in Eilean, Alistair. And if you can't stay here, you and I will find somewhere else in the village to live," says my aunt.

"NO!" Mum, Valentina and I shout in unison.

"I have no choice. Alistair, come on. Children, you can come and see us... whenever... you..." Her voice breaks.

Oh no, tears. I HATE to see people crying.

"If she goes, Duncan, I'll go too!" cries Mum.

"And me! And Luca too!" Valentina adds, holding on to my sleeve just to make sure.

I'm quiet. I don't actually want to leave my dad. He looks a bit taken aback. I don't think he was expecting this total *mutiny*.

"At least listen to Alistair," pleads Mum.

"It seems I have no choice."

He turns, as cold as a loch in winter, and walks solemnly up the stairs. Uncle Alistair follows, and the little shadow follows him. It's not on his shoulder now, it's walking by itself, and it looks a lot like...

Wait. A little girl? Seriously? I try to take a better look, but she blurs, and she's gone. I must have been dreaming. I blink again. Nothing.

I can't go and listen at the door, they'll know. So I can't tell you what they said to each other. But I can tell you what *we* say, my mum, Aunt Shuna, Valentina and I.

"Come to the kitchen, for a snack and a chat. Mum's standard answer to emergencies is to give us food.

Valentina is still looking towards the stairs. She does that sometimes, staring into a corner even though there's nothing there. A bit like cats do.

"Come on, darling," says Mum, and Valentina reluctantly walks into the kitchen with us.

We all sit around the table with the red polka-dot oilcloth on it. Valentina and I have Nutella on toast; Mum and Shuna have a cup of tea.

"When we're finished, can I go and play with the wee girl?" says Valentina all of a sudden.

"Who?"

"The wee girl that came with Uncle Alistair. The one without shoes."

3. DISAPPEARING ACTS

Alistair Grant's *Scottish Paranormal Database*

Entry Number 351: Donald Campbell
Type: Post-mortem manifestation
Location: Inverawe House
Date: 1756-the present
Details: Donald Campbell has been sighted in
Inverawe House many times over the years. He
was murdered in 1756. His brother Duncan had
inadvertently given the Campbell word that
Donald's killer would not be punished. Donald
appeared to Duncan three times, asking him to
break his word and hand in the killer, but Duncan
refused. In revenge, Donald told his brother
where and when he would die.

Shuna and Mum look at each other.

"What are you talking about?"

"The wee girl with the white dress and no shoes. I
don't know her name," Valentina says insistently. "You
saw her, Luca, didn't you?"

I shake my head slowly. My instinct says it's better
to keep quiet. I'd like to give Valentina a sign that yes,
I've seen her too, that we can talk about it later – but
I don't dare. Mum would pick up on it. Instead I give
Valentina a tiny wee nudge under the table. She freezes.

"Is that your new imaginary friend?" asks Aunt
Shuna hopefully. It's not easy to keep up with my
sister's unstoppable mind.

"Yes! Yes, she is. The wee girl with no shoes. My imaginary friend!" Valentina says brightly.

"Yes, she told me about her too!" I chip in.

They decide to buy it. Phew.

"Anyway. You want to know about your Uncle Alistair," Shuna begins. "Twelve years ago, the year before you were born, Luca, your Granny and Papa disappeared. Vanished. It was the night of your dad's graduation – there was a big celebration for him here. We have to assume that your grandparents died. Your dad insists that it was your uncle's fault. He hasn't wanted anything to do with him ever since."

"What happened?" I ask. There's always been a big mystery around Dad's mum and dad. About the only thing I know about them is that they had a band: the Grants of Eilean Ceilidh Band. There's a picture of them on the mantelpiece: my Granny Beth is playing the piano, and my Papa William is playing the fiddle; it was taken at the ceilidh dance here that night, after my dad's graduation. There are people all around them, and they look happy.

My mum always puts fresh flowers from our garden in front of their photograph. She says that's what they do where she comes from, in Italy. They put pictures of their dead relatives in a nice display, and little vases of flowers in front of them. I like having my grandparents remembered this way.

"Nobody knows, Luca. They simply disappeared."

"And why was it Uncle Alistair's fault?" pipes up Valentina.

"Well. It's hard to explain..."

"Did Uncle Alistair say sorry?"

"Yes, Valentina," said Shuna. "Many times. I have forgiven him, but your dad hasn't."

"There's no point for all this to go on, Shuna," says Mum, waving her hands in the air. When she's upset, her Italian accent gets stronger and sometimes her words get jumbled up. "I know he's made a mistake, a huge mistake, but Duncan has to forgive him, like you did."

"I know. Hopefully this time... What brought him here anyway? Why now? He hasn't phoned or emailed me in ages..."

Mum makes one of her "just between ourselves" faces at Shuna and starts talking in a funny voice, a bit like a ventriloquist. "He says his house is... *imhested*. You know, a *ost*." She mouths the words she doesn't want us to understand, but it's easy enough to work out the word "infested". I can't quite make out the second word, though. Ost? Host?

"Seriously? That's why he's come?"

"Yes. Another one of his daft stories!" says Mum, rolling her eyes. "If he wants to come home to Eilean he only has to say. He doesn't need to make up stuff!"

"Better not mention this *ost* thing to Duncan, anyway," whispers Shuna.

Honestly – do they think we're so engrossed in our Nutella that we can't hear what they're saying!

"Infested by what?" asks Valentina brightly, her face all lit up, hoping for some weird creatures.

Mum says, "Rats!" and my aunt says, "Ants!" both at the same time.

They look at each other.

"Rats or ants?"

"Both."

"Cockroaches?"

"Those too."

They're lying. I look from one to the other. They've both got that shifty expression adults get sometimes. There's definitely something else going on, something they don't want us to know about.

"Luca, Valentina, listen to me carefully now," says Mum, covering our hands with hers. "Alistair is a good man. A bit strange, I suppose, with all his crazy stories, but a good man. I've always been fond of him. You know now that your dad is still very angry with him. We need to help them. They're brothers. We must help them to get close again."

"Yes. Everybody deserves a second chance," says Aunt Shuna.

Valentina and I nod. There's no arguing with that.

The crystals hanging on the back door rattle and chime.

"That will be Linda for her aromatherapy." Gary's mum. *Ugh.* Mum goes off to her sanctuary, leaving behind a waft of vanilla.

Aunt Shuna stands up.

"Goodness, I hope everything's ok up there." She shoots a worried look in the direction of the ceiling.

As if on cue, we hear footsteps on the stairs.

There are my dad and my uncle, stony faced.

Dad takes a deep breath. He's like a king about to issue a decree while his court looks on.

"Alistair can see the children. He can come up to the house once in a while. But he cannot stay under this roof."

"Do you have anywhere to stay?" asks Aunt Shuna at once.

"Not yet, but..."

"Duncan, Alistair is staying here tonight." Shuna is firm.

"I said he can't stay under this roof."

"Just one night, Duncan. One night! Or do you want our brother to go to the Eilean Arms? Do you want our brother to have to sleep in a *hotel* when this is our family home?"

"Shuna, it's ok..." Uncle Alistair hurries to pacify her.

"No, it's not ok."

"Fine. One night, and then you find your own place."

I can tell that Dad hates being over-ruled.

"Thank you. I'll find somewhere to rent as soon as I can. You know, with an office as well." My uncle smiles nervously.

"An office? What will you do?" asks Shuna.

"I've set up a little... pest control business in London. I'd like to do the same up here. We remove... disagreeable creatures. Rats, snakes, and the likes."

Valentina's eyes widen at the mention of snakes.

"You can't be very good at it, can you, if you have to abandon your own infested house," says Dad coldly.

"Yeah, well. That wasn't the only reason I came." Alistair looks first at the floor, then at Dad. "I wanted to put it right." He speaks in a very small voice.

Put *what* right?

"That's not possible." Dad's voice is firm.

"You don't know that!" Uncle Alistair blurts out. Shuna reaches out for him, a soft hand on his arm.

"That's enough. You are under this roof on *probation*. Keep my children out of trouble. Keep them out of your crazy stuff."

Alistair nods. "I'll make it up to you." He sounds a bit choked.

"I hope so."

And with this, my dad goes back upstairs – the emergency over, he doesn't stay with us any longer than necessary. Shuna hugs Alistair very, very tight again, murmurs something about a special dinner, and runs into the kitchen.

We are left, Alistair, Valentina and me.

"Come on, children," whispers Alistair. Or he *tries* to whisper. His voice is still like a foghorn. "Come and meet Camilla."

"Is she your daughter?" I ask.

"Not exactly. Just a ghost I know."

What?

"Luca, Valentina, come and set the table!" Shuna calls us from the kitchen.

"Later," says Uncle Alistair conspiratorially.

And that's how it all started.

4. WE FIND A SISTER – A DEAD ONE

"Luca! Luca, wake up!"

It's my sister's voice, coming from far away.

"Mmmmmmm...."

"*LUCA, WAKE UP!*" she whispers urgently. Funny how in the middle of the night a whisper feels like a scream. I look at the clock on my bedside table. Three in the morning.

"I'm sleeping... go back to bed..." I mutter, roll over, and... I leap up!

Someone who is not Valentina is standing beside my bed, staring at me. Someone... see-through. Someone floating!

Oh *Mamma Mia*! I open my mouth, but my sister dives on me to cover it with her hand.

"PFFFFPFFPFF... PFPFPF!! PFF!"

"Don't scream, Luca, you'll wake Mum and Dad!" Valentina's hand is still clasped across my mouth. I nod.

"Pffmm." I nod again, frantically. What *is* that? *Who* is that?

"You won't scream?"

"LET ME... I mean, *let me go*!" I whisper, remembering my promise. My heart feels like it's jumping out of my chest.

"Luca, this is Camilla."

I blink, over and over again. The shadow that was perched on Alistair's shoulder, the one that looked like a little girl when it walked upstairs with him and Dad, is here. It *is* a girl. Transparent, sort of blue-grey, and *suspended in mid-air*.

"How do you do," she says, and her voice sounds a bit echoing, as if it's coming from the bottom of a well. She's smiling. Her long dark hair is in two braids. She's wearing a white lacy sort of dress, and she has bare feet. She looks about eleven years old: my sister's age.

All I can think to say is: "You have no shoes on."

"They came off when I drowned," she says cheerily. *Oh.*

"Camilla was thrown out of her house!" says Valentina indignantly.

"They said it was infested. The family that bought my house," Camilla explains. "It took me a while to realise they meant *me*. I was the infestation."

"She'd been living there for, like, a hundred years! She was there *long before* them!" Valentina is outraged.

"Shocking!" I get carried away.

"I'd never been out of my house before. I mean, not since I became a ghost. I was so scared..."

Valentina puts a comforting hand on Camilla's shoulder.

"Then your uncle, Alistair, found me crying my eyes out, and he took me in. He could actually *see* me!"

"So can we!" says Valentina happily.

"I *know*! I have a real family now. Alistair, you and you!" she whispers emphatically. The two girls hug, Camilla's transparent arms around Valentina's pyjama-clad ones.

"Camilla," I begin, and then I stop. I'm actually *talking to a ghost*. I take a deep breath. "My mum said that Alistair's house was infested. Obviously Alistair wasn't talking about you..."

She shakes her head vigorously. "No, not me! I don't *infest* anywhere. Never in my life! It wasn't me. It was a horrible scary man. He wanted to throw us out. And he did! He did dreadful things..."

"You mean, a dead man? A ghost, like you?"

"Yes. Alistair has this... business, you see. It's called the Really Weird Removals Company, RWR for short. People with ghosts, and other things bothering them – they can email him, and he tells them he'll get rid of the problem, but he actually *helps* the things he's getting rid of. He's saved a lot of us."

"So that's his pest control business?"

"Well, that's what he calls it when he can't say what he *really* does."

"I see..." Valentina and I exchange a glance. "So he doesn't get rid of rats and cockroaches?"

"Well, we had a mouse once. He put it in the garden," Camilla tells us.

"I'm not sure that counts..."

Weird Removals? Saving ghosts? And *other things?* What things, exactly? I can't wait to ask Uncle Alistair about it.

"Well, anyway, he tried to help this ghost who was bothering some people. Rupert Cleaver, he's called. But he's horrible and crazy. He left them and came into our home and started tormenting us!" Her whole body quivers and blurs for a second. "That's why we're here. We had to *escape.*"

"This Rupert Cleaver... what did he do to make you run away?"

"Oh, it was just *awful!*" says Camilla dramatically. She's so emphatic. It's as if she speaks in italics. "He filled our bath tub with BLOOD!" As she says this she floats upwards a bit, quivering, then comes back down again.

"Yuk!" Valentina and I whisper in unison.

"Yes! And he put these awful wriggly maggots all over our kitchen, and he started jumping out of cupboards and drawers, just to scare us. Alistair couldn't even brush his teeth without Rupert popping into the bathroom mirror and making faces. It was *exhausting.*"

"Could you not have gone somewhere else in London? Why come all the way up here?"

"We tried, several places, but he kept following us."

My sister and I look at each other. We have the same thought.

"Could he have followed you up here?" asks Valentina, her brown eyes as big as saucers.

"No. You see, Rupert *hates* water! That's why we tried to put big full basins everywhere, and jugs and cups and glasses and whatever we could find. Alistair nearly set the house on fire when some water spilt onto the TV. I was watching *Eastenders*, it was *really* annoying. But it didn't work completely. It only slowed Rupert down a bit. And it made him even angrier! But we reckoned the sea would put him off."

"Oh!" whispers Valentina.

"Yes! The sea is too much for him. And a *choppy* sea as well! I had never seen a sea like this one when I was alive. We used to go to Margate sometimes, in the summer. It was like a giant bathtub, really. But this! It's like... it's like the sea is *dancing*!" She twirls. She's a cheery ghost, that's for sure. I can't help but smile.

Then an idea comes into my mind. A pretty good idea. Yes. I think I'll ask her.

"Camilla, I was wondering, as we are friends now—"

"Can you be my *brother* instead? I didn't have any brothers or sisters when I was alive..."

"Can I be your sister too?" asks Valentina eagerly.

"Of course! My brother Luca. My sister Valentina." She laughs, a faraway sound, coming from somewhere else, some *time* else.

"So what I wanted to ask you is—" I try to continue.

"Children! What on earth are you doing awake at this hour!" A wedge of light seeps in from the door, and Mum's face appears in it. My heart stops. How are we going to explain this?

"What's wrong?" she adds, looking suspiciously from Valentina to me.

"I... we..."

"I heard you talking... Valentina, what are you doing in Luca's room in the middle of the night?" Then I realise: Mum can't see Camilla, still floating in mid-air, perfectly still. I start breathing again.

"I had a nightmare," gabbles Valentina.

"Oh, wee soul!" Mum sits down on my bed and puts her arms around Valentina. "Are you ok now?"

She nods. We look at each other.

"Come on *tesoro*, I'll take you to bed. Night Luca, thanks for looking after your sister."

"Night Mum, night Valentina."

Valentina throws me one last wide-eyed look before disappearing out my bedroom door, followed by Camilla.

My question will just have to wait. The house quietens down again, the lights go off. There's no way I can go back to sleep. Not with a ghost in the house. I am lying in the darkness, thinking, when a faint glow starts lighting up the room again. Camilla materialises slowly, sitting cross-legged at the foot of my bed.

"So what did you want to ask me?"

"Well, you know the way Alistair and Valentina and me, we can see you, but my mum and dad can't?" I'm talking as if having a little ghostly girl sitting on my bed was perfectly *normal*.

"Yes."

"Why is that, do you think?"

"I don't know. Some people see us, most people don't. It's just the way it is. I could make myself visible to other people if I wanted to. I tried a few times... I was lonely and I wanted a family. But I stopped doing it because they always got really scared. They screamed and went all pale. Nobody wanted to speak to me," she adds sadly.

"That's a shame. I'm sorry..."

"I have Alistair and the two of you now!" Camilla looks so happy, it makes me smile.

"So you can make yourself visible to anyone, if you want to?"

"Yes."

"In that case, would you do something for me?"

"Sure!"

"Would you... would you scare someone for me? Appear to them and scare them? I know it sounds like a mean thing to do, but this boy has been awful to me for ages, he says horrible things about my mum and dad, and he hits me when we play shinty, and..."

"Shint what?"

"Shinty. It's a sport we play up here in the islands. It's a bit like hockey. But better. This boy on the team, he makes my life miserable. He's a lot bigger than me."

"He sounds horrible. A bit like Rupert Cleaver, only Rupert is dead! What's his name?"

"Gary."

"I'll *terrify* him for you. Where will I find him?"

I think for a moment.

"At shinty practice. Next week. I'll find a way you can catch him alone."

I feel a bit guilty. Not much, just a little.

"All sorted then. Goodnight Luca. I'm going for a floatabout. Bye bye." Camilla disappears through the window. I watch her flying down the street and over the roofs, towards the beach, her little shape glowing blue-green like a St Elmo's fire.

"*Night, Camilla,*" I whisper, more to myself really.

My life is getting weirder by the minute. But a good sort of weird.

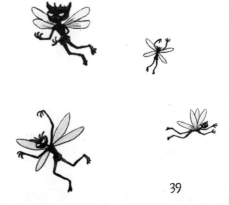

5. THE OCTOPUS IN THE LUNCH BOX

Alistair Grant's *Scottish Paranormal Database*

Entry Number 291: Saltwater slug
Type: Cryptozoology
Location: Tobermory, Argyll
Date: 1973
Details: In October 1973, fishermen Gordon and Bobby Shearer, father and son, dragged up an unknown creature among their usual catch. It was sausage-shaped, grey in colour, three feet long and eleven inches in diameter. It had no eyes and no sign of a mouth, but two holes at either extremity. Because of its resemblance to a slug, they called it "saltwater slug". The event is recorded in the *Tobermory Gazette* and in the personal archives of Mr Shearer.

I'm sitting at the kitchen table, stirring milk into my Coco Pops and thinking about things.

"Hurry up, pet, you'll be late." Aunt Shuna has a spring in her step today. She looks so happy. I can see how much she's missed Uncle Alistair, all these years.

"Ok." I finish my breakfast quickly, throw my coat on and grab my bag.

"VALENTINA, I'M GOOOOING!" I call up the stairs. My sister and I always leave for school together, but we split up on the way, walking with our respective friends.

Valentina runs down, her hair in two braids – my mum always has a struggle to tie her hair back for school, but this morning she actually asked for it to be braided. Camilla's influence, I suspect.

"*Have you seen Camilla this morning?*" I whisper as we open the door. It's a clear chilly spring morning, and the air is fresh and salty.

"No, she was out all night." We start talking at a normal volume as we reach the street, but I still glance behind us in case someone's listening.

"I've asked her a favour... to scare Gary for me."

"Great idea!" Her face lights up. "Though I could have done that for you."

Valentina has offered to pour her insect collection into Gary's shinty bag, but I didn't want her involved in case she got into trouble. "Well, Camilla will do it in style... I mean, your way would have been amazing too!" I add quickly, not wanting to hurt her feelings.

She shrugs.

"Where's Uncle Alistair?" I ask.

"He went out really early, Aunt Shuna said. He's looking for somewhere to rent. Dad's only allowing him to stay one night."

"Mmmm. And he needs an office. For his removals business."

"I'm going to help him with that."

I smile. Valentina is the most determined person I know.

Suddenly, Adil is standing at my shoulder. "Hi, listen, am I in trouble with your mum?"

"No, of course not!" I laugh. Adil is perpetually scared to put a foot wrong.

"Bye Luca, bye Adil!" My sister crosses the road to walk with a friend.

We're strolling down the street past the multicoloured houses, chatting away, when suddenly somebody jumps out of a doorway in front of me.

"MORNING LUCA!" Uncle Alistair booms, scaring us to death. "COME WITH ME!"

"Good grief!" That's Adil getting a massive fright. I told you he never swears.

"MY NEW OFFICE!" Bet they can hear Uncle Alistair in Glasgow. He leads us towards a doorway. "Come in, come and have a cup of tea!"

"This is great, Uncle Alistair... but I can't, I have to go to school."

"Ach, come on, just for a second. And bring your friend."

We walk into a small front room. There's a table with a computer on it, a noticeboard brimming with photos, a small bookshelf filled with books, and a huge map of Scotland on the wall with little red pins stuck all over it. Wow, he did all that between last night and this morning?

"That's fantastic!" I say.

"It is, yes, though I say so myself. Milk? Sugar? Or would you prefer that lovely stuff your mum drinks, espresso, as thick as anything, so you could cut it with a knife! Actually, I only have instant – is that okay?"

"I don't drink coffee or tea."

"Orange juice?" Uncle Alistair asks, opening the small fridge. Adil and I catch a glimpse of rows and rows of small bottles: blue, yellow, muddy green, and a swirling one with little silver speckles in it. My uncle grabs a carton of orange juice and closes the fridge quickly.

Adil taps at his watch and mouths, "*We're going to be late!*"

"Sorry Uncle Alistair, we have to go. Why don't I walk down after school? I'm free this afternoon."

"Sure, sure, brilliant, see you then." Adil is looking at the photos on the noticeboard. Uncle Alistair sidles up to me and bends down to whisper in my ear. "*On your own. I have stuff to show you.*" I nod conspiratorially.

"*We met Camilla last night,*" I whisper back.

"*Did you?* Oh great, great. She went for a floatabout earlier and I haven't seen her since. She does that sometimes."

"What *is* this?" says Adil, twisting his head to one side and squinting.

"Oh, that. That's a saltwater slug. A big one."

"A saltwater... slug?"

"Yes, well, we're going to be late! Let's go!" I grab Adil by the sleeve of his duffle coat.

"THANKS FOR COMING, GUYS! SEE YOU LATER!" Uncle Alistair shouts. Ouch. Why can he not speak at a normal volume? It'd be rude to ask, so I don't.

The school day goes slowly, as slowly as a... as a saltwater slug. I'm way too old for Eilean Primary, I'm well ready to go on to high school and start my life. I want to be a writer, like my dad. I'm going to be as famous as him.

Lunchtime.

"What's that crap, Luca?"

Here comes Gary and his mates. I sigh.

I munch on my saffron risotto. Yes, this is the kind of thing I get in my lunch box: saffron risotto, penne with olives and capers, spaghetti with a walnut sauce. My friends get ham sandwiches, cheese sandwiches, maybe a tuna wrap... But my mum is passionate about food and I love what she cooks. Of course, Gary and his friends make a habit of laughing at the contents of my lunch box every single day.

"Saffron risotto, Gary. And your point is?" I raise my head and I catch a glimpse of Valentina framed in the door of the lunch hall, watching Gary with a deadly look in her eyes, before joining her friends at the primary 6 table.

"You people eat strange stuff, it makes me sick."

Us people? Adil leans over.

"I happen to find your ham sandwich disgusting, Gary. Everything is relative." My heart warms. Adil wouldn't say boo to a goose, but he always tries to stick up for me. Gary shoots him a look that means Adil is also included in the "you people" category.

They move away and sit at the table near the door, well away from us – in case we contaminate their lunch, no doubt. Barely a minute goes by when we hear a scream. Gary jumps up and throws his lunch box off the table.

"WHAT'S THAT!?!?" he shouts, with a look of horror on his face.

His lunch box is lying open on the floor, and in it, even from here, I can see a slimy, very dead octopus.

Mrs Craig and Mrs Duncan run to the scene, the janitor is called, and Gary is taken into the office, shaking. The head teacher, Mr McLaughlin, tells everyone it was a very silly, cruel trick to play and that whoever is responsible should be ashamed of themselves. Everybody looks down, but some of us can't hide our satisfaction. There are quite a few people who get routinely tormented by Gary and his friends.

My eyes meet Valentina's across the hall. A little imperceptible smile is curling her lips.

"Where did you find a dead octopus?" I ask her on the way home from school.

"I know people," she says loftily. Her white-blonde hair is loose again and it's flowing in the chilly breeze.

"Donald?"

"Yes." She beams. Valentina loves going down the harbour. She scans the catch, hoping to find weird creatures. Her dream is to find something really strange, photograph it and be featured in *Cryptozoology Today*. Donald Anderson is one of the fishermen who look out for bizarre fish for her. He's a kind man, who sort of adopted her as a granddaughter, because his own grandchildren live in Canada.

"I told you not to get involved," I tell her. "I don't want Gary to start picking on you."

"He's welcome to try," says Valentina. She has that dark look again. She reminds me a bit of our dad. It makes me think I should worry more for Gary than for her.

We're walking to Uncle Alistair's new office in Osprey Road. It's the light-blue house, tall and thin, between a white one and a yellow one. I can't wait to find out what he wants to show us.

We knock at the door. No reply. We knock at the window. Still no reply.

"Uncle Alistaaaaaaaaaaaaair!" shouts Valentina, looking up at the second-floor window. Nothing.

"I'm sure he told me to come here after school..."

We hear hasty footsteps, and the door opens.

"HELLO CHILDREN, COME ON IN!" Uncle Alistair's reddish hair is standing on end, and there's powder all over it. It looks a bit like snow. His nose is bright red and sniffly.

Wait a minute... are those ice crystals in his nostrils?

He sees us looking, and mutters, "Sorry, yes, bit chilly in here. Heating broken... and... and I was defrosting the freezer. You know the way it is with freezers!" He laughs. Loudly.

What next? "I stuck my head in a bucket of ice cream"?? I manage to shoot a look at Valentina, and she shrugs.

Uncle Alistair clears his voice and moves to one side to let us in. Camilla is floating in mid-air in the doorway. She waves, a big sunny smile on her face.

"Hi Camilla!" we say in unison.

We all walk – well, those who don't float – into the front room. Uncle Alistair is dusting the snow off his shoulders.

There's a bunch of furs scattered around. Thick white furs, tiny speckled ones and a huge grey hairy one that takes up most of the sofa. They're covered in snow, and the hairy one is matted with ice.

"What's all that?" asks Valentina.

"What?"

"The furs."

"What furs?"

Valentina and I look at each other. You can't really miss them...

"These!" Valentina holds up the corner of the grey hairy one.

"Oh, THOSE! They are... rugs. From Ikea."

"Over on the mainland?"

"Yes... They delivered them. And I got this too, look! It's a... a... Wukkatakka bookshelf. Yes. They delivered it in two batches, one yesterday and one today. You know the way it is with these Swedish couriers, they like batches, don't they? They LOVE batches! Batches and funny names for furniture! These rugs are called... Varmundsnug. In the catalogue, I mean." He's beginning to witter.

"Why are the rugs covered in snow?" asks Valentina briskly.

"Because it's snowing in Sweden." Uncle Alistair looks away.

Valentina can't help laughing silently.

"But never mind about all that stuff. Got this for you." He waves a tin in the air. "Thought you'd be hungry after school."

"What is it? Ikea meatballs?" Valentina smirks.

"No. That'll be in the next batch. These are BEANS. And I've got sausages to grill too. I won't be a second.

Take your jackets off, make yourselves at home!" He disappears into the kitchen, leaving us with Camilla.

"So, last night, we were talking about the scaring thing," says Camilla. "Yes? Where? When? I can be *very* scary when I want to be. Look!"

She floats up towards the ceiling, and it happens. Quick enough to make me want to scream in terror.

Camilla's face gets all white, even whiter than it normally is, her eyes become two black empty holes, her dark hair comes undone and floats all around her head like a fan. And then she opens her mouth wide, and makes the spookiest, scariest, most blood-chilling wail I've ever heard in my life.

I freeze. My knees have gone to jelly and my heart is racing. The scream has frozen in my throat, I can't make a sound.

Then, as quickly as she turned monster, Camilla turns back into herself again. I let myself fall on the sofa, panting. I think I'm going to pass out.

Valentina claps her hands enthusiastically. "Ooooh, that's perfect! That's *really* scary!"

"I know! I even scare *myself!*" chirps Camilla.

I'm still too petrified to speak.

Uncle Alistair walks back in.

"There you are: beans and sausages, the perfect after-school snack. It's important to eat healthily," he tells us, solemnly. "Have a seat."

I'm not going anywhere; my legs are still jelly. Alistair hands us each a tin cup with beans in it and a thin sausage sticking out, like a 99 ice-cream. And a glass of juice.

Then he notices my ashen face.

"What happened? *Camilla?*" he says reproachfully.

"He *asked* me to! We're going to scare a bad, bad boy in his school!"

Uncle Alistair turns to me. "Luca. Camilla can be a bit frightening."

"A bit, yes." My voice is small and shaking.

Valentina is happily tucking into her beans and sausage like nothing has happened. "You found a great place!" she tells Uncle Alistair, enthusiastically.

"I did, didn't I?" He beams.

"What are all those?" She gestures to the piles of books all around Uncle Alistair's computer. "Ikea catalogues?" We laugh.

"Those, children, are for research," says Uncle Alistair, ignoring our teasing. "I'm working on the Scottish section of the *Paranormal Database*. The Scottish Executive commissioned it. It records, you know, apparitions, hauntings... sightings of all sorts of supernatural creatures, past and present. Cryptocreatures is a personal favourite of mine. I love cryptozoology."

"I love cryptozoology TOO!" cries Valentina.

"Well, like uncle, like niece!" She and Uncle Alistair look at each other fondly. "By the way, I don't think your dad needs to know about the *Paranormal Database*..."

We nod in agreement.

"And your... your removals business?" I ask.

"Oh yes. That. Well, it's not really like I told your parents..."

"We know."

"You know?"

Camilla clears her throat conspicuously.

"Oh, I see. Well, you were going to find out sooner or later. The Really Weird Removals Company. Yes. RWR, for short. We are the one-stop shop for safe removal and/or rescue of any supernatural creature, from the humble fairy to the mighty troll." He sounds like an ad on TV.

"Cool. When do we start?" says Valentina.

I choke on my beans.

"Sorry, it's not stuff for children." Uncle Alistair looks regretful.

"Camilla does it."

"She's dead already, so there's not much that can happen to her at this stage."

Camilla nods emphatically.

"We'd give you a hand, Uncle Alistair," Valentina insists. "Seriously. You wouldn't be sorry!"

My uncle gets up and goes to the window, looking wistfully out at the pale blue sky.

"I'd love for you to be part of it. But this is dangerous business. If something happened to you, I couldn't forgive myself, and your mum and dad would never forgive *me*..."

I can see his point.

"Like Dad never forgave you about Granny and Papa?" Valentina pales, realising what she's just said. "Sorry, Uncle Alistair, I didn't mean..." she scrambles.

He looks rather shaken.

"It's ok, Valentina. It's ok. Yes, just like that. In fact, that's why I'm back, you see? To try and sort it out. To get Duncan to forgive me at last..."

There is a brief silence.

But Valentina can't stay quiet for long. "Forgive what? What happened to them? To Granny and Papa. Nobody ever told us."

Uncle Alistair shakes his head. "I will tell you. But not now. Not yet. As soon as I've found a way..." He busies himself with some books piled up on the coffee table. His hands are shaking. Poor Uncle Alistair.

Valentina is not defeated yet. "*Please* let us be part of RWR. We know what we're doing." I throw her a puzzled stare. *Do we?*

"You've *got* to count us in," she continues. "We're part of the deal. The whole Eilean deal, I mean. And we can See. We're like you, Uncle Alistair!"

He takes a deep breath.

"The sausages are burning..."

"We trust you. You'll look after us. Keep us out of danger."

"It's not that simple."

"You can't do all this removal business by yourself! We know every nook and cranny of this place. We can *help* you!"

Uncle Alistair holds his hands up. "Listen. If you die, I'm dead. I mean, your mum and dad will kill me. I'm sorry, I can't do this. I can't take you with me."

Valentina is devastated and I'm vaguely relieved. She's about to open her mouth to protest, when a loud howling interrupts her. We both jump up. What creature makes that sound? A wolf?

"No need for alarm, children. It's just letting me know I have an email." He turns to the computer.

"Old Petru Vasilescu sent me the podcast. We were in Transylvania together for a while, before he went a touch crazy and started believing he was a bat. But I digress." He leans towards the screen. "Oh... excellent. Splendid. Smashing."

"Wonderful. Amazing," mutters Valentina, rolling her eyes. She's sulking.

"Looks like the first case is in, children!"

"And we can help?" Valentina perks up.

"No."

And that's the end of it.

6. WE GET OUR FIRST GIG

Except it's not.

"Mmmmm." Uncle Alistair points at the screen. "See what you make of that."

Valentina doesn't need to be asked twice. She stands up like a shot and starts reading the email aloud, over Uncle Alistair's shoulder.

To SOS@reallyweirdremovals.com
From KWMcMillan@bmail.com

Dear Alistair,
It's Kenny McMillan here – do you remember me? I'm

a distant cousin on your father's mother's side. I'm writing to you because here in Hag we have a big problem, and we need your help.

It's the stone fairies. My own grandfather always said they were a nuisance, but they have got out of hand now. They scare the children. They turn the milk. Precious things disappear. They steal from letter boxes – anything they can get their hands on. They trip people up – poor Bill broke his wrist last Wednesday. They tripped a woman carrying her baby down the stairs of the post office. Thank goodness they were both fine, but she was terrified. They rip books in the library and make a mess in church. The kirk elders are in such a state!

We've tried everything, Libby and I – Libby's my wife, I don't believe you ever met her? We put salt on the doorsteps and the windows, then pine needles and garlic too. We left bread and milk and cream in bowls all around the place. We left copper kettles and pots in the woods, and little mirrors, and even jewellery. As you'll know, they love copper. But nothing works. Nobody knows what to do. We're at the end of our tether. I went into the woods and asked them to stop, but they didn't even acknowledge me. When I turned away, one of them – how can I put this? – did something rude on my head. I went home stinking, and we had to wash my clothes five times before the smell went away!

But yesterday, it all turned even worse. My neighbour Jimmy and I were out mushrooming, and Jimmy got bitten. It was agony, but worse was to come. Fairy bites, as I'm sure you know, carry weird illnesses and they make you do strange things. Now Jimmy has forgotten who he is and he's disappeared into the woods. Today I saw him behind a bush, naked as the day he was born, talking to things we can't see.

Worst of all is that the stone fairies want our baby granddaughter, Ella, for their own! We can't deal with this alone, and I was reminded of you last week by a friend of my cousin I remember when you were just a wee boy, and you blew up your parents' garage–

"Did you, Uncle Alistair?" Valentina asks, her eyes twinkling.

"Not on purpose. It sort of... happened," he mutters. For a moment, he looks like a little boy caught doing something naughty. Valentina giggles.

I don't think your dad's eyebrows ever fully grew back. Happy memories!

Anyway...

Alistair, please stop the fairies making our lives a misery, protect Ella and get Jimmy back to normal. Only you can do it.

Best regards,
Kenny McMillan

"This sounds so cool, Uncle Alistair. I'm sure we could be useful!" Valentina hasn't given up yet.

Uncle Alistair appears lost in thought. For a few seconds, there's silence – all I can hear is my heartbeat.

Finally, he speaks.

"This could be a good first case. For you, I mean. The stone fairies might bite, but they don't kill. Usually."

Oh, that's a relief, I think – not reassured in the slightest.

"Does that mean we can go with you?" exclaims Valentina, her eyes shining again.

"On probation..."

"YES!" Valentina claps her hands.

"Let's see how it goes, we'll take it from here." Uncle Alistair is trying to sound all wise and restrained, but I can see he's excited about having us with him.

I'm excited too – and a bit scared. Valentina is entirely without fear, as usual.

"But if you get killed, don't come and haunt me. It's not like I haven't warned you," continues Uncle Alistair. I'm not completely sure he's joking.

"So, here we are, the Really Weird Removals Company! RWR!" Valentina beams, looking around happily.

"Cool!" squeals Camilla, doing an airborne cartwheel.

"Here we are indeed. Right." Uncle Alistair claps his hands, sounding suddenly businesslike. "Let's give Kenny a suitable reply." He cracks his knuckles and sits at the desk. "There. What do you think of this, ladies and gentlemen? And... er... gentleghost?" he adds, careful not to leave Camilla out.

Valentina starts reading aloud.

Dear Kenny,

How awfully nice to hear from you, though in such troubling circumstances. We'll be with you on Saturday. You don't need to put us up; we'll be camping in the woods. Better to be near the action. I'd be grateful if, once the case of the fairies is closed to your satisfaction, you'd make a voluntary donation to the RWR to cover our expenses and aid our survival.

Thank you and best regards,
Alistair Grant, on behalf of the RWR

P.S. The garage thing. It was an unfortunate accident that could have happened to anyone.

"The RWR means *us!*" Valentina grins.

"Just for this once!" Uncle Alistair reminds her. "Now all we need to do is convince your dad to let you go."

"Under no circumstances can you go with your uncle. No."

"Duncan–"

"Please, Dad–"

"I said no, and that's my last word."

If Dad says that's his last word, there's only one person who can turn it into his *penultimate* word, and that's my mum.

"Mum, please... Camping is great, it's... *educational!*" I try.

"We'd be seeing Kenny! He's our cousin – distantly!" Valentina hugs Mum enthusiastically. "And, really, their infestation is terrible!" she adds, for good measure.

"Everybody on this island is your dad's distant cousin!" laughs Mum. "Why is it that they need your uncle again?"

"Rats."

"As big as ducks," I chip in.

"And you know I love mysterious creatures!" Valentina clasps her hands together.

"What's mysterious about rats?" Mum laughs.

"Rats can be *very* shifty," Valentina says solemnly.

"Right, right, leave it with me." Mum, still chuckling, runs upstairs after my dad.

Fingers crossed.

I feel awful, lying to my mum and dad like that. But I've just got to go with Uncle Alistair. It's as if something's calling me. As if this is something I *must* do.

Aunt Shuna shepherds us into the kitchen, where dinner is about to be served.

Camilla's hovering over the stove.

"She seems soooo nice, your aunt. I wish she could see me!"

"What was that, Valentina?" asks Aunt Shuna.

"Pardon?"

"What did you say?"

"It wasn't me, it was–" Valentina puts her hand to her mouth and makes a face at me.

Had Aunt Shuna heard Camilla speaking?

"I just said... I said, '*Mmmm*, my favourite, fish fingers and chips!'"

"With your mum's home-made ketchup."

I *know*. Mum *makes* her own ketchup. Boils a ton of tomatoes with vegetables and sugar and vinegar, and makes the most delicious ketchup ever. And she makes the fish fingers herself too, with freshly caught fish from the local fishmonger, and the chips she double-fries with rosemary and coarse salt. It's as if we live in a restaurant.

But Camilla isn't in the least interested in home-made ketchup. She is birling round the kitchen, trying to attract our aunt's attention.

"Shuna! It's Camilla! I'm here! Look up here!"

"Is there a radio on somewhere?" asks Aunt Shuna.

Valentina wags a warning finger at Camilla.

"Maybe. It must be coming from outside," I say, trying to sound breezy.

As we sit there waiting for Dad to make a decision, I can't help wondering why Alistair, Valentina and I can See, when my dad and his sister can't. I wonder if my grandparents could?

On the way back to our house from his office, Uncle Alistair explained to us that the Sight allows you to see things like they *really* are, not like they appear to be.

"The thing is, some of the creatures I work with look perfectly normal, perfectly human, but they're not."

59

He told us a story about walking down the street one day in London, a man stopped him for information. The man had a map in his hand, and was looking for Grosvenor Square. My uncle gave him directions, then watched him walk away – and noticed that his bottom half was a horse! Everybody else could only see a businessman. How cool is that?

A word of advice though, if you're up here in Scotland, and you see *anything* half horse, half human, just run as fast you can. It's bound to be a kelpie and, believe me, you don't want to meet one of *those*. Have a look at the *Paranormal Database*, there are a few kelpie sightings recorded in there, and quite a lot of people – mainly children – have disappeared around the places they were seen. Just to let you know.

My thoughts are interrupted by Mum's footsteps on the stairs.

"I spoke to your dad." We can tell from the look on her face that it wasn't an easy conversation.

"We can go on Saturday?" Valentina and I ask in unison.

Camilla, who's sitting on the table, leaps to her feet.

"You can go see Kenny and Libby in Hag with your uncle, yes." We jump up and down and Camilla cartwheels along the top of the dresser. Mum holds up her finger in warning. "This time!" she adds, just to specify it won't be a common occurrence.

"Great! Thanks Mum!"

"Ok, ok. But if there's any trouble..."

"Why should there be trouble? It's not like we're going to hunt monsters or anything like that..." I say.

"Stone fairies are only small," adds Camilla, trying to be helpful. Thankfully neither Mum nor Aunt Shuna can hear her.

"Duncan needs time to trust Alistair again," I hear Aunt Shuna say to my mum.

"I know. If the children spend time with him, and Duncan sees they're perfectly safe, I'm hoping he'll come round and let his brother back into the family. It'll be a slow process." Mum is thoughtful.

"To think they were so close." Aunt Shuna's voice is sad.

"Were they? It doesn't look like it now."

"It's true. Wherever Alistair was, there was Duncan. So different in personality, and yet... they were best friends."

They are quiet for a while. Then Mum sighs.

"He says to bring dinner up." My mum and dad never fight, they always seem to understand each other, but these days he's cooped up in his study all the time and I know she gets upset about it.

I'm not sure if his writing is really worth it, being apart from us as much as he is. Yes, he was called "the new J.K. Rowling" when the first *Reilly* came out, and people actually set up websites and fan clubs about his work, and now a film is being made, but...

When I have a family, I'll spend time with them. For sure. Even if I'm a famous writer. Which I will be, one day.

"Darling, put that phone away." Valentina has taken out her mobile, which is strictly forbidden at the dinner table.

"Sorry Mum. Just texting Uncle Alistair."

"Ok, let him know, and then put it away. After dinner we need to get your waterproofs out, and your sleeping bags..." I can see she's excited for us. "Wish I was going! I love camping, and I haven't seen Kenny in years! Since you were a baby, Valentina."

"Why don't we go too?" suggests Shuna.

We hold our breath. *Say no say no say no...*

"I've promised Morag I'll look after her mum on Saturday. She's flying to Glasgow for a shopping trip." My mum was a nurse when she lived in Italy, so neighbours and friends often ask her for help. We only have two doctors and two nurses on the whole island.

"Oh well, another time."

Phew.

Valentina's phone beeps.

"Sorry Mum, I think it's Uncle Alistair, can I look?"

"Right, on you go."

"Oh, he says to bring a few chocolate bars!" Valentina laughs, and hands me the phone.

```
Try and get your hands on
hairspray. Stone fairies hate
it. C u Sat at 8 don't sleep
in. A.
```

We exchange a look.

A few minutes later, once we're tucking into our tea, Valentina says casually, "Your hair looks lovely Mum. Are you wearing hairspray?"

Mum looks at her as if she has grown horns.

"Hairspray? No..." she runs a hand through her soft brown curls. "You know perfectly well I never do. What are you up to, Valentina Kirsty Grant?"

Uh-oh. The full name has been used. It means that my mum's radar is up.

"Nothing! I was just saying your hair looks nice!" Valentina looks outraged at Mum's tone.

"Right..." Mum says, meaning: my eye is on you.

To be fair to Mum, Valentina has done some crazy things in the past. Once she spread seaweed all over the garden – and I mean sacks of the smelly stuff – because she wanted to attract poquitos. According to Valentina, poquitos are a cross between lizards and sea birds, and they live somewhere in western Patagonia. She had read about them in *Hidden Beasts and Forgotten Animals*, a book she'd found in my dad's study. She was sure that if they happened to be flying over us, they would be attracted by the smell of seaweed.

Another time, she stole my dad's aftershave and poured it all over the doorsteps and windows because strong smells keep out poisonous snakes. That tip came from *Reptiles of the Americas*, apparently. There are *no* poisonous snakes in the Hebrides, but then you can never be too careful, she argued.

And that's not all. Last year she skipped her dance class and dragged her friend Rachel down the beach in the middle of winter, hoping to spot the migration of northern mermaids towards Iceland. (Apparently they meet there for a yearly festival. I'm not sure which book she got this from.) Rachel got home blue with cold, her teeth chattering, shaking all over. She caught a terrible flu, and her mum didn't speak to us for weeks.

So yes, when Valentina comes out with something unexpected, my mum worries.

"Do you have any hairspray at all?" Valentina asks now, her eyes wide with innocence.

"What for?"

"My *hair*, of course!"

"How dare we doubt her, Isabella," laughs Aunt Shuna.

"Well, whatever you need it for," Mum says, "I don't have any."

"I have some. I use it in school to seal chalk pictures so they don't smudge." Fixing chalk pictures, stunning stone fairies – you can't go wrong with a can of hairspray. "If you really think you need hairspray on this camping trip, I'll be happy to provide it," says Aunt Shuna, smiling.

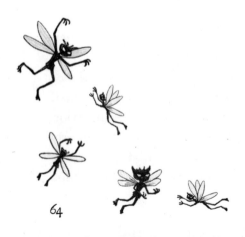

7. SECRETS

Alistair Grant's *Scottish Paranormal Database*

Entry Number 147: St Kilda's first settlers
Type: Fairy
Location: St Kilda
Date: 1824
Details: Duncan Swan and Charles Thornton, writers
and journalists, conducted a series of interviews
with native St Kildans, in order to compile a
guide to St Kilda's folklore and traditions. On
the island they discovered a colony of cliff
fairies, with bird-like wings and curved claws to
hold onto the rugged stone face. The natives kept
the fairies' existence a secret, fearing possible
threat from curious mainlanders.

By the end of the week, everything is ready. The
canisters of hairspray take pride of place in our
backpacks, together with waterproofs, and there's
about twenty plastic containers of food my mum
prepared (chicken with almonds and raisins – a
camping staple – together with walnut brownies,
smoked salmon terrine and cranberry cheesecake –
I'm *not* making this up).

I'm so excited, I can't sleep. I decide to write my
diary for a bit. I've been keeping it since I was eight.
I like writing – and also I always hope that one day
I'll be able to show it to my dad and he'll be pleased
with my work. You know, be impressed by my writing.

I record everything important: what happens in school, what I do with my friends, my thoughts and opinions about things. And since Uncle Alistair arrived, I have a lot to write about!

After a while, faint music seeps into my room. Maybe it's from some car in the street, or maybe Aunt Shuna has her radio on. It's not fiddle practice, so it can't be Dad, or Valentina. We sometimes hear Dad playing in his study; he says it's good for inspiration. And Valentina has been learning the fiddle since she was seven.

Whatever it is, I can't concentrate on my writing. I sneak into my sister's room. She's playing her Nintendo DS with Camilla, snuggled up under the duvet. Petsnake is snoring (loudly) in his cage.

"Hi... It's a bit noisy in my room."

"Noisy?"

"Someone must have the radio on."

"Come in, we're playing 'Julia, Passion for Fashion.'" Valentina lifts the duvet to make room for me and hands me a wee bag of Maltesers, her favourite.

"Thanks." I throw a couple of them into my mouth. "Camilla, just to make sure, are you still up for getting Gary off my case?"

"I can't wait. This is what I'm planning..." She starts floating upwards.

I can't bear it. "NO! No, seriously, don't, it freaks me out. Don't. Just stay... normal, please."

Camilla comes to rest on the bed again. "Next Thursday, after shinty practice, make up an excuse for him to go back to the playing field after everybody leaves."

"Like, that there's a brand new phone abandoned on the grass, maybe? He so greedy, he'll go back to get his hands on it, I bet."

"Super cool!" says Camilla. "And then I can freak him out!"

It sounds strange to hear these expressions from her. I mean, she's hundreds of years old and now she speaks like someone on TV.

"I just wish I could be there to see it!" sighs Valentina.

"You can! Come and meet me from shinty practice. We can sneak round the back and enjoy the moment."

"Awesome!"

"Awesome!" echoes Camilla. "It's all sorted."

The girls turn their attention again to Valentina's DS.

I lie back, munching on Maltesers, cosy under the duvet as the wind howls outside our window. It feels good to be home with Valentina and Camilla, and Dad in his study, and Mum and Aunt Shuna watching TV downstairs. All is as it should be.

By the time I'm back in my room, the music has gone and I drift away into sleep. Tomorrow we're on our first mission.

I'm jumping with excitement as I hear Uncle Alistair calling us from the street on Saturday morning. His voice is like the foghorn we often hear on winter nights. Valentina and I run out with our backpacks and a huge insulated cool-bag full of food. Each. My mum couldn't help herself. My diary is tucked safely into my backpack, of course. I have to record our first adventure as members of the RWR *as it happens*. Valentina has slipped a few books about strange creatures that she borrowed from Uncle Alistair into her backpack, to do a spot of reading in the woods.

"SURPRISE!" booms Uncle Alistair as he steps aside to reveal a bright blue van. Camilla is inside already, waving at us.

We stop in our tracks. "Wow!" and "Great!" we cheer politely. Alistair seems so happy about it, and we don't want to hurt his feelings. But the truth is, it's a sorry-looking thing: faded paintwork, a few bumps, rusty bits all over and a zigzagged radio antenna.

On the side, though, there's a beautiful, shiny, thoroughly stunning sign:

RWR, PEST CONTROL
No pest is too big or too small!
Tel. Eilean 218444
reallyweirdremovals.com

"*Will it get us there?*" whispers Valentina apprehensively, while Uncle Alistair loads the boot.

"Hopefully," I reply.

It's an amazing spring day: the sky is so blue, the sea calm and silky, and everything's in bloom. The perfect morning. Alistair puts the radio on. Paolo Nutini, great!

"*Nothing's gonna bring me down...*" Valentina and I hum cheerily.

"*NOTHING'S GONNA BRING ME DOWN, YEAH!*" shouts Uncle Alistair at the top of his voice.

"Uncle Alistair?" asks Valentina tentatively when it's safe to speak.

"Yes Vally. Fire away." Only Uncle Alistair would dare call my sister "Vally". I brace for an explosion but she doesn't seem to mind.

"Why do you always shout?"

"OH YES. Sorry! Sorry about that." He laughs cheerily. "There's a story behind it..." Of course. With Alistair, there's always a story behind it. "Do you know what a mandrake is?"

"Yes!" we say at once. Valentina is a crazy fan of Harry Potter. "It's that plant that if you pull it up, it screams and makes you faint unless you're wearing earmuffs," she says.

"Exactly. More mature mandrakes can also kill you, actually. However, I survived the encounter. Just. Only thing is, when I woke up, I had lost most of my hearing. They were LOUD, I'm telling you. I haven't even played the fiddle since then. I just can't hear myself playing."

So he plays – well, he *played* the fiddle. Like my dad and Valentina.

"You can't play anymore! That's terrible!" Valentina shudders. She loves music, while I can take it or leave it. I'm more into books.

"*Can you hear this?*" I whisper.

"I don't know what you're saying, because I'm driving

and I can't look at you. If I could look into your face, I'd read your lips. I can lip-read people a hundred yards away. An old Hecton I know taught me that."

"What's a Hecton?" asks Valentina.

Uncle Alistair swerves madly. "Look, Vally! Highland cows! Look how hairy they are!" he points frantically.

My sister shakes her head. "Uncle Alistair, I'm not three years old. What's a Hecton?"

"I can't say. So don't ask."

Something in his voice convinces Valentina that it's best to leave it.

We've been driving for about forty minutes, and here we are, at the outskirts of Hag, on the other side of the island. That's how small Eilean is.

Hag is not right on the sea, it's a wee bit back, on the top of a small hill. Just beside it there's a pinewood sheltered in the fold of the hill, the only place on the whole of the island with trees. We drive along the edge of the wood until we find Kenny McMillan's house: it's black and thickset and quite forbidding.

"Here we are, and there's where we'll be camping," says Uncle Alistair, pulling on the handbrake.

Kenny is standing in the doorway: he's very tall, with grey hair and a kind face.

"Come in, come in! Libby has lunch on the table for you. I made a cake. It's a dairy-free chocolate cake. We can't keep any milk fresh, as you know... Oh, hello." He's completely unfazed when Camilla follows us indoors.

Valentina and I exchange a meaningful look. So Kenny McMillan has the Sight...

"You can *see* me!" Camilla is delighted.

"Of course he can, and so can I. Hello, welcome to you all, I'm Libby," says a friendly looking woman with very thick glasses. She holds out her hand. "Alistair, good to meet you. Good heavens, this can't be Luca Grant, can it? Luca, is that you? I remember you when you were this tall, or should I say this *short*! And who would this be?"

"I'm Valentina."

"Of course! You were a baby when I saw you last. And you, my dear, are..."

"Camilla!"

"You're very welcome. Come and have something to eat, you must be starving."

We shouldn't be, after the enormous breakfast Mum made us eat an hour ago. But we don't complain as we tuck into ham sandwiches, crisps and delicious dairy-free chocolate cake.

"Will it be safe for the wee ones, Alistair?" asks Libby, concerned.

"Probably," he says flippantly.

They don't seem reassured.

"I didn't want to take them! They forced me." Uncle Alistair shrugs.

Kenny and Libby are obviously not sure whether he's joking or in earnest.

"That's right, yes. We forced him," says Valentina seriously. "We're his new staff."

Alistair looks rather pleased at that.

"By the way, I must ask you to swear to total secrecy. Nobody, *nobody* around here must know what the RWR really is and what we do."

"Fair enough," says Kenny. "We won't tell. We have quite a secret ourselves."

Pause for dramatic effect. We wait for more.

Nothing comes.

"And what would that be?" cajoles Alistair.

"You'd better come and see."

We follow Kenny and Libby upstairs into a wee bedroom with a white cot in the corner. The curtains are drawn.

"Here's our secret," Kenny says in a low voice.

We all tiptoe into the room, which suddenly gets very crowded, and look into the cot. There's a baby asleep in it, wearing a pink babygro and a wee pink hat. No surprises there.

But then Libby gently turns the baby on her side, and we can all see something that other people can't see. A little pair of translucent wings.

Short intake of breath from me and Valentina.

"Can you all See?" whispers Libby.

"Yes," says Alistair.

Libby carefully removes the baby's pink hat, and there they are, two little pointed ears.

Another intake of breath.

"This is Ella, our granddaughter."

"Amazing..." I whisper. I look at Alistair, who's smiling mysteriously.

"Can I touch her?" asks Valentina.

"Of course. Just be careful you don't wake her up."

Valentina strokes Ella's little cheek gently. "She's so sweet!"

Once we're out of the room and downstairs again,

Alistair stands in front of Libby. He lifts his hands towards her face and, ever so gently, takes her glasses off. We all freeze. What is he doing?

Without the thick lenses, Libby's eyes shine incredibly. They're bright green, emerald-like. No human could have eyes that colour. Then Alistair tucks a lock of her white hair away from her face, to reveal a pointed ear.

"I thought you might figure that out," says Libby, smiling. "I've always known *you* could See, even when you were a wee boy."

"You're a fairy!" I exclaim, before I can stop myself.

"I've been living as a human since I was sixteen, since I met Kenny..."

"I've always loved going into the woods, picking mushrooms. One day, I went out looking for mushrooms and I found... her." Kenny smiles fondly at his wife.

"Kenny and his family pretended I was a friend from America. I had to fake an American accent for a while!" she laughs. "I've never looked back. All our children are half-fairies. Our son lives as a human, and our daughters as fairies, in the woods behind the cottage. But a few months ago one of my daughters brought us baby Ella. The stone fairies want to kidnap her, they want her as one of their own..."

"The same way that they steal human children?" interrupts Alistair. "I see."

"My daughter thought that maybe we could protect her. But ever since we took the wee one in, the stone fairies have given us so much trouble. We just can't take any more." Libby's beautiful eyes fill with tears.

"I fear they'll come for Ella, and we won't be able

to stop them," says Kenny, his face full of apprehension. "They'll bring her up wild, like one of them. Stone fairies don't speak, they grunt. They're always up to no good. And our poor daughter, she's beside herself, missing Ella..."

"I get the picture. I'll make them stop," says Alistair.

I swallow. He sounds very confident.

"Come on, children, let's go. We need to do some exploring before we set up camp." He hustles us into the hallway. "Kenny, Libby, lock all the doors and windows. There'll be fireworks tonight."

"Wouldn't it be safer if the children stayed in the cottage with us?" asks Kenny.

"Sorry, no, I need them. I'll offer them in exchange for Ella."

"WHAT?" we exclaim in unison. I feel a bit sick.

"Come on now!" Uncle Alistair's voice is matter-of-fact.

On the doorstep, Libby hugs us all. "Take care... stay safe..."

Valentina looks resolute as she walks on. "Let's GO GET THEM!" she mutters to herself.

I try to mould my face to imitate her expression, but I'm actually terrified. Why did I get myself into this?

We're about to climb into the van, when...

"Oh no!" exclaims Kenny. "The stone fairies have slashed your tyres!"

"Of course!" says Uncle Alistair cheerily. "I was expecting this! We'll walk."

With a last wave to the McMillans, we walk on, some with a spring in their step, others (me) dragging their heels.

8. THREE THINGS I NEED TO KNOW ABOUT SCOTLAND

The night is very black. There are a million stars above us. I lie using my hands as a pillow, wrapped in my sleeping bag, and I'm happy. Freaked out and terrified, but happy.

"According to this, stone fairies are allergic to walnuts." Valentina is reading *Magical Creatures of the Woods*, a heavy tome bound in bright blue leather. Camilla is sitting beside her, glowing faintly in the darkness, reading the book over her shoulder.

"Some are, some aren't. Can't rely on that one," Uncle Alistair says briefly.

"And they can't stand any hair product, like you said."

"True," says Alistair, gesturing to the cardboard box full of hairspray and the like, some of it Aunt Shuna's. "But that's just a temporary measure."

"So what are we going to do?"

Uncle Alistair raises his eyebrows. "I told you, I'll offer the two of you in exchange for baby Ella."

I gulp. I'd been hoping I'd misheard his earlier statement. Even Camilla looks shocked.

"You wouldn't do that," says Valentina defiantly.

"You sure? They'd treat you ok, and you'd be free in three hundred years," he says, his expression deadpan.

"MFFFFFF mfffff mmffff," says Jimmy.

Yes, you read right. We found Jimmy – Kenny's neighbour who got bitten by the stone fairies – wandering in the woods in his underpants, frozen. He can't remember a thing. We brought him to the van to warm him up but he keeps trying to run away, so we've wrapped him up warm in a jumper and an extra sleeping bag, which Alistair had brought just for him, and we've tied him up. He half drank, half drooled the mug of tea we gave him. Now he's lying down, mmmfffffing on the ground between us.

"You wouldn't swap us," I protest, sitting up.

"Mum and Dad would be pretty angry if you lost us," points out Valentina, as if she's not that worried.

Uncle Alistair sighs deeply. "Don't worry. You're safe with me. I'm not going to lose anyone else, children." His voice has a sad note, all of a sudden. His shoulders have stooped, and he seems far away.

Valentina and I look at each other.

"Of course. We know we're safe with you," whispers Valentina, taking his hand.

"Uncle Alistair," I ask, "I know you don't want to tell us what happened, but... why does Dad think it's your fault that Papa and Granny disappeared? Aunt Shuna said it was an accident..."

He shook his head. "It *was* my fault. I shouldn't have done what I did. I have no excuses. But what happened... couldn't have been predicted. So Shuna is right too, in a way. It was... a fluke. A terrible fluke..."

While he's talking, a strange sound builds up in my ears. I shake my head. It's like my ears are ringing, in a weird way.

"It should not have happened..."

The sound is getting stronger, more defined. It's a melody, similar to the music I heard in my room a few nights ago. I shake my head, thumping my ears with my hands. There can't be music here, in the woods. It must be in my head. Nobody else seems to hear it.

"...Duncan is right to blame me. But you know, I'm trying to make it right, Luca... I'll make it up to all of you..."

That very moment, something hits Alistair's forehead – hard, right between his eyebrows. The melody stops at once.

Alistair is stunned for a second, his eyes crossed, and then he jumps up, holding the missile. "It's a walnut!" he cries. "So much for that book, Vally."

We look around, unsure what to do next, but aware that something has started.

"HAIRSPRAY!" Uncle Alistair booms all of a sudden. We each take possession of a can and crouch expectantly. Camilla is floating above us, a can in each hand.

A pause.

A moment.

A lifetime.

And then they arrive: black, nasty, persistent – like flies, all around us, in horrible little clouds. We spray and spray and spray. A few lie stunned on the ground, others run away, while some hover around us, biding their time, darting this way and that every time one of us takes aim. I can see them clearly now, their little scrunched-up, malevolent faces, their wisp of black hair and their ghastly *eyes*, shining like pieces of night. They're as small as my hand, but there are a lot of them. An awful lot. *Awful* being the key word.

"STOP!" cries Alistair. His cry is not panicked, it's commanding.

The stone fairies actually stop too.

Valentina is on one knee, her hairspray can ready to shoot. Her blonde hair is sticking out, solid, into what looks like a cloud around her head. The fairies must have ruffled it as they buzzed her, and the hairspray in the air has made it rigid. If I weren't scared to death, I would laugh.

"All right. You win. I have brought two children for you. In exchange for Ella. Look."

Oh, *Mamma Mia*, as Mum would say. What is he thinking?

"Look. A boy and a girl! For you! Let Ella be."

The cloud of fairies buzzes, swerves, breaks into two battalions. In between, a single fairy emerges. It's wearing a little copper ring around its head and carrying a metal sceptre. Wait a minute. That's not a sceptre. It's a *teaspoon*.

"Fine. We'll take them," the stone fairy king says, in a voice that sounds like someone sharpening knives, with a touch of soil in it. Sorry, can't describe it any better. You'd have to hear it.

I swallow. I can feel Valentina moving imperceptibly. I'm still the fastest runner in my school, and no matter what, I'll take Valentina with me.

But Uncle Alistair notices us getting ready to run for it. "Come here, children," he says, and opens his arms wide, ready to put them around us.

I don't move.

But Valentina does. She stands up and actually goes to him.

I can't believe it! I have no choice now. I've got to go too. I can't abandon Valentina.

I walk over, and my legs are like lead.

I look into Uncle Alistair's face. Unreadable.

His arms are around our shoulders now. He squeezes them slightly. Just once.

"At my three, take a step back. Just one step. No more, no less. Clear?" he murmurs.

We nod.

"One, two, three." The three of us take a single step back in unison.

I feel strange. A sort of... electric current has gone up my back and into my arms, as if I'd stepped on a plug with wet feet.

My head spins for a second, and I can't see.

"Come and get them!" I hear my uncle shout.

The cloud of fairies swoops towards us at once. I shut my eyes as Uncle Alistair grabs our hands and with all his might throws himself, and us, sideways.

One instant the stone fairies are there. One instant they're gone.

Gone completely.

Except one, one solitary single fairy, buzzing around in amazement. Then he flies away, into the darkness of the woods, and we're alone.

There's silence all around, nothing more than the peaceful night. All I can hear is our panting, and my beating heart.

And an owl.

"You're safe!" exclaims Camilla, and jumps over to throw her arms around Valentina's neck.

"What happened? Where did they go?" asks Valentina.

"Somewhere far away," says Uncle Alistair flippantly. "Best get going. Let's bring Jimmy back and hopefully they'll give us a reward. The van won't pay for itself, you know," he mutters.

"Wait a minute!" I shout. I actually stamp my foot. "Tell us what happened! Where have they gone?

We were standing there..." I take a step towards where we stood "...then we took a step back, and—"

"NO!" cries Uncle Alistair and grabs me by the sleeve, pulling me back. "Don't go there, you'll disappear too."

"I know what it was! A fold in time! Like in *Time Travel: A new direction!*" Valentina claps her hands with delight. "I read about it at your place."

"Exactly!" says Alistair.

I smile. And then I laugh, a bit maniacally. "A time fold! So the fairies have gone... somewhere else! Another time! But where? When?"

"No idea. It's not like a time machine. You can't program it. It sends you where it sends you. And once you're there... chances are, you won't come back." He looks into the distance.

"How did you know it was here?"

"It wasn't here. Not before I arrived. I put it there."

"You can create time folds?" Valentina says incredulously.

"No, I didn't create it, I just carried it here. Some time folds are fixed, and they can't be moved. Some are portable."

"Portable? Do you mean you've got one with you and you can use it whenever you like?"

"Exactly. I placed it there earlier on. I need to take it back now." He pulls out a small crystal from his pocket, a very plain-looking one, opaque, greyish. It barely shines. You would never guess its immense power.

Uncle Alistair passes the crystal over the time fold, over and over again, careful not to step in it. The air blurs a little, it sort of *shifts*. And then it's over.

"Feel it." He hands the crystal first to Valentina and then to me. It feels ice cold. "Ready for next time," he says, putting it back into his pocket. Then he gives us a broad smile. "I'm starving. Time for breakfast."

"Mmmmmffffffffffffff!"

We've forgotten all about Jimmy.

"Come on, pal," says Uncle Alistair, untying him.

Jimmy looks around, as if he's woken up from a long deep sleep. "*The fairies! They bit me!*" he says, his voice panicky and frightened. "Don't let them... Where are my clothes?" Now he looked bewildered, and a bit embarrassed.

"It's ok now, they've gone," I say, putting my arm around his waist and helping him onto his feet. "Come on, let's get you home." He takes a while to calm down, but he relaxes when we promise him food.

Dawn is breaking now, and the sky is all pink and yellow, with the black pines silhouetted against it. My island is so beautiful.

The McMillans are already awake, and they greet us with pale anxious faces as we make our way up the path. Then they see our smiles, and Jimmy, and they relax.

"The stone fairies won't be troubling you again," booms Alistair.

"Thank goodness!"

"Come on in, everybody! Jimmy! It's great to see you back safely! Come in and eat." Libby sits her old friend down in front of the range. Then she turns to Camilla. "You won't be wanting any food I suppose, but come and sit with us." Camilla looks overjoyed; I'm quite moved to see how happy she is to be counted in. She's so used to being invisible.

Twenty minutes later, we all sit down to a cooked breakfast. After wandering in the woods naked for over a week, Jimmy has quite an appetite. "No acorns for Jimmy. Acorns YUK! Acorns BLEURGH!" he explains as he attacks his fourth sausage. He's still a bit confused.

"Alistair, how on earth did you do it? What happened?" asks Kenny.

"Long story." Clearly, Uncle Alistair wants to keep his methods under his hat.

"A lot of hairspray," says Valentina. She's sitting with Ella on her knee.

Libby smiles and shakes her head.

Kenny is silent for a moment. "You wouldn't have wiped them out, Alistair. You wouldn't have done that," he says.

"Who says?" asks Alistair.

"Your eyes," Kenny replies simply.

"The RWR is not about killing," says Libby quietly. Her eyes are shining very green, very lovely. "Or we wouldn't have called you."

"No, we never kill anyone. Not even the dangerous ones like Rupert Cleaver," chirps Camilla.

"You must have sent them somewhere else," says Kenny firmly.

"Some*time* else," corrects Alistair, and a look of understanding passes between them, across the pile of pancakes on Alistair's plate. Nothing more need be said.

Kenny and Libby's half-fairy son happens to be a mechanic, and he changes our tyres while we stand in the chilly morning air. It's quite surreal to see Ross McMillan's translucent wings, dark blue as opposed to Ella's tiny silver ones.

"I can see his wings. How come I never saw people with wings before? Are they the only ones on the island?" I ask my uncle.

"No, they're not the only ones. It's that your Sight is getting stronger." He looks at me fondly. It's a great feeling. My dad never looks at me that way. "Can you see them, Vally?"

"Yes, I can see them too." Valentina beams.

"Your gift is strengthening. Evolving. You're doing amazingly well, children..."

We bask in his words like a cat basks in sunlight.

As we're getting ready to go, Kenny takes Valentina and me aside for a minute. "Remember this." He's looking very solemn. We look into his clear blue eyes, and listen carefully. "Here are three things you need to know about Scotland. One: there are places in this country that can take you to another time. Like the one Alistair used with the stone fairies, only some of them are a lot more powerful. Put one step wrong – or right, depending on the point of view – and you'll find yourself deep in the great Caledonian forest, or looking a dinosaur in the eye, or hiding with a bunch of desperate Jacobites. So be careful where you walk.

Two: there are... *things* all over Scotland that nobody knows about. At the bottom of the lochs, on the moors, in the sea waters, there's more than anybody could ever imagine. Keep your eyes open and I promise you, you'll *See*.

Three: only a few chosen people can See all this, and they come from all over the world. But only if you *belong* here, only if you are really and truly part of Scotland, only if this is truly your home, will you be able to See what hides beneath Artan Mor."

As we drive across the moors I mull over his words and wonder what he meant. I could ask Alistair, but I won't. For now, what he said is just for Valentina and me to know.

We stop for petrol at the outskirts of Eilean, and I smile as I notice a little girl standing in front of the wee shop, a packet of crisps in her hands and a pair of translucent green wings on her back, moving gently in the breeze.

9. WHERE A BULLY GETS WHAT HE DESERVES

Alistair Grant's *Scottish Paranormal Database*

Entry number 616: The white lady of Glen Avich
Type: Ghostly apparition
Location: Glen Avich
Date: August 1781
Details: In August 1781, the manifestation of a white lady in her bedroom caused Lady Ramsay of Glen Avich to die of fright. Similar sightings of a lady in a white dress have been recorded at different places across western and central Scotland; sometimes the lady is threatening, sometimes silent and forlorn. It is the author's opinion that there's more than one white lady, as such apparitions have also been recorded elsewhere in the world.

"It looks dreadful, Luca. That... that... rotter." Adil stares at the caman-shaped bruise on my right cheek.

"It *feels* dreadful, I can tell you." Guess who did it.

"It'll look even worse tomorrow."

"Thanks Adil, that's just what I needed to hear."

"Are you ok, Luca?" asks Mr MacDonald.

"Yes, I'm ok." I manage to sound breezy. "Things happen."

"Do they? I mean, I didn't see it, and everybody swears it was an accident, but you seem to be at the end of Gary's caman a lot. Is anything going on?"

"He doesn't like me much," I admit reluctantly. Mr MacDonald must be aware of the friction between us.

"I'll have a word with him. This can't go on."

"No, seriously, don't. I'll sort it myself." I've got a plan now, and Mr MacDonald getting involved could just make things worse.

Mr MacDonald takes a breath. I can see he's trying to figure out the best thing to do. "Ok. You try. But if it happens again, I'll have to step in. Deal?"

"Deal," I say. It *won't* happen again. I'm sure of that. Because Camilla is in the room with us, floating against the ceiling, with a very, very black look in her eyes. I wonder what she has planned.

"Valentina's here," she says, and flies swiftly away. Since we came back from the McMillan's, Camilla and Valentina have discovered that they can actually speak to each other *in their heads*. They can send messages to each other, like some sort of telepathic texting.

Adil and I make our way back to the changing rooms. Gary is lagging behind, to gloat over my purple-and-blue face.

"Poor Luca... did they give you a lollipop?" he mocks.

"No, no lollipops. But I nearly got myself a mobile phone."

"What are you talking about?"

I shrug my shoulders. "There was a phone out there, on the grass. It looked fancy. I wanted to pick it up and hand it in, but my head was spinning..."

"I didn't see it," intervenes Adil.

"Did you not?" I feign surprise.

"We better go get it, someone might be looking for it." Adil is honest to a fault.

"No, it's ok, you go with Luca, I'll get it and hand it in." Gary has a sly look in his eyes.

"Sure." Of course. As if Gary would ever return it. He'd just put it in his pocket and not think twice.

"Adil, you go on home, I won't be long," I say quickly.

"I don't think it's safe to leave you to walk back alone..." he mutters, puzzled. We always walk home from shinty together.

"My sister's coming, I just texted her."

"Are you sure?" He is concerned.

"Positive."

He buys it. I make sure I see him leaving the sports centre before slipping out myself, still in my shinty gear. Instead of turning right, I turn left, towards the back of the playing fields. In the distance, I spot Valentina's blonde hair shining in the pink light of sunset. Camilla's white dress looks all pink too. They're hiding behind a concrete pillar.

I run to them, hoping that Gary won't spot me. He's on his hands and knees in the grass, checking every inch for the imaginary mobile phone.

"What happened to your face?" exclaims Valentina, horrified.

"Let's just say it's another good reason to do this."

Camilla touches my face gently, with her transparent cold hands. "I'll sort it."

Her eyes are so empty and dark that I feel my knees giving way. I hesitate, just for a second. Then my face throbs again, and I steel myself.

"He's in the playing field. Go."

Camilla dissolves before our eyes.

Gary is about a hundred yards away. Greedy, dishonest, and a real bully, I say to myself. I won't change my mind. We're going through with this.

Camilla starts taking shape, hovering above Gary's head. I catch a glimpse of her face, and I don't like what I see. I *really* don't like what I see... I hesitate. I'm about to call Camilla back, when...

"*Don't!*" whispers Valentina fiercely, grabbing my shoulder. "We have to do this. There's no other way to make him stop."

Camilla keeps circling him, like a vulture. Her braids have come undone, her eyes are empty pools of darkness, her hands like claws. I can see her thickening, becoming more and more solid in order to make herself visible... I just hope and pray that Mr MacDonald has gone home...

Gary is still on all fours, scouring the grass.

"She's asking him if he found it," whispers Valentina, reading Camilla's mind. My sister is excited, elated, I can see it in her face.

We see Gary looking up, surprised, straight into Camilla's eyes, and then falling on his knees in terror, his hands covering his face. We can hear his screams from here.

"She's asking him if he enjoys tormenting you," says Valentina, reading Camilla's mind.

Gary's now shaking his head, over and over again. Camilla's face is the stuff of nightmares, her dress looks ragged, floating in the darkening light... her claw-like hands are poised to touch him...

"She says that if he ever bothers you again, she'll take him with her to the land of the dead!" Valentina laughs.

I'm horrified. What a dreadful thought. I just feel terribly sorry for Gary.

I watch Camilla circling him again, once, twice. Then she strikes. She falls on him at incredible speed, her black hair streaming behind her like a bat's wings, her eyes getting bigger and darker...

Gary screams again, covering his head with his arms. In a heartbeat, Camilla is gone.

He keeps on screaming for a couple of minutes.

Somebody must have heard, because staff from the sports centre are running out over the field. Gary's crumpled up in a heap. I feel awful.

"So, did I do ok?" Camilla materialises by our side. Her black hair is still flowing around her, and her eyes are still empty, but mainly she looks like herself again.

"You did great," I say, but I'm shaking. "Let's go. Don't run, just walk." I pull Valentina back. "A lot of people will wonder what happened. Let's not look suspicious."

Gary is being helped inside. He's struggling to walk.

"I want to hear what he says!" cries Camilla, as she floats away.

Valentina and I head down towards our house.

"You look terrible, Luca," laughs Valentina.

"I know. It's just that she was so... so *scary*," I whisper. "I felt sorry for him."

"You felt sorry for *him*?" she whispers urgently, her brown eyes blazing. "Does he feel sorry for you when he hits you?" She points at my face. "Or when he laughs at Mum and throws your lunch on the floor?"

"No he doesn't. That's the point. I'm not *like* him. If I were, I wouldn't feel awful now!"

"Luca, you drive me crazy... wait! Camilla is talking!" Her eyes focus on the distance for a second.

I look behind, just to make sure nobody's listening.

"Gary said he saw a ghost. A white woman screaming..." Valentina giggles. "They've given him some juice but he threw it up!" She laughs. I feel even worse. "He's as white as a sheet... his mum and dad are coming to get him. He can't even stand!"

"Shhhh..." I shush her as two fishermen pass us by, still in their fishing gear.

"Camilla is coming back to our house now," Valentina whispers, as soon as it's safe to speak.

"Tell her to go to Uncle Alistair's. We'll see her there."

"Mum will go mental if we're out too late."

"Just twenty minutes."

"COME IN GUYS! I'M IN THE BACK!"

It's pitch dark, except for the orange glow from the lamp-post in front of the house. We make our way in, and venture up the dark corridor that leads to the back rooms. We've never seen any other room but the front one. I peek into the door on the left – a small storeroom. It's empty but for piles of cardboard boxes, sealed with sellotape and marked "PRIVATE!" and "DO NOT TOUCH!"

I open the next door quietly, slowly... It's very dark, but there's a green light glowing faintly behind a black shape at the opposite end of the room. I blink, trying to make out what it is, and I walk in hesitantly, followed by Valentina.

"COME ON IN, WHY ARE YOU TIPTOE-ING LIKE BURGLARS?"

We jump in fright.

Uncle Alistair switches on a table lamp. He's wearing a long white coat and big goggles. The green light is coming from a little bottle in his hands, containing something that looks like liquidised frogs.

I look around. The room is a cross between a chemistry lab, like the ones you see in films, and a kitchen.

Beside the door there's a huge fridge with two little magnets on it: a piper with a tall hat, a kilt and a caption that says "Greetings from Scotland", and a tiny pizza. There's a gas stove, a microwave and jars full of strange powders in muted colours. A row of hooks, with an oven glove and a few kitchen towels hanging from them. And a few normal-looking pots, like the ones my mum and Aunt Shuna use to cook in, hung tidily on the far wall. There are three tables, one against each free wall. One has nothing on it; one is covered with the same kind of bottles I saw in the fridge in the front room, some blue, some yellow, some swirling and silvery. And the third...

Is that a Viking helmet? With two very real-looking horns sticking out? And something else... it's like a huge saucer, decorated in bright colours. It's a *shield*. A Viking shield, with a red-and-white eye painted on it. I try to get a closer look...

"BLOOMING SINKING SHIP!" Uncle Alistair jumps in between me and the table. "Forgot about those... Nothing to see here. Move on, guys... come through to the living room." And he shepherds us towards the door, hastily.

"*What was that?*" I whisper, knowing he can't hear me unless he's reading my lips.

"No idea!" mouths Valentina. "Another Ikea delivery?"

"Aaaaanyway. Wanted to show you this." Uncle Alistair goes to stand beside the computer, pointing to the screen dramatically. "Ta daa! Our new shiny website: reallyweirdremovals.com. This will bring us heaps of business. And it links to the *Paranormal Database*. You like?"

"It's great!" I say, genuinely impressed. A website all for us. It looks so... so *professional*!

"That. Is. Cool," says Valentina.

"Hello!" Camilla materialises right in front of us, and I jump out of my skin.

"Camilla! That was INCREDIBLE!" Valentina hugs her.

"What was?" asks Alistair, screwing a cap onto the green bottle he's still holding in his hand.

"Camilla scared Gary. You know, the boy that was hitting Luca and saying horrible things."

"Right. I see. Oh, that's why the black eye." Uncle Alistair removes his goggles. "Was that him?"

"Yes."

"Did *you* ask Camilla to do it?"

"Yes. But then I wasn't sure..."

"Why were you not sure?"

"Because Camilla was terrifying..."

"Thank you!" chips in Camilla cheerfully.

"...and I felt sorry for him. It was weird."

Valentina rolls her eyes.

"What do you think?" Uncle Alistair asks Valentina.

"I think Gary deserved it. Look at Luca's face!"

"Mmmm."

"What do *you* think, Uncle Alistair?" I ask hesitantly.

"I think you should have come to me first."

"Sorry, we didn't put Camilla in any danger..."

He roars with laughter. "I would have told you how to make the whole experience even worse for him!"

Valentina and Camilla laugh. I smile too, in spite of myself. I'll certainly have something exciting to write in my diary tonight.

"Right, I'll make us all some beans with sausage 99s – are you hungry?"

"Oh, sorry, we can't now. We need to be home by six, or they'll worry. We promised."

"Oh, of course, of course." He looks a bit deflated.

"Maybe we could phone and ask to stay for dinner?" Valentina asks me.

"Dad has promised to be down for dinner tonight..."

"He won't," says Valentina, shrugging. She's right.

"I know, but Mum..."

"It's ok, another time..." Uncle Alistair looks a bit lost.

"You're working. We'd be in your way," I point out.

"I know. But I'm *lnl*," he mutters and looks away.

"Pardon?"

"I'm *lnl*."

No idea what he's saying.

"He's LONELY!" repeats Camilla helpfully.

"Oh."

"I've lived on my own for a long time..."

"Apart from me, but I'm dead and I go out a lot," says Camilla.

"Never mind. Now go, you'll be late," he says, putting his goggles back on, to indicate that the conversation is over.

"Uncle Alistair?" I've got to ask this.

"Mmmm?" He doesn't look up.

"What was that Viking stuff?"

"What Viking stuff?" He doesn't even turn around.

I know to ask no more.

As we walk into the darkness, I look back to see Uncle Alistair framed in the window, waving forlornly. Silhouetted against the light is the shape of two horns: the Viking helmet. I smile to myself. I must have the coolest uncle in the whole of Scotland.

Valentina, Camilla and I are under my duvet, eating Maltesers. Petsnake is snoring, as usual. There's that eerie music again, the one I hear in my head. It's so faint I can barely follow it, but it's definitely there. I seem to be hearing it quite a lot these days and it's beginning to freak me out a little.

"Did Gary mention Luca?" Valentina's blonde head and Camilla's dark one are bent over the same book, *Tales of Beedle the Bard*.

"Not a word. I think he was too scared," giggles Camilla.

I'm writing down everything that happened today. Each night I write in my diary, using a booklight I bought with my pocket money at the Eilean Bookshop.

> Camilla keeps circling him, like a vulture. Her braids have come undone, her eyes are empty pools of darkness, her hands like claws. I can see her thickening, becoming more and more solid. I just hope and pray that Mr MacDonald has gone home...

I take my diary with me everywhere. One day I'll show it to my dad, when the time is right. Surely he

will have to forgive Uncle Alistair then, when he
realises how great he is to Valentina and me, and the
incredible things he's showing us.

Dad will be well proud of my writing. He'll see
that I'm just like him, a born author.

Yes, it's all going to work out, one day soon.

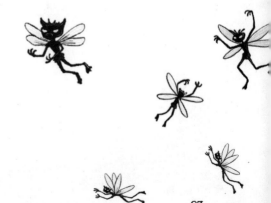

SUMMER

10. THE THING IN
THE CELLAR

Alistair Grant's *Scottish Paranormal Database*

Entry Number 542: The singing troll
Type: Fairy or cryptozoology (disputed)
Location: Bridge on the river Dee, Kirkcudbright,
Dumfries and Galloway
Date: Summer of 1819; summer of 2009
Details: In the summer of 1819, two gentlemen
disappeared, presumably eaten, after their
encounter with a troll. The only witness, a
passer-by, recounted that the troll sang throughout
the attack. 190 years later, in 2009, the singing
troll was accidentally recorded by two schoolgirls
playing with their mobile phones. The recording
eventually became a ringtone that gained a popular
notoriety in some Scottish schools.

The beach looks incredible under the scorching sun.
It's the last day of school. Finally!

Adil and I are sitting on the rocks, our grey uniform
trousers rolled up to the knees, eating ice creams and
looking at the bright blue sea.

A long summer is ahead of me, with games of
shinty and football, books and more books, and, most
of all, the RWR.

I wonder what's next for us after the stone fairies.
Uncle Alistair was brilliant with his portable fold in
time. I've been thinking about where the fairies could

have been sent. Maybe they reappeared in the middle of some ancient battle, or they ended up in the Ice Age, or maybe in some futuristic megacity. The folds in time are also folds in space, so they could have wound up on the other side of the world. Maybe in the middle of Tokyo at rush hour, or among some lost tribe in the Amazon.

I wonder if fairies are all around us? And how many types of fairies are there? Because the stone fairies were very, very different from baby Ella. The magic world – or the world like it really is, not like it appears – is opening in front of me.

I know that Uncle Alistair said he would only take us along with him once, but then he did also say, "We'll take it from there." I'm sure that when the next case comes in, Valentina and I will convince him to let us be part of it.

I'm getting all sleepy and floppy and dozy in the bright warmth, when a shadow appears between me and the sun. I open one eye.

"Hey, Valentina. How's things." I close my eye again. Pink and yellow lights dance in front of my eyelids.

"*Hiya,*" whispers Adil, sitting up at once and sweeping a hand through his black hair, trying in vain to flatten it. He's blushing. Well, I can't see him blushing, but I *know* he is. In the last few weeks he's been all tongue-tied and shy around Valentina. Very annoying.

"Yes, hi. Luca, come with me. Need to speak to you."

"But..."

"Come on, chop chop! Stuff to do! Stuff to discuss! *Uncle Alistair sort of stuff...*" she whispers dramatically. She has her Bossy Voice on. No point in resisting.

"Ok, ok." I get up, dizzy from the sun. We can't talk in front of Adil, obviously. It feels very strange to keep secrets from my best friend. He and I have been inseparable since nursery, and we know everything about each other. We *knew* everything about each other. Not anymore. A million times I nearly told him about the RWR – but then I couldn't bring myself to do it. I'm too worried he won't believe me. After all, he doesn't have the Sight; he can't see anything of what we see. Also Adil can't lie to save his life. He's completely *unable* to tell a lie, even a wee white one. If he knew about us and he was asked, he'd probably blurt it out. And we can't afford for my mum and dad to find out, not until Dad forgives Uncle Alistair. We have to keep pretending it's just a pest control business.

"To the beach, Luca. Bye Adil!" Valentina is already dragging me down to the sand. Her head bobs up and down as she walks on, purposefully.

"Bye, Valentina," calls Adil. "Bye then... Bye. Bye!" He'd keep going, if Valentina hadn't turned her back on him already. Embarrassing. I really don't understand what this is about. I can't picture myself going red and mumbling around girls. Anyway, each to their own.

"I've just been to see Donald, to thank him for the *octopus*," Valentina whispers conspiratorially as we walk towards the waterline. "He said that Uncle Alistair has been up to his boat a few times. He bought *a lot* of fish, and... oh−"

Valentina's phone is making a strange noise. A horrible tune, something between a song, a grunt and a screech. She takes it out of her pocket and starts pressing buttons.

"What was that?"

"A message from Uncle Alistair. Change of plan! He wants to see us. Come on!" She makes a sharp 180-degree turn, and I follow, biting the last remains of my ice-cream cone as quick as I can.

The phone makes that horrible noise again.

"What on earth is that sound?"

"Another message."

"But that weird noise!"

"Oh, that. It's a singing troll. There was a podcast on the net − on, you know, that site Uncle Alistair is putting together, the *Paranormal Database*. Cool, isn't it?"

"A *singing* troll?"

"Yep. Anyway, Uncle Alistair says to pack our bags, we're going to Edinburgh." She waves her phone. "Awesome! I knew he'd want us with him again!"

"If Mum and Dad let us..."

"They will, they will. I'm sure he'll find a good excuse."

"I suppose." We step onto the boardwalk, making our way briskly towards Uncle Alistair's. I'm looking forward to our next adventure, but I leave the sunny beach with a bit of regret.

"So, what did you think of that strange stuff he had in his kitchen? In his... lab-kitchen," I ask Valentina.

"The helmet with the horns, and the shield... and all those bottles."

"No idea. But..." Valentina pauses.

"But what?"

"Remember when he had snow on his head and ice up his nose? And the furs?"

"Yes. He's so up to something."

"Shall we ask him?"

"He'll just make up more daft stories. I don't think he wants to talk about it. Maybe we can try and ask Camilla."

"Ask Camilla what?" Camilla is suddenly floating beside us.

"Hey, welcome back! Where have you been? I missed you!" exclaims Valentina, throwing her arms around Camilla and going right through her.

"Just a floatabout. I went to sea and spent some time with the dolphins – it's great out there..."

I notice that Mrs Armstrong is standing on the doorstep of her hairdresser's shop, looking at us wide-eyed. She's seen Valentina hugging the air and talking to nobody. Well, nobody she can see.

"Valentina!" I whisper, elbowing her and signalling towards Mrs Armstrong, subtly (I hope).

"Welcome back, Luca! I didn't see you all morning!" Valentina tries to recover. We hug awkwardly. Camilla giggles, and Mrs Armstrong keeps staring at us, bewildered.

We hurry away, and let ourselves into Uncle Alistair's house, now known as "Weird HQ". The sign on the door says:

It's a bit of a flimsy cover, more for my mum and dad's benefit than anything else. We're all over the internet, especially now Uncle Alistair has updated our website. Type "Really Weird Removals Company" into Google and you'll quickly see exactly what we do, although there's no mention of me or Valentina. Thankfully, Mum and Dad are completely allergic to technology. My dad actually writes letters to his agent and publishers, I mean *real* letters, stamps and all. He refuses to own a mobile; he uses the home phone. And my mum says that technology is bad for you, because of all the electromagnetic waves.

Sooner or later, though, they'll find out...

"Anyway, Camilla, what we meant to ask you was, those bottles–"

A loud bang, coming from inside, interrupts us.

And an even louder "OUCH!"

"Uncle Alistair! Are you ok?" We run through, only to bump into a very wet, very slimy uncle.

"Blooming big lizards!" he's muttering under his breath, trying to wipe the light-brownish slime off his t-shirt.

"Eurgh! What's that?" I squirm.

"What? Oh, this?" he lifts a hand, a trail of slime joining his fingers to the shirt. "It's jelly. I was making jelly."

"Jelly? That colour?" Valentina stifles a smile.

"It's... mustard jelly."

"Right." We exchange a look.

"Mmmm... tasty!" he licks his finger and winces. "Lovely!"

He's in summer mode, with faded blue shorts and a bright yellow shirt. He looks very tanned. Awfully tanned, for someone who's always indoors working. His nose is actually peeling.

"Are you sunburnt, Uncle Alistair?"

"Am I? Oh yes, a bit. Lovely sunny day!"

"How did you get sunburnt? You're always in here. I've never seen you on the beach."

"I went yesterday, you know, to get a tan. It works wonders for your looks." He glances away.

"You're worried about your *looks*?" Valentina laughs.

"YEAH WELL WE GOT AN EMAIL!" Uncle Alistair booms, all in one breath. He's holding a piece of paper. "Read this." He hands me the sheet.

I suppose we're not to know how he got that weird slime all over himself. It's not jelly, that's for sure. Or how he got so sunburnt. Another Alistair mystery.

I read the printout aloud.

. . . .

To SOS@reallyweirdremovals.com
From NicolJames@coldmail.com

. . . .

Dear Mr Grant,

My name is James Nicol. My wife and I live in a Georgian house in Edinburgh, in Garfield Road. Great location, I hear you say. Fabulous, we say as well. Except that we have something in the cellar. We have no idea *what* it is.

It all started with the light in the basement being shattered in a million pieces. We thought it'd exploded, but now we know better. It's pitch dark down there. I went and bought a torch and tried to go down to repair the light, but as soon as I put a foot on the stairs I heard the most bloodcurdling scream you can imagine—

"Cool!" interrupts Valentina. "A *creature!*"

...it's still ringing in my ear. I needed not one but two stiff drinks to recover from that, and another one at bedtime. And another one around two. We thought of calling the police, but I was scared they'd think we were pulling their leg. What to say? "There's a monster in my basement?"

Since then, we've been hearing strange noises, grunting and grinding of teeth, banging, and the sound of things being shoved against the walls. I tried to go down and have a look, but every time the same shriek stopped me. Then, one day, I steeled myself and made it down three steps. Well, I don't remember anything after that. I know that something hit me and I went out cold–

(Sharp intake of breath from Valentina and Camilla.)

...My wife had to drag me back up. She said that she just heard a scream, a thump (that was my head, I'm afraid) and the sound of heavy footsteps scurrying away.

Thing is, we've been hearing footsteps in the house, too, at night. We've been finding little bones all over the place – bird and mouse bones. Our neighbour's cat has disappeared.

Mr Grant, I fear – no, I'm *sure* – that if we don't do something about it, it'll be us who disappear next.

"It'll be them for sure!" exclaims Valentina, darkly.

We found your website and would be most grateful for your help.

Kind regards,
James and Jean Nicol

"So. What do you think? That, to me, sounds like a troll." Uncle Alistair is very cheerful.

"Yes, to me too," says Valentina knowledgeably.

"We better hurry, it sounds bad," I add, just to make sure that Uncle Alistair intends to take us too.

"Very bad, actually, that troll must be starving, feeding only on mice and birds! We need to take it somewhere it can find bigger prey." Valentina has her priorities right.

"I was thinking more of the human beings!" I laugh.

"Can we leave tonight, Uncle Alistair? asks Valentina.

"Mmmm... well... might rain... homework. 'Nother time," he mumbles.

"What? Rain? Homework? What are you talking about?" asks Valentina.

"It might rain. And you have homework."

"We live in Scotland! We don't mind a bit of rain! And we'll keep up with homework," Valentina exclaims. But I know that rain and homework are not what's worrying Uncle Alistair.

"Do you not want us with you, this time?" I ask, gloomily.

"It's not that. I do want you with me. It's... trolls can be funny business. You know, eating human meat and all that. I just don't want you turned into sausages."

"But you *need* us! And I know you can keep us safe!" Valentina puts a hand on Uncle Alistair's arm. Their eyes meet.

"Can I? You sure?"

"Positive. You always know what to do. You'll return us in one piece."

"One big meatloaf, yes," I can't help saying.

Uncle Alistair looks out of the window for a while. All you can see from the living-room window of Weird HQ is a lamp-post and a tiny dry-cleaners. He stares wistfully at the yellow sign—

Eilean Wash N' Iron Services

– and then he turns around.

"Yes."

"Yes... as in we can come with you?"

"You can. And I'll keep you safe." He wants us with him again! Result!

"Of course you will!" cries Valentina.

I'm a bit more cautious. There's another obstacle ahead.

"Will you convince Mum and Dad to let us go?"

"I'll speak to them. Come on." He strides out of the

place, and we hurry after him. Uncle Alistair has very long legs. When he walks fast, we need to run if we want to keep up. Maybe this is the right time to try and find out about what he's been doing.

"Uncle Alistair," I call, trying to keep up with his pace, "why are you buying tons of fish?"

"How do you know?" He stops suddenly and we bump into his back.

"This is Eilean. Everybody knows everything about everybody!"

"True. It's bait."

"For what?"

"I'll tell you another time."

Something else he'll tell us another time.

"ISABELLA! DUNCAN!" Uncle Alistair calls cheerfully, as we make our way in. My mum is wearing paint-splattered jeans and she has a yellow half-moustache of paint on her face. She's redecorating our guest bedroom. Nonna Rina is coming from Italy to spend the whole summer with us in Eilean, and my mum wants everything to be perfect for her.

We are sent upstairs while Uncle Alistair negotiates with Mum and Dad in the kitchen. We stop halfway, of course, and sit on the stairs, so we can hear what they're saying.

"It's a great opportunity, Duncan. They've never been to the Museum of Scotland." My mum's voice.

"It'd be fun for them," adds Uncle Alistair. "And they'd learn so much. I'll look after them."

"Will you?" Dad's voice is sarcastic. Valentina and I look at each other. This might not work. "You'll look after them like you looked after our parents?"

A moment of silence. Dad has gone for the throat. Poor Uncle Alistair.

"Duncan, Luca will go to high school next year. This museum visit would be great for him..." Mum is trying to smooth things over.

"Maybe *I* want to take them, have you thought of that?"

"And will you?" asks Mum. It's her voice that sounds cold now.

"Well, not in the immediate future... Ach, you know what my writing schedule is, Isabella! Right, you have me in a corner there. Ok. Ok. They can go. But you look after them *for real*, Alistair, do you hear me?"

"Of course I will..." he begins, but Dad walks out of the kitchen. We run upstairs as fast as we can. I'm barely in my room, and pretending to look for my sunglasses, when I hear a knock at the door.

"Come in."

It's Mum. "Sorted. I'll help you pack," she says with a smile.

It'll be a great summer, I know it. This is just the beginning.

II. THEFT OF A MARS BAR THIEF

Alistair Grant's *Scottish Paranormal Database*

Entry Number 1001: Vegetarian troll
Type: Troll
Location: Bettyhill
Date: 2011-present
Details: Mr Shepherd of Bettyhill currently shares his home with a troll. The troll, known as Charlie, occupies the basement and sheds of Mr Shepherd's property. Charlie's diet is uncommon, for a troll. He feeds only on fruit and vegetables, particularly mushrooms. This allows him to dwell undisturbed among the people of Bettyhill.

CAUTION: Do not approach. Though not keen on human meat, Charlie can still attack and maim.

We're standing on the pavement in front of the Nicols' house, a beautiful, grand-looking building. Our eyes are closed, our shoulders hunched, as Uncle Alistair douses us, and himself, in stinky brown liquid from several pickled-onion jars. The smell is revolting.

"You didn't tell us you were going to do this!" I complain. My hair is soaking with the stuff.

"Stop moaning, Luca," snaps Valentina, but I can see she's annoyed too.

"Sorry guys. Everybody knows trolls can't stand pickled onions."

"*How* do they know that?" Valentina is trying to smooth back her wet blonde hair.

"Well, two young lads were coming home from a chip shop in Cromarty, in 1976. A troll attacked and the boys threw the chip bag at him. It had a fish supper and two pickled onions in it. The troll threw up and ran away."

"How do they know it wasn't the fish supper that did the trick?"

"Yes. Well. Could be. We'll find out soon enough."

I can't believe it. We've got pickled onion skins all over us and he's not even sure we won't get eaten. He might just have *seasoned* us!

Uncle Alistair rings the bell. An old lady in a woollen jumper and tartan trousers opens the door. She has a pen in one hand, and a Sudoku in the other.

"Alistair Grant, RWR. I'm here for the thing in the cellar."

"Oh, yes. I'm Mrs Nicol," answers the lady. "Well, you're too late. It's too late for James."

Our faces fall. Oh no! The troll has struck already! Poor Mr Nicol. Mrs Nicol doesn't look too fussed though.

"I'm so sorry, Mrs Nicol," says Uncle Alistair. "Do you have anywhere to go? A relation, a friend? While we sort this for you." He gestures towards the back of the house.

"I'm not going anywhere, young man. I want to see what happens. It's not every day I get this much excitement. Come on in, I've got tea and sandwiches ready. To give you energy," she adds, leading us into the living room. We walk on, leaving a wet stinky trail on the wooden floor.

"Was it raining, outside?" Mrs Nicol asks as she notices our wet hair. Then the smell hits her. She wrinkles her nose. She's too polite to comment, but I can see her wincing.

"Pickled onion. Repels trolls, which is what I think this is," says Uncle Alistair, matter-of-factly. "Mrs Nicol–"

"Call me Jean." She really is very cheery for someone newly widowed.

"Has anybody asked questions... you know, about James? They must have wondered what caused his untimely death..."

"Death?" Jean turns to look at us. "He's not dead! He's at his men's club. He goes every Tuesday. You missed him by twenty minutes."

I'm about to breathe a sigh of relief, when an unearthly growl breaks the silence. We all jump. It's like something from beyond the grave, piercing and deep at the same time. I feel chilled to the bone.

"That's our cat. She ate a whole Mars Bar this morning – stole it off the wee boy next door and ran away with it. She's been in agony since." A ginger cat with a red collar pads slowly across the room, makes an attempt to jump onto an armchair, then tries again, and again, until she (just) makes it. She abandons herself on the cushions and emits another terrible growl. We all wince.

"Have a seat, I'll get your refreshments."

A few minutes (and a few groans from the cat) later, Jean comes back with a plate of sandwiches, tea for herself and Uncle Alistair, and blackcurrant juice for us.

"Jean, I *must* advise you," says Uncle Alistair, in between morsels, "it would be better if you left the house while we do this."

"Out of the question. I've got to see... *it*."

"It could become dangerous."

"I've prepared a small kit, just in case," Jean says with a smile, and produces a handbag from under the coffee table. "Let me see. Yes. A rolling pin," she takes out the objects as she lists them, "a pan, some rope, my perfume – to spray into his eyes – and some mints."

"Mints?" I ask.

"My throat gets awfully dry."

"I'm sorry, Jean, I must insist." Uncle Alistair puts down his empty cup. "You cannot be here while we do what we need to do."

"I know it's dangerous, but James and I –"

"I don't think you know how dangerous this *really* is. Someone I know had a run in with a troll on the outskirts of Dublin two months ago. They found his hat and a sock. And *nothing else*."

Jean's eyes widen.

"I suggest we wait for Mr Nicol to return, and then we put you both into a taxi to wherever you want to go. We'll phone you when we're finished."

"Well, Mr Grant. I suppose you know best. As soon as James is back we'll go to my sister-in-law's house, over in Morningside. What a shame, to miss all the excitement! Our life has become so boring since the Elliotts moved. They were hippies, you know –

strange clothes, long hair, lots of peculiar friends: I could have spent all day watching them from the kitchen window. I had the perfect vantage point. It was so entertaining."

Another growl interrupts her. It's the cat again. She sounds different, though.

A meow. High pitched, sort of strangled.

We all look at the armchair where she's sleeping.

Where she *was* sleeping.

She's disappeared.

Uncle Alistair springs up.

"Where's the cellar?"

"This way!" exclaims Jean, who's gone a bit pale.

"We haven't got the stuff out of the car!" I say, panicked.

"No time!" hisses Uncle Alistair.

We all hurry after Jean. She stops in front of a black wooden door.

"*Here*," she whispers.

All noise has ceased. There's perfect silence. Uncle Alistair takes Jean gently by the shoulders and pulls her behind him. He stands in front of the door.

Suddenly, it opens, just a little... And then shuts again with a bang. Something has been thrown through, nearly hitting Uncle Alistair in the face.

It's a small red collar, with a bell.

The cat's collar.

12. WHERE I NEARLY GET EATEN

Alistair Grant's *Scottish Paranormal Database*

Entry Number 156: Ghostly guardians
Type: Post-mortem manifestation
Location: Seil, Argyll
Date: May 2005
Details: In May 2005, a team of archaeologists digging on the Isle of Seil in Argyll recorded seeing ghostly warriors. The warriors were Pictish in appearance, with long hair and beards, wearing helmets and carrying swords and shields. Many believe such warriors remain in order to guard buried treasure.

Jean gasps and leans down to pick up the collar.

"*Oh, no,*" she whispers sadly.

"Stay back," Uncle Alistair urges her.

We all take a step back.

Nothing happens.

"Luca, Vally."

"*Yes,*" we whisper.

"Go get the equipment from the car." Uncle Alistair throws me the keys to the van.

We run out as quickly and as silently as we can. I open the boot, and take out the white cool-bag with the orange flowers that my mum lent us. She didn't know what it was for, of course. She wouldn't have lent it otherwise. I hand it to Valentina, who runs back in with it.

I'm left to manage the cage. It's really heavy; I'm sweating as I lift it out of the boot. It falls onto the pavement with a CLANK!

A dog-walker, who's just stopped at a bush for a quick wee (the dog, not the walker), looks at me.

"Yes, it *is* a cage, you saw right," I mutter grumpily under my breath. It's just too heavy for me to carry, and we're in a rush. I'm about to run back in and call Valentina, when she runs out again. Together, with great effort, we manage to lift the cage and bring it into the hall.

"*What's happening?*" I whisper to Uncle Alistair, making sure he can see my face and read my lips. "Nothing yet."

"Where's Jean?"

"It got her."

I feel the blood drain from my face. Valentina and I look at each other. She is as pale as I feel.

"Just joking! She's in the living room, I told her to lock herself in." Uncle Alistair smiles mischievously. Valentina rolls her eyes. My heart starts beating again.

"Valentina, you go upstairs, too. Luca, get the cage ready—"

"I'm not going upstairs!"

"Do what I say! Now!" whispers Uncle Alistair, loudly and urgently, as he opens the cool-bag and takes out a few dead, plucked chickens. He scatters them in a trail from the cellar door to the cage, with the last one right inside it.

"Ok, ok!" Valentina grudgingly makes her way up the stairs. She crouches on the landing, her face between the bars of the banister.

"Everybody still. Cage ready?"

I nod. I'm holding its door open, ready to shut it as soon as we get the troll inside.

I can feel my heart thumping like it's going to jump out of my chest. There's perfect silence, except for our heavy breathing...

Then Uncle Alistair opens the cellar door.

"HELLO-HOOOOO!" he booms.

Nothing.

"HELLOOOO-HOOOOOOO!!! THERE'S FOOD HERE!"

A thumping sound, heavy footsteps up the stairs, a terrible smell – strong enough to cover even the pickled onions – and there he is, emerging from the darkness of the cellar. The troll.

"A moor troll!" booms Uncle Alistair. He seems delighted.

The troll is dressed in what look like rabbit skins; he has a huge head and huge feet and hands, and his skin is all leathery, with a greenish-yellowish hue. He has a few straggly yellow hairs on the top of his head and pale, nearly white eyes. He blinks in the light, towering over Uncle Alistair – he must be at least seven feet tall.

"There you are! See? I was right. It *is* a troll!" shouts Uncle Alistair triumphantly.

Great, I think. You were right, yes. Hooray.

After a few interminable seconds of blinking, the troll throws himself on the first thing he sees:

Uncle Alistair. Uncle Alistair ducks, covering his head with his hands. Valentina screams, I'm about to run to his aid, when the troll stops in mid-air.

He scrunches up his face and makes a gagging noise, then roars in anger.

"I smell bad, don't I? But look! This is good! THIS SMELLS GOOD!" shouts Uncle Alistair, grabbing a chicken by the leg and waving it in front of the troll's face. "FOOD!"

The troll roars and grabs the chicken, and then bites a great big chunk off it. I can see his teeth: huge, pointed, black. Slowly, deliberately, he devours it, making a horrible, disgusting crunching noise. I feel my stomach churn. I could throw up, but I stop myself.

"There – there's more! Good boy, good boy!" Uncle Alistair entices him on, and the creature grabs the next chicken on the trail and starts chewing. Then the next one. And the next one.

And then the troll sees me.

His pale eyes are looking straight at me. My legs give way. I have to hold on to the cage to stay standing.

"LUCA!" I hear Valentina's terrified scream, and it seems to come from far away.

The troll crouches slightly to gain momentum. I know what he's about to do: he pounces towards me, all seven feet of him. I fold over myself, hiding my face, praying for my life.

When he's near enough to smell the pickled onions, he stops in his tracks, just a few inches away from my face. I can smell him, too: a mouldy, revolting stench that seems to come from the depth of a bog.

The troll scrunches up his face again and makes the same gagging noises, and again he howls in anger.

It's my moment.

"Here boy... here..." my voice is coming out all small. I grab a chicken and lift it up, dangling it in front of him. I'm shaking so much that the chicken trembles too. I throw it into the cage.

The troll puts his head through the cage door. Not one, but *two* plucked chickens lie inside. He can't resist. He's taking a step... I'm ready to close the door and lock it, when...

"Jean, I'm hooooome!"

The front door opens. And there's James Nicol.

It takes James a few seconds to grasp the situation. He blinks, just like the troll did when he came out of the dark cellar. In front of him there's a huge, foul-smelling, seven-foot-tall creature who's watching him like he's a plate of haggis, neeps and tatties. With a whisky sauce and all.

James screams. I scream. Valentina screams. Uncle Alistair screams. The troll growls.

We all run towards James, with different intentions: three of us want to save him, one of us wants to eat him.

Thing is, the one who wants to eat him is a lot faster than us, and his legs are a lot longer. He'll bite James's head off before we can reach them...

"AAAAAAAHOOOOOOOOOO!"

All of a sudden, the troll stops, takes his foot in his hand and starts hopping. Jean has come out of the living room, the handbag in one hand and the rolling pin in the other.

"Do. Not. Touch. My. Husband," she says, in a low deep voice. Her eyes are blazing.

We are frozen. Jean lets the rolling pin fall as she rummages in the bag. She takes out a small bottle, then jumps around a bit until her hand is even with the troll's face, which is lowered because he holds his sore foot.

"Take this!" A hissing sound. Jean sprays her perfume right in the troll's eyes. He growls again, covering his face with his hands. He's now blind and rolling on the floor in pain.

"And *this*!" Jean takes out her final weapon, the frying pan. With a scream you wouldn't think could come out of an old lady, she raises the pan and lowers it with all her might on the troll's head. There's a resounding BANG. He's out cold.

"RESULT!" says Valentina jubilantly.

James slides against the wall, and sits down with a sigh.

"Help me, Luca!" Uncle Alistair and I drag the troll into the cage and lock the door. We both sit on the floor as well, exhausted.

"Mint?" says Jean.

"We can't set it free, it's too dangerous! It *eats* people!"

The troll is still unconscious, but is starting to move a little. We're about to cover his cage in sheets, and take him out into the van.

Uncle Alistair's plan is to drive somewhere north, as far from civilisation as we can, and free him on a wild moor to feed on wildcats and deer. But I have my doubts that he'll stick to animals.

"Uncle Alistair, you've seen him in action. Sooner or later he'll get someone."

"Yes, perhaps. Kill him, then."

"WHAT?"

"Kill him. There you are." Uncle Alistair hands me his dagger. Yes, he keeps a dagger in his sock, believe it or not. Just in case.

I take it, my hand shaking.

"Luca! You can't!" I hear Valentina's voice from somewhere far away. The wind is roaring in my ears.

Where? Where do I hit, to *kill*?

The troll's eyes open. He sees me and the dagger, and curls up. He lifts his head to one side, and we look at each other.

His pale eyes are full of terror, and... resignation. Like he knows he's about to die.

That second, that precise exact second when my eyes meet the troll's, I know that I can't do it. That I can't kill anyone, anything. *Ever*.

I hand the dagger back to my uncle, who gazes at me with something very similar to pride.

I have no words to describe the stench in the van on the way back. A mixture of mouldy troll and pickled onions. I think I'll never eat again.

We drive north for hours to the middle of nowhere: a place Uncle Alistair chose for its remoteness.

When we get there it's past midnight, and it's pitch black because there are no lamp-posts or houses for miles around. The sky is clear and covered in a million stars.

Uncle Alistair gives us another drenching in pickled-onion liquid to make sure that the troll won't attack us, then hands out a torch each.

We stand in a semicircle as he opens the cage. The troll blinks at the harsh light of our torches, and hides his face in his hands. He's scared.

"*Come on. Come out. It's ok,*" I whisper. He looks up, tentatively. It dawns on him that he's being set free. He jumps out of the van, and my heart is in my throat as he stands there among us, all seven feet of him.

Then something weird happens.

The troll puts his hand in the rabbit skin he has around his hips, and he takes something out. Without a sound, he extends his huge pale-green hand, curled up in a fist, towards me. Then he unfurls his fist to reveal a little shiny thing inside. I can't make out what it is.

Cautiously, I take the object from his hand.

The troll looks at me, then at Valentina, then at Alistair, as if he's saying goodbye. He turns around and takes a huge leap into the darkness.

Valentina and Uncle Alistair step beside me to look at the troll's gift. It's a small medallion, beautifully carved with waves and spirals. It looks like it's made of pure iron, and very, very ancient.

"Troll treasure," says Uncle Alistair. "Very rare. Keep it safe."

I put it around my neck and tuck it inside my sweater, proudly. Then we climb back into the van and try to snatch a few hours' sleep while Uncle Alistair drives back, across the dark moors.

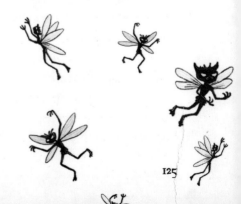

13. SOMEONE LIKE US

"Another sunny day," I say to myself, as I open the blind in my room, and then the window, to breathe in the fresh salty sea air.

The summer has truly arrived in Eilean. Hordes of tourists are walking up and down the main street and stopping on the pier to take pictures of the seals, and the beach is full of families swimming and sunbathing. Heaven.

We're going to spend the whole summer at home. Sometimes we fly to Italy to see my mum's family, but this year Nonna Rina has come to us instead.

It's barely nine o'clock, but I know for sure that my mum and Nonna are already cooking. Nonna Rina loves anything to do with food: food shopping, reading cookbooks, watching cookery programmes on the TV and, of course, cooking. She's always concerned that we are too thin, and feeds us huge portions at every meal.

"*Ciao Luca, vuoi la colazione?*" she says with a smile as I step into the kitchen. It means, hello and do I want my breakfast?

"*Si Nonna, grazie!*" Mmmm. Home-made bread and honey, brioche and chocolate milk. Valentina is already sitting at the table, tucking in happily.

"Morning, children." Mum comes in from the shop, laden with grocery bags. "I met your Uncle Alistair on the way back. He says if you want to, go over and see him this morning."

Great! Something's up. A new adventure.

I look at Valentina. She's smiling from ear to ear. We've only been back from Edinburgh two days. In spite of several showers, our hair still smells of pickled onion, which we had to explain by saying we stayed above a fish shop and ate a lot of the stuff. We'd also stopped at the Museum of Scotland quickly on the way to the Nicols', to gather some brochures and postcards and a few pocket-money toys, so we could get away with our cover story.

Valentina and I eat breakfast as quickly as we can, managing to consume everything on the table, and then we run out.

"*Ciao Nonna, ciao Mamma!*"

"But they haven't eaten a thing!" I hear my Nonna saying. Valentina and I look at each other and laugh. We could never eat enough for Nonna.

Both Valentina and I are wearing t-shirts and shorts; it's great to step out and feel the sun and the fresh air on my skin. We run all the way to Weird HQ, and we're breathless when we get there.

"GOOD MORNING CHILDREN!" booms Uncle Alistair, loud as ever. He's at the computer, and the *Paranormal Database* is on the screen. Camilla is lying on the sofa, reading a book. She can't hold the book, or turn the pages, of course, because her hands just go through them, but, she's explained, she can move things with her mind. Only very light things though, like paper or sand or feathers.

"Come into the kitchen, I'll make sausage rolls," shouts Uncle Alistair. We follow him. "I got a call this morning," he begins, while cutting and buttering bread. "Luca, sausage roll?"

"No thanks, I couldn't eat a thing more," I reply. Not after Nonna's breakfast.

"Yes, please!" says Valentina, and bites into one.

"Anyway. Two mermaids were spotted in the river Clyde last night, in Glasgow. It's far, far too crowded a waterway for them. We need to go get them and take them somewhere safe."

"If someone else sees them, they might be taken to a zoo, or worse!" Valentina's brown eyes are full of concern.

"Don't forget that very few people can See them. Most people only see some big fish. The mermaids' real danger is not so much being spotted, but the motor boats." Valentina gasps. "There's a lot of river traffic on the Clyde. Imagine the mermaids as people with not much experience of cars wandering in the middle of a motorway. We need to leave as soon as possible."

"They'll never let us. Nonna has just arrived, she wants to spend time with us..." says Valentina, torn between wanting time with Nonna and the adventure in prospect.

"How long will she be here for?"

"Three weeks."

"What if I return you by tomorrow at lunchtime?"

"It's worth a try" I say, but I doubt it will work.

"Why not? It's a great opportunity to take Nonna to Glasgow. We can go shopping. The Buchanan Galleries, lunch in Prince's Square..." My mum's eyes are shining.

Disaster. How, how are we going to handle this? How can we save the mermaids with Mum and Nonna in tow?

It's impossible.

"That's settled, then," says Uncle Alistair, beaming.

Is it? I look at him disbelievingly.

He winks at me.

A couple of hours later, we are ready. Uncle Alistair, Mum, Nonna Rina, Valentina and I, all packed up like sardines in the van, with Camilla floating alongside us. We can hardly close the boot for bags. We all have a small one each, but Uncle Alistair is bringing a heavy, clunking trunk, which, I suspect, contains more than a change of underwear and a toothbrush.

On the ferry to Glasgow we stand in a line on the deck, looking out for dolphins and seals. Nonna is wrapped up in a woollen coat and kitted in a hat and scarf, drawing a few amused glances from the tourists in shorts and t-shirts. When my Italian family come over to Eilean, they always look like they're going on an Arctic expedition.

Uncle Alistair is standing a bit away from us, making phone calls. The wind is blowing hard on the deck, so I can't hear what he's saying.

"He's spending a lot of time on the phone," I say to Valentina. She shrugs.

"You just never know what he's up to!" she replies philosophically.

Glasgow is busier than ever, this lovely summer evening. On the way to the hotel, my mum and Nonna are beside themselves with excitement, planning all they're going to do tomorrow in the big city, and I'm enthralled at the hustle and bustle of the streets in the evening. The shops are open, the sky is still light and it seems that half the city are out enjoying themselves.

Valentina and I are so excited to be staying in a hotel. We stay up as long as we can, chatting with Camilla, but soon we're too tired to stay awake. I'm in deep sleep when a sudden noise wakes me with a jolt.

"LUCA! WAKE UP!"

I sit up at once. Uncle Alistair is in our room, and he's standing beside my bed, fully clothed, with his big black clunking bag in one hand and his phone in the other.

"What is it?" I groan.

"Time to go. Come on, get dressed. I'll help you downstairs."

"Eurgh..." I'm really tired after the long day. Valentina must be too, but she shows no sign of it, getting dressed quickly, her eyes shining in anticipation.

My head spins from the rude awakening as we head out. I hope and pray that Mum and Nonna won't notice we're gone, or we'll be in the worst trouble of our lives.

We drive to the river in our blue van. The night is warm and windless; the city is now deserted, except for occasional late-night party-goers. Orange light from the lamp-posts reflects on the black streets, and the sky is tinged with orange too, not like our beautiful black velvety sky on Eilean.

We get to the river-bank. The Clyde is grey, flowing slowly, its waters completely opaque. I can't see how we'll ever find the mermaids. Do we just sit here and hope they appear?

We watch intently while Uncle Alistair opens his huge clunky bag and takes out a few blue-ish bottles – they're the ones I'd seen in his fridge! He lines them up on the pavement, carefully, one by one.

Next out of the bag is something that looks like a whistle. Uncle Alistair puts it in his pocket, ready for use.

Finally, he presses a button on his phone. The screen glows green in the darkness.

"We're here. Ok," says Uncle Alistair in what he thinks is a whisper, but is really quite loud. It's so funny when he *tries* to speak quietly.

A few minutes of silence. We stand, waiting.

Then, all of a sudden, we're blinded by a strong white light. It's so bright that I can't make out any shapes, though I shade my eyes with my hands. Slowly, as I get used to the glare, I make out the shape of a van, a black one, three times the size of ours. Two shadows appear, silhouetted against the light. I blink, over and over again. It's a boy and a girl, and they're walking towards us.

Uncle Alistair greets them, his arms outstretched.

"Sorley! Mairi!" he exclaims, hugging them.

"Alistair, great to see you again," says Sorley.

"These are Vally and Luca, my niece and nephew."

"Cool, nice to meet you." Sorley smiles.

"Nice to meet you, guys," echoes Mairi.

"Wow!" whispers Valentina in an awed voice.

"Wow!" echoes Camilla. They're mesmerised by Mairi.

She's about fifteen and has bright red hair tied back in a ponytail and huge shiny grey eyes. She's wearing jeans tucked into big boots, a waterproof jacket, and she has all sorts of equipment hanging off her: binoculars around her neck, a rope under her arm and a walkie-talkie around her wrist. She looks exactly like the action heroine Valentina and Camilla long to be, and her outfit is like one they'd invent on Valentina's DS. No wonder they're gazing at her like they're dreaming.

Sorley is slightly older – he must be about eighteen. He looks so cool, like he should be on TV, or in a music video. He's wearing skinny jeans, a zip-up fleece and yellow baseball boots. His black hair is long and windswept, and his eyes are a deep ocean-blue. When I grow up, I want to be *exactly* like him.

He's carrying a big black bag under his arm, and he's smiling brightly. He seems delighted to see us. Mairi, instead, is scowling a bit. She's not giving anything away, which, in a way, makes her even cooler.

"Bait ready, then." Sorley puts his bag down on the concrete carefully, just beside Uncle Alistair's bottles.

Bait, I think, remembering that was what Uncle Alistair said to me when I asked him about the fish he got from Donald.

"The best fish juice in the Western Isles. With a touch of... something else," Uncle Alistair replies. Sorley smiles and nods. He knows what Uncle Alistair is talking about. Some secret ingredient, probably.

The next ten minutes rush by amid frantic activity. Valentina, Camilla and I stand fascinated, watching them work. Sorley zips open his bag and takes out a wetsuit. He quickly takes his clothes off, revealing trunks underneath, and slips the wetsuit on. He disappears into the van, re-emerging with two oxygen tanks and a mask. Meanwhile, Mairi is standing at the edge of the concrete wall with her arm raised. The thing around her wrist, which I thought was a walkie-talkie, starts beeping: a rhythmic, quiet beep.

"What is that?" whispers Camilla.

"I don't know, but I want one!" sighs Valentina.

"*There they are*," whispers Mairi, as the beeping gets louder. They? Is that the mermaids?

"What's that at your wrist, Mairi?" I ask.

"A radar," she replies, without looking at me.

Sorley opens the sliding door at the side of the van, while Mairi disappears into the driving cabin.

"She's driving! She's DRIVING THE VAN!" Valentina is beside herself. "I'm SO going to ask Uncle Alistair to teach me to drive."

"He certainly will!" exclaims Camilla. Yeah, right, I think to myself.

They stand close to each other, admiring Mairi as she pulls and lifts and presses buttons in the cabin.

There's a small metallic *whirr*, and something like a forklift folds out inside the van. Sorley and Uncle Alistair jump in and slide something square and transparent onto the metal arms. Another *whirr*, and the arms slide out and come to rest slowly on the pavement, then retreat.

The big square object looks like a huge aquarium. I'm getting a clearer idea of what's about to happen.

Mairi turns off the lights, and for a second everything is dark again, until she jumps down from the van with a hand torch.

"Camilla!" whispers Uncle Alistair, and gives her a nod. Camilla knows what to do. She floats down towards the black waters, her translucent little body becoming smaller and smaller as she glides downriver.

"Whenever you're ready," says Sorley to my uncle.

"Luca, Vally?"

"YES!" says Valentina excitedly. She's so delighted to be called upon, that she's nearly jumping up and down.

"Pour the bottles into the water."

We kneel down, and pour the contents of the bottles into the black river, one by one. The liquid coming out is blue-ish, viscous and smells strongly of seaweed. Yes, if anything looks – and smells – like mermaid bait, this does.

From my kneeling position I see Sorley's black-clad, wet-suited feet beside me, and I gasp slightly when he sits on the bank and jumps into the water.

Mairi is standing on the edge again, her arm raised and her radar beeping steadily. Uncle Alistair is by her side, blowing his metal whistle. No sound is coming out of it.

A few minutes pass when everybody is still. Silence, but for the rhythmic beeping of Mairi's radar. Uncle Alistair keeps blowing the whistle noiselessly. A little fluorescent light, marking Sorley's position, is floating on the still waters.

Suddenly, I can make out a silver glow in the distance, coming closer. It's Camilla on her way back.

"They're nearly here!" she announces.

We hold our breath. The radar on Mairi's wrist is beeping faster, faster, faster, until the beeps merge into a thin, high-pitched sound. At that point, she switches it off, and she switches her torch off too. Sorley's light has also disappeared. Everything is dark and still and quiet.

"*Look!*" mouths Uncle Alistair.

Two heads and two silvery tails appear and disappear rhythmically in the black waters, swimming closer and closer to us. They are now against the concrete wall, dipping their heads into the pools of Uncle Alistair's blue liquid, lapping it up. Their long hair floats on the water like seaweed. It's too dark to make out their faces.

Then Sorley switches his underwater torch back on, and I see them.

14. WHERE I NEARLY DROWN

The mermaids turn towards Sorley, who's floating in the soft light of his underwater torch. Their skin has a light blue-green hue; their hair looks like seaweed and it's all tangled up. Their eyes are deep, deep black, and full of fear. They have beautiful faces – human in every way, but with elongated eyes and full lips that are vaguely fish-like.

"Don't worry," says Sorley kindly. "We're not going

to hurt you." The mermaids seem to be listening intently. One of them tips her head on one side. Sorley's tone is warm and soothing: "It's dangerous here. The river is very busy. You'll end up hurt. If you come with us, we'll take you somewhere safe."

The mermaids look at each other, and then disappear underwater. Valentina and I gasp.

"They've gone!" whispers Valentina, alarmed.

"They're just talking it over." Mairi's tone suggests this is obvious and we don't know anything.

And indeed, after a few minutes, the mermaids re-emerge and swim near Sorley, warily. I think they're coming round.

"We'll get you up on land," Sorley starts explaining, when a low buzzing interrupts him. I barely register the sound, but Mairi gasps softly in the darkness, and then Uncle Alistair shouts at the top of his voice:

"WATCH OUT!"

Two searing white lights are bouncing over the water at full throttle. It's a speedboat, fast and deadly, swallowing mile after mile of river – there's nothing we can do, there's nothing Sorley can do – it's upon them. It cuts through the river right where they were floating, leaving behind only darkness and the low buzzing sound fading away. Mairi is the first to shake herself.

"Sorley! SORLEY!" she screams, bending over the parapet.

"Mairi..." Uncle Alistair has a hand on her shoulder. My heart is beating so fast I think my chest will explode.

"Sorley!" she calls again, and her voice sounds hoarse and broken. It can't be. It can't be...

We all peer in the black waters. They're terribly, terribly still. I can hear Valentina's ragged breath, and Mairi's soft sobs.

"Uncle Alistair! What are we going to do? Surely there's something we can do..." I ask, and then, seeing his stricken expression, I realise that things are bad. Really, really bad.

Then a squeak, a strange sound – something between a dolphin's voice and the deep alien song of a whale – breaks the silence. It's a mermaid.

"I'm hurt," she's saying.

Wait a minute.

I understand their language?

"The mermaids!" shouts Uncle Alistair.

"Sorley! Sorley!" call Mairi and Valentina, their hope rekindled.

"Stupid light! It went off!" A human voice comes from the water. It's Sorley! He's alive!

"Sorley!" I can see tears shining on Mairi's cheeks.

"I'm fine! Phew, that was close! I'm going to look for the mermaids," he calls, waving his hand in the semi-darkness. I can barely make out his floating shape; the speedboat must have broken his torch.

"We heard one calling!" Uncle Alistair shouts in Sorley's direction. And she's hurt, I want to say, but how can I explain I actually understood her words? I look at Uncle Alistair sideways. Would he know that I might understand the mermaids?

"*There they are!*" whispers Mairi, pointing down to the water. Two green heads are swimming towards Sorley, very close to each other.

And again, the pitiful sad cry of the injured one. "Help!" she's imploring. She's holding onto her friend, arms around her neck.

"Are you hurt?" Sorley asks. And then, louder: "Mairi! Get the first aid kit!"

"Sure!" Mairi calls back, with an edge to her voice that makes me think she's actually saying, "Thank goodness you're alive!"

"Please let us help you. Let us take you up on land and see to your wounds." Sorley reaches out to them. "You'll still be in the water, and we'll take you somewhere with no motorboats and no human beings. Well, just a few. A few like us."

The mermaids look at him for a long still minute, the injured one resting her head on her friend's shoulder. They confer briefly, in voices so low that I can't make out what they're saying. But they seem to decide to trust us; they float closer to Sorley.

"Yes. We'll come with you," they say.

I heard that!

I can't help gasping.

"You ok?" Valentina nudges me.

"Yes. Yes. It's just that..."

"Shhhh!" Uncle Alistair scolds, and I have to be quiet.

Sorley waves with his outstretched arms, and Mairi and Uncle Alistair spring into action. The aquarium has wheels, so it's relatively easy to move, and they manage to get it to the river wall. It's secured with a thick rope to a hoist inside the van.

Then everything happens very fast. Mairi and Uncle Alistair push the aquarium over the edge and, using a pulley, gently lower it. I'm standing in the wrong place. The rope hits my arm, I lose my balance, and I fall into the black water.

Water is everywhere – in my nose, in my mouth, over and around me. It's so dark, and so cold, I can't see anything and I can't breathe. I feel like my heart has stopped.

"LUCAAAAAA!"

I hear distant voices but they're too muffled to grasp words, apart from my name. I come to the surface briefly, gasping for air, and I'm underwater again – breathing in water, suffocating... I feel a big splash, and there's someone beside me – I open my eyes underwater – it's Valentina! We'll both drown! I splash and writhe, trying to stay afloat – I can swim, but the water is so icy, so black. Panic hits me. Valentina throws her arms out to meet mine, and we hold hands... I'm running out of air. I can't see, I can't think... My lungs are full of water – will I breathe again?

And then two strong arms embrace me. They're cold, and a bit slippery. I feel seaweed on my face, on my neck, on my hands – but it's not seaweed, it's the mermaid's hair. I can make out her face, her scaly skin, her black eyes. She's singing for me. I think she's trying to reassure me. We look at each other for an instant. It's beautiful and surreal.

"Valentina…" I try to tell them, but when I open my mouth I just swallow more water, and it all goes black. I feel the mermaid tying her arms around my waist, and holding me close to her face. She puts her lips on mine, and blows air into my waterlogged lungs. Then she lets me go… and I can breathe!

I can breathe underwater! My lungs are full of air again. Oxygen makes its way back into my system and I can see. I turn frantically left and right, looking for my sister. Why, oh why did she jump after me? She's nowhere! A few silvery fish dart in front of my face, and seaweed wraps around my arms. I try to hold the mermaid's hand, but it's so slippery, and she's not looking at me anymore, she's looking up to the surface, where a bright light is shining.

Valentina…

Suddenly I make out a small shape, emerging from the darkness right in front of me. It's her! Her eyes are closed, and her face is so white… I hold her close, and I can't feel her chest rising, I can't feel her breathing. She's *not* breathing!

"Don't worry. We'll help you," the mermaid whispers.

I try to reply, but water enters my lungs again. The mermaid's kiss has lost its effect. I can no longer breathe underwater. I'm drifting away…

I wake up spitting water. I'm shivering violently.

"Valentina!" I splutter. "Valentina!"

"She's fine, she's here!" A girl's voice. Mairi.

I turn my head and see Mairi, Valentina and Camilla kneeling beside me. Valentina is soaking wet, her hair falling in long fair strands over her shoulders.

"You nearly drowned, you silly beggar!" she shouts.

"So did you! You crazy girl! Why did you... why did you jump—" I cough up more water.

"Shhhh... breathe!" Mairi urges me. Her face looks softer, kinder than before.

"The mermaids saved me." I manage to say. I sit up, spluttering more water.

"They saved me too," whispers Valentina. "They sort of... sort of kissed me, and then I could breathe underwater. For a wee while. You were out of it for ages, Luca, I thought you were dead..." She's on the verge of tears.

"Where are they? The mermaids?"

"Sorley and Alistair are sorting them out. Securing the aquarium for the journey, and all that," Mairi reassures us.

"You'll catch your death in these wet clothes. But I didn't think to bring a change. I never thought you'd be in the water!" Uncle Alistair is striding towards us.

"Sorry..." I murmur.

"And your sister, jumping after you! So we had not one, but *two* children to save! Terrible, terrible. But you're alright now."

"I'm not a child," grunts Valentina.

"Uncle Alistair..." Maybe I should tell him about

the way I could understand the mermaids' language.

"Later, Luca. We'd better get you safely back to the hotel."

"Ok."

Maybe I won't tell him at all. Maybe I dreamt it?

"See you guys soon, then. Thanks for helping," says Sorley to my uncle.

"You'll certainly see us again soon. I have to show Luca and Vally what you do up there in Loch Glas."

Loch Glas? Is that where the mermaids are going?

"Can I say goodbye to the mermaids?" I ask.

"Be quick, Luca."

They are sitting in the aquarium, arms around each other. One of them has a nasty bruise down her side, and a long strip of missing scales down her tail. It looks painful, but it could have been much worse.

"Don't worry. If Uncle Alistair trusts Sorley and Mairi, you can too." This is what I want to say, but something strange comes out of my lips. A singing sound, an undersea sound. The mermaid language.

How on earth do I know it? When did I learn it?

One of the mermaids puts her hand against the glass. It's webbed, and blue-grey like the rest of her body. I lift my arm, and put my hand against hers on the other side of the glass. We stay like that for a moment.

"*Thank you*," I whisper, and a strange sound of foamy waves, windswept rocks and cold depths comes out.

"I hope to see you again," she replies.

"Me too."

The van sways gently. Mairi has come up, and she's standing at my shoulder, her thoughtful face tipped on one side.

"You're cool, Luca Grant," she says without looking at me.

I climb down, and the van drives away, taking Mairi, Sorley and the mermaids out of the city.

I'm lost in thought as we drive back to the hotel. I can't believe what just happened. I can't believe I can *speak mermaid!*

I think I'll keep it to myself, for now.

It's nearly dawn as we step into the hotel. We sneak into our room. It's such a relief to get out of my wet clothes. Valentina and I shiver together.

"I'm starving," she says.

"So am I."

Only a couple of hours until Mum and Nonna wake up, then we can have the biggest breakfast on the menu.

Besides my hunger, I feel so much better. The freezing cold leaves me. We fall asleep, exhausted.

"Wakey wakey! Time to go and explore Glasgow!"

My mum sounds horribly cheery. It's half past seven. I'm shattered. Valentina is still dead to the world.

"Come on you two. Get dressed. We'll see you in the restaurant in ten minutes."

I'm so tired I feel sick. I drag myself out of bed...

and then I see wet muddy clothes still lying on the floor! My mum can't have noticed them. I hang them over chairs. Hopefully they'll dry a little.

Valentina has purple shadows under her eyes. We drag ourselves out.

"CHILDREN! HELLO! DID YOU SLEEP WELL?" booms Uncle Alistair as we walk into the restaurant.

He's *loud*. Too loud for someone who had two hours' sleep.

Valentina is about to attack the bacon and eggs, when my mum gasps.

"Luca!"

"Yes!" I exclaim, jolted. My nerves are a bit frayed.

"What's that?" She lifts my arm. There's a nasty-looking purple bruise running from my elbow to my wrist.

Valentina stops chewing.

"Oh, that. I bumped into the wardrobe."

"That's some bump, Luca. And you're all scratched..."

She touches my neck. Uh oh. I hadn't noticed that.

"What happened?"

"I had left my diary in the van..." I scramble. "I wanted to write before sleeping. So I went down to get it. It wasn't dark or anything, it was just past nine o'clock. I lost my footing and fell."

"Poor you! We'll get you some arnica cream. Come on, everybody. Glasgow awaits us!"

I take a deep breath. Valentina starts eating again.

We got away with it.

I hate lying to my mum, but if I think of the mermaids – the way we talked, their black eyes and blue skin, and that incredible seaweed hair...

No, I can't give up on the RWR. I just can't.

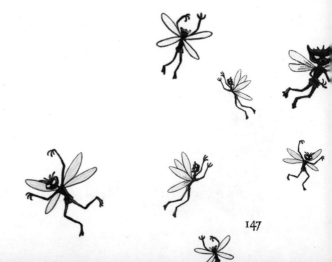

AUTUMN

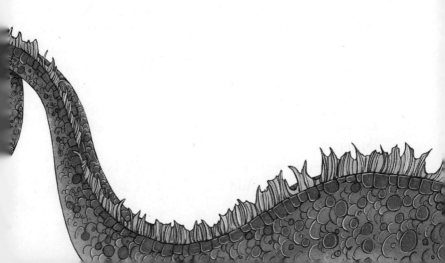

15. FROM THE SEA

It's been a beautiful Hebridean summer, with the sun shining, the sea blue-green and smooth. It's now August – technically still summer, but we can feel the days getting fresher already. There's a chilly wind blowing on the holiday makers, and people have started to cover up. Nonna Rina will be heading home to Italy soon. She's been cooking up extra food and storing it in the freezer so there's no danger we'll starve during the next months.

Next week we'll be back in school. Not Eilean Primary anymore: Adil and I will be starting high school. I'm a bit nervous about it, though since Camilla terrified Gary I've had no more trouble from him and his gang. Still, everything will be new.

There'll be no more trips away with Uncle Alistair for a while. Mum and Dad say I must concentrate on my studies now. I suppose they've got a point, but I'm disappointed anyway.

Relishing our last week of freedom, Valentina and I head out for a morning wander and drop in on Donald down at the harbour. Valentina always hopes to find some weird creatures in the fishermen's catch.

"Donald?"

"Yes, pet?"

"Have you ever seen a mermaid?"

I nudge her. She shouldn't be talking about these things, in case people start to suspect there's something not normal about RWR.

"No, not me. But a friend of my cousin, over in Castlebay, did. Well, he said he did. Willie Grant was his name. Wait a minute. He was a relation of yours, wasn't he?"

"My dad's uncle was called Willie. He died in the war."

"Yes, that one. He used to See things. Some said he was a bit... you know, soft in the head. I suppose he should have stopped talking about those kind of things, because folk were laughing at him. But he kept trying to convince everyone that what he said was true. Mermaids, sea serpents, the lot. Sailor stories, you know? He was in the Navy..." Donald shrugs his shoulders.

Poor Willie Grant. Nobody believed him. He had nobody to share his gift with.

I wonder if that's why Dad has kept these stories from us. He didn't want people to think our relatives were weird, or mad.

"Why, have you seen a mermaid?" Donald is teasing Valentina.

"No way, nothing like that!"

"No, not even a bit!" We laugh nervously.

"Never saw a mermaid in my life!" adds Valentina, just to make sure Donald is convinced.

"Neither have I. Or a... a..."

I freeze.

"*Luca?*" whispers Valentina, following my gaze. Then she gasps.

"Oh, look!" says Donald. "A seal. Isn't she lovely?"

"Help me, Luca!" says the seal. But it's not a seal. It's a selkie.

I can't speak, I can't move a muscle. Surely the selkie knows that I can't speak to her in front of Donald and the other sailors.

"Come down to the beach. I need help. Please..." she adds. Her eyes are amazing. A bit like the mermaids', but blacker, softer.

"See you later, Donald. We're going down to the beach for a bit," chirps Valentina in a shrill voice. I still can't speak.

"Right so, see you later." He waves.

We run as fast as we can along the sand to the rock pools. There are a few children playing nearby, but we manage to find a secluded corner.

After a few minutes, the selkie emerges. She's leaning on a rock, so we can only see half of her.

She looks like a normal woman, with very black hair and very white skin. The thing that gives her away is her eyes. No human being has eyes as black and as shiny as that. Seal's eyes.

"There you are. Hello, Luca, hello Valentina."

"How do you know my name?" asks Valentina.

"I've seen you and your brother playing on the beach many times. I even spoke to your brother, once."

"You never told me!" exclaims Valentina, outraged. "You saw a *selkie* and you never told me!"

"I wasn't sure it had happened *for real*..." I protest. A shiver creeps down my spine, as I recall something that happened long ago, something uncertain, that I had chosen to forget...

One day, when I must have been about four years old, I think, we had a family picnic on the beach. It was chilly. Dad was there with us, which rarely happened, and that made the day stand out.

Mum and Dad were playing with Valentina, and I'd gone to explore the rock pools. I was looking at the little shrimps swimming about in the shallow water, when I felt someone watching me. Strange, I know, but I just felt it, somehow.

I lifted my head and saw a pair of black, liquid eyes gazing at me from the swell. At first I thought it was a seal, but then I saw her long black hair floating in the water, and her arms, crossed in front of her as she leant on a rock. We looked at each other for a bit in silence, then she spoke.

"What's your name?"

"Luca. And yours?"

"Mary Kenny."

"Are you not cold?"

"No. The water feels great." At that moment, someone stepped onto the rocks behind me. "I'll see you again, *Luca*," she whispered quickly, and disappeared into the sea, just like that – like it had all been a dream.

As she dived back, I saw her body.

It didn't look right. It didn't look *human*. I couldn't make sense of it. And that meant although the strange woman was nice to me, I still felt scared. I never told anyone about what I saw, and I decided, without really thinking about it, to just forget it.

But it had happened.

"You're Mary Kenny." My voice sounds a bit croaky.

"You know each other?" gasps Valentina.

"From way back!" laughs Mary. "Can you See me too, Valentina? For what I am?"

"Yes. I'm lucky that way."

"You're lucky indeed. There are many wonders in this sea that most people will never be able to know..."

"I wish I could see *everything*!" says Valentina.

"You will. It's in your eyes... you'll unravel many mysteries," smiles Mary.

"Yes," Valentina agrees, perfectly confident as ever.

"I called to you because I need your help," says Mary.

"Of course!" we say in unison.

"I need to come on land. I've lost something very precious to me."

"Oh... What is it?"

"My mother's wedding ring. A wee boy has it. Euan McAnena."

"Oh yeah. He's our cousin. Everybody here is our cousin, in one way or another! Maybe even you," says Valentina.

"Maybe. Euan collects treasures from the beach. Sometimes I help him. I leave shells in the rock pools where he can find them. And other things... things from the shipwrecks out at sea – golden coins and jewels..."

"Wow." I can only begin to imagine what kind of treasures the sea hides. I feel a longing to visit the shipwrecks.

"Can he See you? Euan?"

"I'm not sure. Sometimes I stay for a bit, you know, watch him gathering the stuff I've left for him. A couple of times he's looked at me... in a strange way. Like he knew it was me leaving him treasure. Like he knows I'm not just a seal. But he's never spoken to me."

"Why did he take your mum's wedding ring?"

"He didn't mean it. The ring slipped off my finger and fell among some little things I'd found for him. I only noticed when he was gone. Look." She lifts her right hand and I spot a white mark around her ring finger.

"Right. How can we help you come on land?" Valentina sits cross-legged on a rock, a determined expression on her face. She has taken over.

"I need clothes..."

"Of course."

"Also, I need help to hide my selkie skin. If I lose

155

it, then I won't be able to go back into the sea, and I couldn't bear that!" Mary shudders.

"We can do that. We know somewhere very safe." Valentina and I look at each other: we're both thinking of Weird HQ.

"Thank you. And there's something more..."

"Sure."

"After I get my ring back, I plan to live on land for a while. But I've never been before. I was born in the sea. My mother never went on land either. I need somewhere to stay... someone to help me. I don't know anything about your world."

"That's not a problem," I say, with certainty. "We have this uncle, Alistair is his name. He can put you up. He has the Sight too, so you can tell him anything..."

"Are you sure? Can I trust him?" There is apprehension in her eyes. A whole new world for her to discover... She's brave. If it was me thinking about living underwater, I'm not sure I could take the plunge.

"A hundred per cent," says Valentina solemnly.

"Should you not ask him first?"

"We'll go ask him right now. But believe me, he'll be delighted. Are you ok with ghosts?"

"You mean people who've died? Yes, I've seen a few, out at sea. Mainly sailors."

"That's good. Because there's a ghost living with him. Camilla. You'll love her."

"I'm sure I will." Mary smiles.

"We'll sort things out and be back tonight." "Thank you. I'll be forever grateful. Come anytime after dark. I'll be waiting."

"This is the coolest thing that ever happened to me," says Valentina as we walk towards Weird HQ.

"More than the fairies?"

"Yes."

"More than the troll?"

"Definitely."

"More than the mermaids?"

"Absolutely."

"More than Camilla?"

"Mmmm... As cool as Camilla!"

"Uncle Alistair! It's us!" we call, letting ourselves in. Uncle Alistair is at his desk.

"Hi, we have something to tell you!"

He doesn't reply.

"Uncle Alistair? Are you ok?"

"YES, YES, OF COURSE I'M OK!" he booms. He turns around. He looks terrible. He looks... sad.

"What happened?" asks Valentina.

"Oh well, it's grown-up things really... You know, stuff goes on..." he has a huge bar of chocolate in his hand. He starts chomping it, looking like he's a million miles away.

A glowing little shadow appears on the sofa beside him. It takes shape. It's Camilla.

"Hi guys! Oh, Alistair... *Not again...*" she whispers, and snuggles up to him, her arms going through him.

"Can someone tell us what's up?" says Valentina.

"Alistair is feeling down again," sighs Camilla.

"Oh, no!" says Valentina, and snuggles up too. There's no way I'm snuggling anyone, so I just mutter, "I'm sorry..."

And then I see it, right in the centre of his desk. My grandparents' photograph. They're smiling; baby Alistair is in my granny's arms and a toddler, my dad, is at their feet.

Poor Uncle Alistair.

"RIGHT! NO MORE BROODING!" he shouts, scrunching up the chocolate wrapper. "What did you have to tell me?"

"We spoke to a selkie, down at the beach. Mary Kenny," I say.

"Oh! A selkie! Your great-great-grandmother Margaret Watson was one. Did you know?"

"See? I knew we must be related to her *too*!" Valentina smiles broadly.

"The Grants have a few interesting relations. I should really show you our family tree... But yes, back to your selkie. Tell me."

"Mary asked for our help. She needs to get back her mother's wedding ring. A boy called Euan McAnena took it by mistake."

"I see. How is she planning to get it back?"

"No idea. She's never been on land before. She'd like to stay for a while..."

"She can stay here," says Uncle Alistair immediately. I smile. He has a heart of gold. "Not sure where she can sleep, though. My spare room is full of boxes. Righty-o, I'm off to Parson's to get some furniture, then."

"I'll help," I offer.

"Come on, Camilla, we're going to get some clothes for Mary from my mum's wardrobe." Valentina heads for the door.

"Sure!" Camilla twirls towards the ceiling in happiness.

"You can't do that. If Isabella sees Mary dressed in her clothes, she'll guess we took them," points out Uncle Alistair. "We need to buy her some new stuff. There." He hands her a small wad of notes.

"We're on it." Valentina is beaming.

"Ok then. Luca, you come with me to Parson's. Valentina and Camilla, you hit the shops."

Half an hour later we're trying to fit a bed frame, a mattress, a pillow, a bedside table and a lamp into the van.

"Hi! What are you doing?" It's Mum, walking down the main street with two bags of groceries.

"Sorting a room for a friend. Mary. She's coming up from London. Starting afresh, a few hard times and all that," explains Uncle Alistair.

"I'd love to meet her. Tell her she's welcome to ours anytime."

"Will do!"

"Is she moving up for good?"

"She's not sure yet. Everything is... at sea, at the moment." I stifle a smile. "Let's just say she's been in stormy waters, recently." I can't help laughing.

"Luca! That's not funny, poor girl... Anyway, I'm off. Call if you need me."

Somehow we manage to get everything into the van, although we have to drive very, very slowly.

Well, Uncle Alistair drives, while I walk beside him, checking that the mattress hanging out of the boot doesn't fall down completely.

I think we can set things up so Mary will be happy on land.

16. TREASURE HUNTING

Alistair Grant's *Scottish Paranormal Database*

Entry Number 57: Ghostly sea eagles
Type: Ghostly apparition
Location: Isle of Shuna
Date: First recorded sighting 1782; latest sighting
spring 2012
Details: On the tiny isle of Shuna, a family of
ghostly sea eagles hunt the cliffs. They resemble
normal birds, but they may disappear in mid-flight.
Many expeditions have tried to get close sightings
of them, but all have failed. The ghostly sea-eagle
cry is very sad, and so intense that it can make
even sailors cry.

The moon is shining on the moving sea, perfectly round.
It looks like a million crystals are floating on the waves.
It's so bright we can see almost as well as in the daytime.

Mary is waiting for us.

"Luca, Valentina... Oh!" She freezes as she registers
Uncle Alistair.

"Don't worry, he's the one we were telling you about –
you can trust him."

"Alistair Grant," says Uncle Alistair, and puts out his
hand. Mary looks at him, puzzled. "You're supposed to
take it, and shake it," he says kindly.

Mary does so, her arm dripping wet.

"And what's your name?" she asks Camilla. "I've seen
you floating around."

"I'm Camilla. Oh, I love it when people can see me!"

"Here are your clothes." Valentina hands Mary a bundle.

"I chose the top," says Valentina.

"And I chose the jeans," chips in Camilla.

"Thank you, girls..."

"Right, Luca, come on." Uncle Alistair and I walk a bit further away, letting Mary get dressed. Suddenly, Alistair stops in his tracks.

"What's that tune you're humming?" he asks.

I wasn't even aware I was humming.

"Don't know what it's called, I hear it sometimes... sort of in my head. Why?"

"Can you hear it now?" He looks so... intense. Like it's really, really important.

"Not now, no."

"Listen to me, Luca." He crouches in front of me, his hands on my shoulders, his eyes burning into mine. "When you hear it next, I want you to close your eyes and... tune into it. I want you to concentrate very, very carefully. If something happens, if you See something, you need to tell me. Ok?"

"Ok. Sure..." What is going on?

"St Anne's Reel."

"Pardon?"

"St Anne's Reel. The tune you were humming. It was a favourite of my mum's."

"Ready!" calls Valentina. Uncle Alistair tears his gaze away from mine. He looks... forlorn. He's got so many secrets, and I wonder if I'll ever fully understand them?

The girls walk up to us. Mary is wearing a blue jumper and jeans and a pair of trainers. She'd look totally and utterly normal, except for her long wet hair, and those seal eyes, bright as the full moon.

She's holding something that looks a bit like a blanket, shimmering subtly in the moonlight. She's hugging it tight, like she doesn't want to let go of it. I look at her face. She's frightened.

"Don't be scared," I try to soothe her. Valentina takes her by the arm, gently.

"Don't worry. You'll be safe with us," says Uncle Alistair, and his voice is soft, like I've never heard it before. That's how he is. A bit weird, but so, so kind.

We head back, with Mary holding onto Uncle Alistair's arm. She's wobbling a bit, because she's not used to walking on dry land. She's gazing about like she's seeing everything for the first time. Which I suppose she is.

When we get to Weird HQ, Mary looks around apprehensively.

"Come in. I'll show you where to put your skin," says Uncle Alistair, and leads her into her room. I smile, as I notice he has hung a pair of blue curtains on the window. It's a nice touch. There's a sheet laid out on her brand new duvet that is blue as well. Maybe Uncle Alistair thought that having everything blue would make her feel more at home.

"There, you can wrap your skin in the sheet and keep it in the wardrobe. So you'll always know it's safe."

"Thank you," says Mary, and she sounds incredibly grateful.

"Would you like some tea, to warm you up?"

She looks at him with wide eyes. "Tea?"

"Never tried it, of course! I'll make you a cup. Are you hungry? Would you like something to eat?"

"I'm starving actually... I couldn't eat all day, I was so nervous."

"Fish, I suppose?"

"Yes, please." Her voice is very sweet, very soft, like waves. Uncle Alistair disappears into the kitchen and emerges with a plate. On the plate is a fish. Raw, cold, straight out of the fridge.

"Thanks," says Mary, and bites the head off the fish, leaving a bloody gutsy grey stump in its place.

I feel like throwing up. Uncle Alistair and Valentina seem unfazed.

"Beans on toast, guys? We all need energy for tonight."

"No thanks," I mutter.

"Yes please! Any sausages going?" says Valentina.

"Sure thing, but let's make it quick. We need to break into the McAnenas' house."

We need to WHAT?

"Ok, no problem." Valentina seems unconcerned.

"Yes, *problem*! We can't go burgling people's houses!"

"It's not technically burgling. The ring is Mary's."

"Oh well, then! Guys, you're crazy..." I take my face in my hands.

"Come on, Luca, it'll be fine. Maybe we should wear black? Paint our faces black too?"

"Put twigs in our hair so we look like bushes?" I add, sarcastically.

"Good idea..."

Oh, no. No nonononono.

"Wait a minute..." It's Mary's soft voice. "Can I not just ask him to give me my ring back? Say that I lost it in on the beach, and..."

"That would mean explaining the situation to him. I'm not sure you want to do that..."

"You'd need to tell him you're a selkie," adds Valentina.

Uncle Alistair shrugs.

"Exactly. Nah, it won't work. I often say, burgling is the solution to many a problem."

Isn't it *just*?

Half an hour later we're crouching in the McAnenas' garden, the five of us. Mary looks petrified. She had to come so she could identify her ring, but I can see how scared she is. Valentina is as cool as ever. Camilla is humming to herself, swaying gently from side to side.

Uncle Alistair is wearing infrared glasses and is dressed top to toe in black lycra, leggings and all. He wanted a ninja suit, but all we could find was Aunt Shuna's old aerobics get-up. His white, hairy legs stick out from the too-short leggings. If anyone sees him like this, it's prison for him. Or the circus, one of the two.

The McAnenas' house is in complete darkness.

"Right. I'm going to silence the alarm," says Uncle Alistair, taking a brightly coloured mass of something sticky from his bag.

"Is that Play-doh?"

"It's EFD, Electrical Failure Device!" explains Camilla. "We used to go through tons of the stuff in London!"

"I stick this on the burglar alarm..." Uncle Alistair points at the blinking light beside the second-floor window "...and Bob's your uncle!"

"Who's Bob? Another uncle of yours?" whispers Mary in her soft voice.

"Er... never mind. You stay there, everyone."

We watch as Uncle Alistair in his lycra aerobics gear grabs two handfuls of ivy and pulls himself up. He's a lot stronger, a lot more agile than I expected. And a lot quicker. In three long vertical strides he's level with the burglar alarm and has stuck EFD all over it. We see the blinking light blink once more, and disappear. Result!

If I weren't so completely horrified by what we're actually doing, I'd be excited by now.

Uncle Alistair jumps down – it's awfully high up, but he doesn't seem to mind – and runs towards us in that bounding way he has.

"Now," he whispers, "Luca, Mary. It's your turn."

"*WHAT?*" Valentina and I whisper.

"Why *me?*"

"Why *not* me?" Valentina is outraged.

"Do what I say. Valentina, you watch for anything stirring outside. Camilla, you watch for anything stirring *inside*. Aaaand... we're good to go!"

He bounds back towards the door, and Mary and I follow, with Camilla floating above us. I turn back to see that Valentina has climbed the brick wall and is sitting there mutinously, arms crossed, watching the road in the orange light of the lamp-post.

Uncle Alistair takes out a little key from his pocket, and he opens the door, just like that, no sweat. Mary and I look at each other.

He really would make the perfect criminal.

"Right, in you go. I'll wait here."

"*What?*"

"Shhhh! It's better this way! I'm a lot bigger than you! I'll wait in front of the door. GO!"

I swallow hard. If we get found out, how am I going to explain this to my mum and dad?

Anyway, here I am and I've got to do it. No choice now.

The McAnena family is sleeping, the house is in perfect darkness. Mary and I tiptoe upstairs, with Camilla floating above us. My heart is in my throat, every creak of the wooden floor clenches my stomach... Once she's on the landing, Camilla gestures to us to wait. She enters the first bedroom, floating right through the door, and comes out shaking her head. Then she floats inside the second bedroom and comes out nodding enthusiastically. It's Euan's room.

I open the door as quietly as I can. I can make out Euan's dark shape, gently rising and falling in time with his breathing, in the bed beside the window.

Mary points silently towards Euan's desk. There are several shoeboxes piled on it, big and small. I lift the lid of one... they're full of treasure. Shells, coins, bits of polished glass, pebbles smoothed by the sea...

Euan sighs and turns over in his bed. We freeze, and my heart leaps. How am I going to explain all this to my mum and dad? But Euan doesn't wake.

We have no time to go through the boxes, and the noise would give us away, so Mary and I pile our arms with them and make our way out. We're tiptoeing down the stairs when Mary, whose footing is still unsure on dry land, trips and lands on her bottom, boxes and little shiny things falling everywhere. The soft thud of her body on the stairs and the plink-plink-plink of Euan's treasure on the wooden floor resound through the silent house.

This. Is. Bad.

We try frantically to pick everything up. I see Uncle Alistair's shape through the glass door, jumping up and down in alarm. Everything is back in the boxes, and we're ready to run when...

A gurgle. A stir. A yelp.

A SCREEEEEEEEEEAM fills the air, and it's the loudest, most piercing noise you'll ever hear: a *baby*.

Footsteps. We're frozen at the bottom of the stairs, as a figure in white walks across the landing making little soothing noises: "There, there... Mummy's coming..." The figure stops in her tracks all of a sudden.

We both jump out of the way, flattening ourselves against the wall opposite the door, clutching our boxes to our chests.

"Hello? Hello? Anybody there?" she calls.

Please pleasepleasepleasepleaseplease don't come downstairs!

At that moment, Camilla swooshes in front of us and up the stairs. I see her float right in front of a picture hanging on the landing, and scrunch up her face in concentration. I know what she's trying to do...

but it's not working. The picture is too heavy for her to move. Camilla's face curls up into itself, and she's PFFFFFMMMMMMMing with the effort... Until finally, the picture falls off and breaks with a shattering noise, and a sea of glass sweeps the landing. The woman in white screams.

"Sharon? Are you ok?" a male voice, struggling to be heard over the baby's screams.

It's our chance. The noise of the screaming baby is so loud, and Euan's mum and dad are so freaked out at the painting coming off the wall like that, that we manage to run towards the door unnoticed, and then out into the night, dangerously balancing a pile of boxes each.

My heart is beating so hard I think I'm going to faint. I crouch against the brick wall at the bottom of the garden, and Valentina and Uncle Alistair bend over us.

"Did you get it?" Uncle Alistair whispers.

"I'm not sure. Too many boxes of stuff. We took everything out." The McAnena house is now fully lit, and the silhouettes of its inhabitants pass back and forth in front of the windows.

"I just hope it is really in here..." whispers Mary, leaning over her pile of boxes and clutching them to her heart.

"Are you ok, Luca?"

"I... am... ok...." I whisper. I'm panting so hard I think I'll faint. "*Never...doing this....again!*"

"Yeah, no, maybe," shrugs Uncle Alistair and jumps on the wall. "Pass me the boxes, guys."

I climb on the wall too, and turn around to reach out my hand to Mary to help her climb, when I see that she has turned her back to us and she's peering in the darkness.

The pyjama-clad shape of a small boy comes out of the shadows.

The boy reaches out his hand, palm up. On it, a golden ring.

"Are you looking for this?"

Mary smiles and nods, taking the ring from Euan and slipping it on her white finger.

"So you could See me all along. I mean, you know who I am."

Euan shrugs his shoulders. "I See a lot of strange things, I just don't tell. I looked for you, to return the ring, but I haven't seen you for a while. Can I have my treasure back?"

We hand Euan the boxes, one after the other. He balances them all in front of his face.

"Thank you. This will be difficult to explain to Mum and Dad. Oh well, I'll find a way. I always do. See you in school, Valentina!" And he walks away.

We are all speechless.

"Well, that was easy!" booms Uncle Alistair, standing under the orange light in his ninja suit. "We should do this kind of thing more often!"

We're back at Weird HQ. Valentina and I are straightening ourselves, getting leaves out of our hair and sweeping mud off our jackets. We told our mum and dad we were going to watch a DVD at Uncle

Alistair's, so we can't look as though we've been hiding in bushes, like we, in fact, did.

Mary disappears into her room, and when she comes back, she has something for us.

"I had wrapped them into my skin, to keep them safe. There."

She hands us one shell each. They're oysters, and inside them lies a perfect, shiny, unbelievably beautiful pearl.

"Thank you," she says softly, "to all of you." Her liquid eyes linger in mine, and I feel like I'm diving in the waves of the sea.

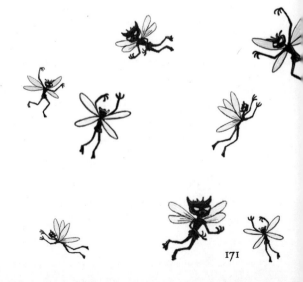

171

17. SHETLAGGED

Alistair Grant's *Scottish Paranormal Database*

Entry Number 202: Storytelling Luh
Type: Cryptozoology
Location: Shetland
Date: 13 April 2007
Details: The teacher of St Magnus' Primary
in southern Shetland, having left the school
playground briefly to attend to a hurt child,
returned to find the schoolchildren sitting happily
around a Luh, who was telling them a story. The Luh
is a kind of werewolf, having the body of a human
and the head of a wolf. He feeds on fish and is
known for his generosity: he enjoys leaving gifts
of fish in front of people's houses.

It's the last day of school before the October week holiday. Valentina and I are sitting at the breakfast table, eating toast and Nutella. I'm struggling to keep my eyes open – the mysterious music I've been hearing woke me up in the middle of the night. Twice.

Uncle Alistair walks into the kitchen, or should I say he *jumps* into the kitchen, in his usual subtle way.

"MORNING GUYS! *ISABELLA!* You look lovely today. What a nice... nice... nice *hairdo!*"

"Thank you," says my mum, suspicious. "You've never been one to notice hairdos, Alistair. What's up with you?" Mum reads Uncle Alistair as well as she reads us.

"Yeah, no, you're right. I was just at the bakery there, brought you some muffins. Cranberry, the ones you like..." Uncle Alistair hands her a pale blue box.

"That's nice. So. What do you want?"

"What makes you think that..."

Mum looks at him.

"Ok, ok." He takes a deep breath. "I need the children. In the October week, I mean. I'd like to take them somewhere. For my work."

We prick up our ears. I can see Valentina opening her mouth, and I kick her under the table. Better leave them to negotiate, for now.

"Oh Alistair, the whole week? I was hoping that we might do something together, if Duncan took some time off... all of us, you and Shuna as well..."

"No, no, just for three days!" Uncle Alistair holds his hands up. "After that, I'd love to do something with you all."

"Where would you take them?"

"Shetland. This farmer found a nest of ferrets in his sheep shed. Not dangerous, just that there's a *lot* of them. Dozens."

We gasp. Shetland! I'd *love* to go! I'm crossing my fingers...

"Ferrets?"

"Deadly for sheep. They carry these viruses..."

"Shetland is a long way away..."

"I know, I know. Ferry to Glasgow, plane to Orkney, plane to Lerwick."

"Oh Alistair, I don't know..." My mum sighs. We hold our breath. "Three days, you said?"

"Yes. Maybe four. At the most. It takes ages to get there..."

"No point in asking you two whether you want to go, I suppose?"

"We'd *love* to go! Please Mum!" cries out Valentina.

"I'll think about it."

"Why? I mean, why think about it," says Valentina, "when you could say yes now?" she looks at Mum with big, brown puppy eyes.

"Even if I say yes, I'm not sure that your dad..."

"Dad is going to spend the whole October Week in his study, Mum. It won't make much of a difference if we're here or in Shetland," I say, and immediately regret it. I wish I could take the words back, because a wave of sadness passes over my mum's face, like the shadow of a cloud on the hills.

"I know, I know. Listen. I'll ask him. Ok?"

"Luca is right, I'm afraid. Go and have fun." It's my Dad. We hadn't heard him coming.

"Seriously?"

"I have to work throughout the October week, anyway..." My mum's face falls. Only now I notice how tired Dad looks.

We cheer. We're going to Shetland!

"Alistair, you'll watch them, won't you?" Dad adds quickly.

"Don't I always."

"Thank you, Alistair," he adds, unexpectedly. "Thank you for doing so much for them."

"Thank you for letting them come, Duncan."

If only Dad could forgive him. Let him back into

the family, properly. A look passes between the two brothers: it's like they see each other for the first time in a long, long while. For a moment, I feel change might be possible, sometime in the future. But then Dad seems to shake himself – he turns away, and the spell is broken. Uncle Alistair's face falls in disappointment.

So many times now Alistair had told us he's trying to make it right. But how? And when?

"So what are we doing? *Really?*" I ask.

We're on our way to the ferry, driving in our little blue van. The van always looks like it's on its last legs, coughing and spluttering, sitting at the car repairer's day in and day out. But somehow, it keeps going.

"We're investigating a series of kidnappings. *Sheepnappings*, to be more accurate."

Valentina and I look at each other.

"Fifteen sheep disappeared with no trace."

"We're going all the way to Shetland for *that?*"

"Let me think... a murder of sheep... a wolf? A werewolf! Yes, it must be!" exclaims Valentina.

"Maybe. Shetland is home to a few fine werewolves. But let's not draw conclusions. Luca, can you get my jacket, just beside you? The Blackberry is in my pocket. Look among the last emails, the name is Moller."

"There. Is it... Andy Moller? *Help needed in Scalloway?*"

"Yes. Can you read it aloud please?"

"Sure. Here it goes...

To SOS@reallyweirdremovals.com
From asheepisforever@bmail.com

Dear Mr Grant,

My name is Andy Moller. I'm a Shetland man, born and bred. I have a few hundred sheep near Scalloway, not far from Lerwick. In the last few weeks, many of them have disappeared. Vanished, just like that. We all know who did it. It's a Luh, of course...

"What's a Luh?" asks Valentina.

"A werewolf."

"Just like I said!"

"...but we can't find head nor hair of him. Not a trace. I'm not for this Internet malarkey at all, but I found ReallyWeirdRemovals.com and I thought: just the thing. We need your help, because every night some more sheep disappear, and we don't seem to be able to stop it. If you want to take the job, we'll reward you, of course. Drop me a line, or phone me..."

"...And so on and so forth, best regards, blah blah," I finish.

"Thing is..." says Valentina, looking thoughtful, "...I read a bit about Luhs in that book –"

"*Moonlight and Me: Memoirs of a lonely Luh?*" interrupts Uncle Alistair.

"Yes, that one. It said that they aren't aggressive at all..."

"That's true. Which is why I doubt that Andy knows what's really going on. Werewolves can be aggressive, but Luhs feed on fish."

"Do you think it was something else?"

"I do. And I think some poor Luh is going to get the blame for it."

"We need to help him!" Valentina is vehement.

"I've never seen a Luh. But werewolves..." Camilla has just materialised between us. "There's one who hunts in Kensington Gardens..." she shivers at the thought, and floats up a bit as she does so. "You don't want to cross his path, believe me."

"I know a couple too. And yes, you don't want to cross their path," says Uncle Alistair grimly.

It's my turn to shiver.

The Moller farm consists of a whitewashed cottage in the middle of nowhere, a shed just next to it and fields of green grass all around. The cottage is only a few hundred yards from the sea, and from the stone-floored kitchen we can hear the waves breaking against the shore. It's a comforting sound. The music of the sea is home to me.

Andy Moller is a short stocky man with red cheeks and jet-black hair, bushy eyebrows and enormous hands. After a warming cup of tea and biscuits, he stands up and points to the door.

"Let me show you what I laid out. For the hunt." Hunt? I look at Uncle Alistair, but his expression is unreadable.

Andy leads us into a tiny shoebox-like building at the side of the main cottage. It's a gloomy sort of place, full of cobwebs and farming equipment. A mouldy smell pervades the air, and it's so damp I start shivering.

As my eyes adjust to the gloom, I see what's lying in the middle of the floor: a net, what looks like a snare and a hunter's knife in its sheath. Valentina is looking on, pale and horrified.

Andy gestures at the weapons.

"Will this be enough? I've got guns, as well. My grandfather shot two, in his day."

"Two... what, if I may ask?" Uncle Alistair's tone is polite, but I can feel an edge to it.

"Luhs, of course. This thing is to catch them."

"Luhs feed on fish! They don't steal sheep! There's no need to shoot him! Or trap him! Or... skin him!" cries out Valentina.

Andy looks at her like she's crazy.

"Do you want half men, half wolves around your house, Missus? 'Cause I don't!"

"They don't harm anything! Or anyone!" Valentina is on the verge of tears.

Uncle Alistair crouches beside the hunting equipment, and picks up something invisible with his fingers. "A Luh hair," he says.

"See! I told you it was a Luh! And it was in my house! I'm telling you, it'll make a good rug for my living room..."

"You know what this means, children?" says Uncle Alistair quietly, lifting the black hair between his fingers.

"That the Luh knows Andy is after him. He's seen the net, and the snare. And the knife," I say, shivering once more – and not because of the cold this time.

Valentina gasps. Poor Luh. Alone and frightened. About to be turned into a rug.

Uncle Alistair gets up swiftly. "Something else is taking your sheep, Mr Moller. It's not a Luh."

"Like what, then? Whatever it is, it's not human. He leaves no traces..."

"We'll see. Would you be so kind to take us to the site of the disappearances?"

"Aye. It's just down the road."

An hour later, we're still walking. I was glad to leave the gloomy shed, but outside it's bitter. We're soaked to the bone, and the salty wind is blowing us off our feet.

"Didn't think it was worth to take the Jeep. Not for short distances," shouts Andy, over the noise of the wind and rain.

"Nah, not worth it!" answers Uncle Alistair cheerily.

"They're crazy," mutters Valentina under her breath.

"I'm freezing," I reply. We're wearing our waterproof jackets with hoods up, hats, gloves, scarves and wellies. But the rain is still finding its way inside our clothes, and our hands and feet are icy cold.

"I'm freezing too."

"Me too," whines Camilla.

"You're a ghost, you can't be cold!" Valentina points out.

"I know... I just feel for you."

"HERE!" shouts Andy over the wind. "It happened RIGHT HERE!" He stops abruptly.

We look around. Grass. Grass. And more grass.

"There's *nothing* here!" I point out.

"Exactly. I had a few sheep grazing here the other day. Gone. Not a trace."

"Children, help me," says Uncle Alistair, taking three magnifying glasses out of his brown leather rucksack.

"*A magnifying glass?*" whispers Valentina. "*Does he think we're Sherlock Holmes?*"

"Shhhh!" I frown and shake my head. Thankfully, Uncle Alistair can't hear whispers, unless he reads your lips.

"Look for clues. Any clues. Possibly, black or grey hairs."

We get on all fours, reluctantly. We are *soaked*.

"Nothing?"

"Nothing" we reply, mutinously, rain pouring down our faces. Andy is looking on, frowning. His monobrow looks even bushier.

"Thought so. Take this." Uncle Alistair takes something out of his bag. It's like a plastic... spray bottle thing, like the ones you'd use to clean the kitchen. There's one each.

"Spray."

We look at each other. Valentina shrugs her shoulders.

We start spraying.

"A bit more here. Over there. Just a bit more... There. Done."

"And now?"

"And now we wait."

A few minutes later, the grass starts glowing blue.

"I thought it could be that," smiles Uncle Alistair. "When you said no traces..."

"*That?*"

"A ghost, of course."

"A ghost? On my land! How do I shoot a ghost?" barks Andy.

"You really are obsessed with shooting, aren't you?" says Uncle Alistair pleasantly.

"I can't stand him!" murmurs Valentina.

"I'm afraid that ghosts can't be killed. They're dead already."

"So how do I get rid of it? I can't keep losing sheep! It's costing me money!"

"We ask the ghost: 'Please, stop doing this.'"

"What? And that's going to work?"

"Worth a try," says Alistair, and walks away. Valentina and I run after him.

"Ghosts can be vanquished," I say, making sure I'm out of Andy's earshot, "maybe you could do that."

"I could, but I won't. I don't vanquish, I don't shoot, I don't kill and I don't destroy. Anything, ever. Unless they're about to destroy me. And even then, I'd think twice."

"Of course, but there's that poor sheep too..."

"The sheep are ok."

"Are they? How do you know?"

"Just a hunch. Camilla!"

"Yes?"

"You know what to do."

Camilla nods, a determined expression on her little face, and she floats away in the pouring rain.

Andy's wife, Hilda, has set up a lovely welcome for us. She lists the menu: a delicious stew with potatoes called "reestit mutton", sea trout with buttery toast, and a mouth-watering treacle cake.

"I hope you're enjoying our Shetland hospitality," she says warmly. Hilda has white-blonde hair, blue eyes, and an open smile.

"Very much, thank you, Mrs Moller," I reply.

"Mmmmm. Mmmmm...." says Valentina. "This fish is amazing." She's at her third helping.

"I'll give you some to take back," says Hilda, generously.

"Yes, please. My mum would love all this. She's a great cook too."

"I'll give you the recipes as well."

"Thank you!" we say in unison.

"I'm back..." A little voice comes from under the table. Camilla.

Alistair nods, without looking down.

"I think I found the ghost."

"*Speak later!*" whispers Alistair as soon as Hilda turns her back, and Camilla perches herself on the windowsill, waiting patiently.

The Mollers have invited a few people, to give us a proper Shetland welcome. There's music, chat and whisky for everyone – orange juice for Valentina and I – until the small hours.

The music is amazing – a few fiddles and an accordion, played brilliantly. Valentina and Uncle Alistair clap and tap their feet, smiling broadly. They both have music in their blood, I think.

The musicians take a break – more food prepared by Hilda – and Alistair takes us outside for a minute, to speak with Camilla.

"So. Who's this ghost?"

"A grumpy man. With a cap and wellies, and a long red scarf. He didn't say his name; he says he wants to speak to Andy."

"Did he seem reasonable to you?"

"S'pose."

"Where shall we find him?"

"He says Andy knows."

"Where did *you* find him?"

"I didn't. He found *me*. In a field. Not sure which field, the place is full of them."

"Fair enough. I'll tell Andy tomorrow."

It's past midnight when we make it to our room. Our beds are soft and wonderfully warm. We fall asleep to the sound of the sea and the wind whistling around our window, with the fiddle music still drifting from the living room. Fiddles and the sea, a real Shetland lullaby.

18. BROTHERS

The next morning, while we're having a lovely breakfast of herring on toast, Uncle Alistair clears his throat.

"Andy, we found your ghost. Actually, he found us. He wants to speak to you." Andy's face turns a pale shade of green. "An old man, with cap, wellies and a long red scarf. You must know who he is. Or at least have some idea. He says you know where to find him."

"A long red scarf?" he mutters. His face goes white, then bright red, then green again.

Uncle Alistair looks at him with narrowed eyes.

"I think you *know* what all this is about, Andy."

Andy swallows. He seems about to faint. Hilda helps him to a chair.

"What's going on, Andy?" she says.

"Never you mind, Hilda. I'll sort it," he says brusquely, but puts his hand on hers.

We're driving in Andy's dark-green Jeep, through lush, shiny green fields. The sea seems all around us. We can see it from every direction.

"A bit drizzly, isn't it?" Andy says. It's *pouring*. Lashing down so hard that you'd get soaked in minutes. And possibly drown.

"A bit," says Valentina.

"A touch," I say.

"A shadow," says Alistair.

"Yes, a shadow," agrees Andy.

"No, I mean, a *shadow*! There!" Uncle Alistair is pointing somewhere beyond the thick curtain of rain.

Andy brakes suddenly, and we all get propelled forward, our breath taken away by our seat belts.

"It's him!" whispers Andy. He's green again.

"Where?" asks Valentina. We peer. The rain is so heavy, we can hardly make out anything.

"There, there, look! In front of us!" Andy is now properly panicked.

I can see him now. A human shape, greyish, blurry, like Camilla gets sometimes. The rain seems to go through him, yet somehow it flows around him as well, so that he looks like he's *made* of rain.

He's stopped right in front of us, blocking our way.

The rainy shape lifts his arm, and waves.

"He's telling us to follow him," says Uncle Alistair.

"Yes. Yes," whispers Andy, and starts the car again, following the flying ghost.

"You know what this is about, don't you?" asks Alistair.

Andy nods. I can see he's terrified.

To be honest, so am I. An avenging ghost on a stormy day. Just about the *last* thing I want to see.

We drive for another wee while, until we get to what looks like an abandoned, half-ruined whitewashed cottage. Andy stops right in front of it.

"Right, let's go!" says Uncle Alistair.

"Right on!" echoes Camilla.

"Coming!" says Valentina.

Andy and I say nothing. We stay glued to our seats.

"Come on! We need to sort it. Andy, let's go."

We obey. My legs are like lead. We all run to the door of the cottage, looking for shelter from the pouring rain. The noise is so strong, I can't hear a thing.

Andy tries the door. It's open. We all walk in, leaving wet footprints on the wooden floor.

It's a dark, cold, ruined shell of a place, with debris everywhere and spider webs hanging from the ceiling. Still, there are pictures on the walls and a sofa. Curtains. A sink and a stove with a kettle on it.

There's no doubt. This rundown place is somebody's home.

"Iain!" cries Andy.

The ghost is called Iain?

"Iain, it's me. Andy."

A door opens slowly. Slowly.

We all hold all breath, expecting the shadow to come out...

A man.

Standing in front of us, there's... *another Andy*.

Andy and Other Andy look at each other, like in a mirror. They're identical twins.

"What do *you* want?" says Other Andy – I mean Iain – gruffly.

"Alistair Grant!" says Uncle Alistair, taking Iain's hand and shaking it. "And this is my nephew, Luca, and my niece, Vally. Goodness, we're soaked! Any chance of a cup of tea?"

"Why are you shouting, Alistair Grant?" grunts Iain.

"Because I'm deaf," answers Uncle Alistair, without missing a beat.

"Right, fair enough. I'll put the kettle on. Take a seat."

We look at each other. Andy is looking down. His chin is shaking.

"Iain..."

"What? Are you going to ask me how I'm doing? How I've been doing in the last twenty years?" cries out Iain.

"I... I...."

"Nice of you to ask. Not so good, since Mary died."

"I'm sorry..." mutters Andy.

"Wait a minute. You're twins, and you haven't spoken for twenty years?" cries out Valentina.

"It was *his* fault!" shouts Andy.

"It was *his* doing!" cries Iain.

"Are you *crazy*? You're brothers! And you," she points at Andy, "live in that lovely, warm farm, with a really nice wife... while your twin is living in a *ruin*, on his *own*?"

Andy looks down, sheepishly.

"Hold your horses, Valentina. Let them explain," says Uncle Alistair, and sits down on the dusty sofa. "This cup of tea?"

"Coming," grunts Iain, and busies himself. Everybody is looking towards the two men; I'm the only one who's in sight of the window, and the only one who notices a shadow passing quickly in front of the glass. The shadow has a weird shape... Like a human being, but his head is... wrong. I take a sideways step towards the window, and look out, just in time to see a strange creature, with the body of a man and the head of a wolf, running away towards the open fields. It's the Luh! I'm about to alert Uncle Alistair and Valentina – better not let Andy know that the Luh is here – when Valentina tugs at my sleeve.

"Where's the ghost?" she whispers.

"Look up," says Camilla.

We all look up. I gasp, and Valentina lets out a small scream.

Right over our heads, there's an old man. Lying on the ceiling, so to speak, like you would lie on the floor. Looking down on us. He's glowing faintly blue.

"What is it?" cry Andy and Iain, in unison. It's uncanny, they even have the same voice.

"I take it that's your dad?" says Uncle Alistair matter-of-factly, pointing up.

"AAAAAAAAAARGH!" cries Andy, and faints.

"Oooooooooooooooooh..." whispers Iain, and passes out.

"They always were easily scared," says the ghost, and floats down to sit beside Alistair.

Uncle Alistair throws some cold water on the twins' faces, and they come to, spluttering.

"I knew you'd listen if I started taking your sheep! You always cared about sheep more than you cared for human beings!" booms the ghost. He sounds a bit echoey, just like Camilla.

"That's not true! Are they ok?" mutters Andy.

"See?" says the ghost, looking at us. "What did I say? Cares more about the sheep than about us! Mark my words! Yes, they are fine and well, Andrew. In the old shed. And how's my Hilda? She always was a dear one, too good for you! The daughter I never had!"

"She's fine, Dad."

"Good. You *promised*, Andrew," says the ghost, and he's so upset, he blurs a little. "You promised on my deathbed you'd make up with Iain. But you didn't."

"I'm sorry."

"And look at him now! Since Mary died, he's on his own! Look at the way he's living!"

"Dad..." mutters Iain, eyes downcast.

Uncle Alistair is watching the scene intently. He has a strange look in his eyes, an expression I can't quite understand. Like someone who's lost something, and wants it back.

"I'm going to have to go soon," continues the ghost, "for good. Before I go, I need to know you're reconciled. I need to know Iain is not alone."

"What did you fight about, anyway?" asks Valentina.

"We went to an auction..."

"A livestock auction..."

"And Andy took the best ram —"

"And Iain nearly stole it –"

"I had it first!"

"It was mine!"

"A RAM! TWENTY YEARS OF SILENCE FOR A RAM!" booms the ghost, and his voice is so powerful that it shakes the windows. We all put our hands to our ears.

"There goes the rest of my hearing," says Uncle Alistair, grimacing. "Look, the two of you. You need to talk this through, ok. Why don't you go for a wee walk? To get some space?"

"No!" I shout. Everybody looks at me. "I mean… it's so wet, outside." I raise my eyebrows, looking straight at Uncle Alistair. The Luh is out there – if Andy sees it… Hopefully Uncle Alistair will catch my drift.

He does, of course.

"Luca is right! It's very wet indeed! IT'S A FLOOD! Off you go to the bedroom then, come on!" he shepherds them through, like a sheep dog.

"But we…" Andy begins.

"SEE YOU IN A BIT!" booms Uncle Alistair, and closes the bedroom door right in his face. "What is it, Luca?"

"The Luh. Outside!" I whisper.

"Pfff, Luhs!" The ghost, now floating in mid-air, dismisses us. "Harmless creatures. My dad was obsessed with them, and so are my sons. Nonsense, I say, NONSENSE!"

"Yeah, well. Tea?" offers Uncle Alistair, politely.

"I WISH!" says the ghost, and his voice resonates like an echo.

Uncle Alistair does make tea and we clear a space on the sofa and warm up gradually, chatting about Shetland life and the afterlife for an hour or so.

"Here they come!" exclaims Valentina. The door that Alistair shut on Andy opens and the twins walk out, both red in the face.

"I'm sorry, Dad," blurts out Andy.

"I'm sorry too," sobs Iain.

"We made peace."

"We did."

"At last!"

"At long last!"

"IAIN!"

"ANDY!"

They turn towards each other, go in for a hug, get all flustered, and settle for a handshake, their eyelashes moist and their eyes shiny.

I look at Uncle Alistair. He's drying a tear. I think I know what's going through his mind: the twelve years in which my dad refused to speak to him.

"Don't dare fight again or I'll be back!" the ghost admonishes. He's slowly disappearing, getting more and more transparent. He seems to be becoming water, dripping on the floor from every bit of his body. A real Shetland ghost, I think, turning into sea and rain.

"Never!" the twins say, in unison.

"It's time for me to go, now... Thank you, Alistair Grant! Thank you children!" says the old man. One last look at his sons, and he dissolves right in front of our eyes, leaving a little puddle of rain and a bit of blue liquid, the same colour as the night sky.

On the way back, Uncle Alistair is very quiet, and lost in thought. A conversation between Aunt Shuna and my mum came back into my mind.

"To think they were so close."

"Were they? It doesn't look like it now."

"It's true. Wherever Alistair was, there was Duncan. So different in personality, and yet... they were best friends."

I just hope things can be that way again. I hope it can all be sorted out, just like for Andy and Iain.

It's time for us to go. We're packing up our van, when I notice something beside it. It's a parcel, all wrapped up, to protect it from the rain.

I unwrap it. Inside, there are three beautiful sea trouts.

A gift of fish, from a Luh who's happy to be off the hook.

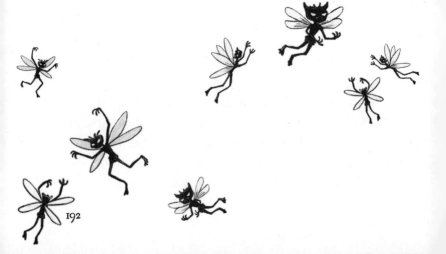

19. PICTURES OF A SEA SERPENT

Alistair Grant's *Scottish Paranormal Database*

Entry Number 410: Zeuglodon
Type: Cryptozoology
Location: Off the coast of North Uist
Date: 1612
Details: The first recorded sighting of a sea
serpent in Scotland is found in Lord James
McTire's memoir, dated 1612, kept in the McTire
Private Collection at Loch Glas. Sea serpents, or
zeuglodons, are ancient reptiles of the sea. While
they may look frightening, they are timid, peace
loving and wholly vegetarian.

We're all in the living room, the fire's dancing, crackling and hissing, and the rain is tapping on our windows. My mum and Aunt Shuna are sitting on the sofa reading books, my sister is watching *Harry Potter and the Goblet of Fire* for the twentieth time, and I'm writing in my diary about our Shetland adventure. It's perfect.

Well, *nearly* perfect. It would be even better if my dad was with us, instead of upstairs with Reilly, but you can't have everything.

Suddenly, a horrendous, hair-raising noise comes from Valentina's pocket. It's the singing troll. I mean, it's her phone.

"Oh, a text from Uncle Alistair." I prick up my ears. "He says if we want to go see him later on, he's got a job for us. You know, for his pest removal business," she adds hastily, for my mum's benefit. A look passes between us.

"Great. Go see him," says Mum.

We run upstairs for our jackets. I'm ready straight away, and dying to know what Uncle Alistair *really* wants, but Valentina is rummaging about in her room.

"I'll just be a minute, Luca. I'll catch you up," she says.

"What are you doing?"

"Private stuff!" she replies loftily. "Wait for me in the hallway."

"Fine, fine..." I raise my hands. As I'm walking down the stairs, I turn around just in time to see her tiptoeing into my parents' bedroom, clutching a wooden box. I wonder what she's been up to...

"What did the text say, exactly?" I ask Valentina, as we walk down towards Weird HQ, wrapped in our waterproof jackets, hoods up and hands in pockets.

"Not much. Just that he has a job for us."

"Cool."

"HELLO GUYS!" he says, as we walk into the living room. I don't know how Mary, living with him, puts up with his volume of voice. It's ear-piercing.

"Hi Uncle Alistair!"

"LOOK AT THIS!" he shouts, straight in my ear.

I take his phone from him. It's a picture. A blurry picture of... a sort of dinosaur. Like those Nessie pictures – the ones that for some reason are always blurred and taken from far away.

"A monster!" says Valentina cheerfully.

"Just don't call him 'monster' to his face – he might take offence. He's actually a very, very ancient kind of sea reptile. Cryptozoologists would call him a zeuglodon, or sea serpent."

"So... he's not a magical creature. He's an animal, really," I remark.

"Yes. That means that everybody can see him. Which is extremely dangerous for him."

"Where is he?"

"At the moment, in Loch Brue."

"That's just down the road from us!"

"Exactly. I got an email from a Connor Moran, a fisherman down that way. He's the one who took the picture. Not the best photographer, as you can see... There."

He takes the phone back from me, pushes a few buttons, then he hands it back.

"Read his letter."

....

To SOS@reallyweirdremovals.com
From CMoran123@bmail.com
....

Dear Alistair,

I found you on the web; I can't believe you're just here in Eilean. I think this might interest you. Sorry about the quality of the picture, I only had my camera-phone with me. I don't even know what to call this – a dinosaur?

"Wrong!" chirps Valentina.

Anyway, whatever this is, it's been here for a few days now. I have no idea where it came from, but I know it needs help before the scientists come and get it. This is, as you know, a small loch, and it won't be long before someone spots the creature and calls the papers. After that, you know what'll happen, and it's not good. Thankfully it's not summer, or it would have been spotted already. The bad weather buys us a bit of time. Give me a phone when you're coming up.

Sincerely yours,
Connor

"How on earth are we going to do this?" I ask. "He's enormous!"

"Not really. He's only about nine feet long."

"Still too big to fit in our van!"

"That's not a problem. Remember Sorley and Mairi?"

"YES!" cries Valentina.

"Of course!" I say enthusiastically.

"I've called them already. They'll be here by tonight."

"Cool," sighs Valentina.

I don't say anything, but I'm so happy to be seeing them again. Especially Mairi.

Sorley has given us regular news of the mermaids since that night in Glasgow. They now live in a loch called Loch Glas, which is next to Sorley and Mairi's home, and they are doing great. Sorley is always vague about where he and Mairi live, and the whereabouts of this loch. I'm curious. I think there's more to Sorley and Mairi than meets the eye. They have *a lot* of sophisticated equipment, just for a start. And they seem incredibly skilled, like they've been doing this supernatural rescue thing forever.

"We're setting off tonight. I'll come and get you."

"We can't just leave in the middle of the night!" I protest.

"Well, we don't need to say we're trying to get a zeuglodon to safety. We can say it's a photographic expedition. We're going to get pictures of some animal that we're more likely to see at dawn... white otters? What do you think?"

"White otters? Do they exist?" asks Valentina.

"Only in Tasmania. An albino variety. Still, your mum and dad don't know that..."

"Might work," I venture.

"No danger in taking photographs. Unless, of course, you fall into the water, eh Luca?" Uncle Alistair elbows me.

"Very funny," I mutter.

"It's Friday, after all. It's not like we'll be missing school. And it's only down the road," insists Valentina.

Everything on Eilean is only down the road.

"Come on. Let's head back to your place via the chip shop. I'll bring supper over and speak to your mum and dad."

"The chip shop? You've got plenty of fish here!" I say, laughing. Since Mary has moved in, there's always a bucketful of fish in the fridge. The kitchen smells like Donald's boat. She *is* trying other foods though. Last week, at ours, she devoured my mum's home-made pasta. But then, who wouldn't?

We walk out to the rainy street. Alistair strides incredibly fast as usual. He has very long legs and is always in a hurry. We struggle to keep up.

"So... how did the monster... I mean..."

"Sea serpent. Or zeuglodon."

"How did the zeuglodon... get... into... Loch Brue..." I'm panting.

"Was it a fold in time?" shouts Valentina above the noise of the rain.

"No, this animal is very much from our time. It must have swum through an underground stream. There's one that goes from Loch Brue to the sea. This is not the first time we've had sightings of mysterious creatures there."

"Oh... wow..." I wonder what else hides in our lochs.

We have to interrupt the conversation because we arrive at the fish shop, its neon lights illuminating the dark street. As soon as we take hold of our warm, yummy-smelling paper bags Alistair is off again, at the speed of light.

"Quick, before it gets cold!"

"I've never heard of an underground stream on Eilean..." I manage to blurt out, scrambling after him as fast as I can.

"Hardly anyone knows about it. There's a map that tells you all about this stuff... underground streams, caves, wells, fairy mounds, even a few folds in time, the lot. The Secret Map of Scotland. I'll show you one day."

"HELLO! SUPPER'S HERE!"

"Oh hello, thank you! How thoughtful. Did they help you then?" asks my mum.

"With what?"

"The pests. The ones you mentioned in the text."

"Oh, those! Yes. Yes. They certainly did, Isabella. This time it was ants. An invasion of Purple Ants. Nasty business."

"Are they dangerous?" exclaims Mum, in alarm.

"Dangerous? No, not at all. Just... smelly. They let off a terrible smell when they feel threatened. Had to carry an air freshener around my neck. Cats love Purple Ant smell, for some reason. I had a few of them following me all the way home, trying to chew my trousers. But enough about me! Will I set the table for you?"

"That'd be great, thanks. I'll go and call Duncan."

Ten minutes later, we're all sitting around the table. Yes, Dad too, believe it believe it not, like Aunt Shuna says.

"I'm hoping to steal your children again, this weekend," says Alistair casually.

"To go where?" asks Dad.

"In this weather?" adds Mum.

"Just down the road. Loch Brue. There've been sightings of white otters. I'm hoping to take a few pictures. The first light is the best time to do it."

"White otters ? Does such a thing exist?" says Aunt Shuna.

"Oh, very much so. Truly interesting creatures."

"All these strange animals... Valentina must be

loving this," smiles Mum, looking fondly at Valentina, who beams back.

"It just gets better and better!"

"We have a lot of fun, together. The children are... they're great." Alistair is looking at somewhere over my dad's shoulder. I can see he means what he's saying.

"When would you be leaving?" asks Dad.

"Tonight. Well, tomorrow morning, really. Before dawn."

"Goodness. That's early," says Shuna.

"Like I said, the first light is the best moment to take pictures of that kind of creature."

"Right," smiles my mum.

"You don't believe they exist, do you?" Uncle Alistair smiles back.

"Actually, I have an open mind. I don't think for a minute that we know all that there is to know, or that we see all that there is to see." A look of mutual affection passes between her and Uncle Alistair. It makes me happy to see them getting on so well.

"Well, there are some things that I'd rather not see. And that I'd rather my children didn't see..." intervenes my dad, darkly.

Does that mean that we can't go?

"Loch Brue is beautiful, Duncan. They'll have a ball. Please tell me that you won't go camping, though! In this weather!"

"We'll stay with a friend of mine, don't worry. Connor Moran. He happens to be a relation of ours, a distant cousin."

"Everyone is a distant cousin of ours on this island!" laughs Shuna.

"Can we go, then?" asks Valentina.

"If you show us the pictures you take. I've never seen white otters before," says my dad unexpectedly.

I smile at him, and he smiles back. And I'm happy.

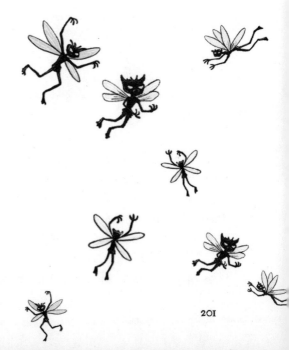

20. WHISPERING

It's a very early start for us. It's still pitch dark, and
we're already on the road. It'll only take us an hour
to drive to Loch Brue through the moors, but Uncle
Alistair is not taking any chances: Sorley and Mairi
are meeting us there, and we can't risk being late.

"Are we meeting Connor Moran there?"

"No, I didn't phone him. I'd rather not get him
involved in this. I'll email him back to say thanks for

getting in touch and ask him to keep an eye out and tell me when he sees the sea serpent next. Which, of course, will be never."

"So we won't be staying with him tonight? We don't have any camping stuff..."

"Don't worry about that. We have somewhere to stay."

There's a small dirt road that takes us to the loch. We follow it to the end, then park by the side and venture into the cold and damp. There's a strong smell of dead leaves in the air, and the scent of water. Strange how water has a scent, and how it changes if it's the sea, a loch or a river...

Loch Brue is still and black in the moonless night. It's just over an hour till first light. Uncle Alistair takes a waterproof sheet from the boot, and spreads it out for us. We sit in silence, broken only by the wind in the trees, enjoying the beauty of the night sky. It's so peaceful. Camilla glows softly, floating above us, humming gently to herself. Sometimes I hear that music, St Anne's Reel, as well as Camilla's humming, but mostly there is quiet calm and the water lapping just beyond our feet.

"Did you bring your bag?" whispers Valentina, noticing the little velvet bag hanging from my belt. Uncle Alistair has given a blue one to me and a red one to Valentina, to hold any treasure we might receive along the way. In mine I put the troll's medallion and Mary's pearl. I also have my rucksack with me, to carry my diary and some other bits and pieces. I like to have my diary with me – because I want to record things as they happen, and because with all the incredible things I've written recently, it's best if the diary doesn't fall into the wrong hands.

"I thought it would be good to have the treasure bag with me when we go on missions. You never know."

Valentina nods. "Good idea. I'll bring mine next time."

After about twenty minutes we hear the sound of a car in the distance, and then footsteps on the dirt road. It's them. Like us, they are not carrying torches, just in case the zeuglodon sees the light and decides to stay away.

"Hello everyone..." says Sorley quietly. We all exchange whispered greetings. Mairi and Valentina hug in silence.

"Hi, Luca."

"Hi." Her hair is down on her shoulders this time. I've never seen a shade of red like it.

"Stand by the trees up there, guys. We need to get the truck right on the shore. The trolley can only go so far."

Trolley? I suppose that's for the sea serpent.

We stand aside and they drive the truck as close to the shore as they can. It's not the black van they had in Glasgow; this one's much bigger. Sorley and Mairi open the back and slide out a huge metal trolley. They push it near the water. It has ropes coiled on both sides that they free up, extending them on the grass.

"Luca, Vally, it's feeding time," calls Uncle Alistair.

"Using us as bait?" I say, sarcastically. I wouldn't put it past him.

"Can't. Zeuglodons are vegetarian," he replies.

Otherwise, he *might*?

"Lucky for us!" I say, and I mean it.

Valentina and I get the bottles from the van. These ones are deep green, unlike the blue ones we used for the mermaids. We all start pouring them into the loch, the green liquid disappearing into the black waters. They smell awful, like rotting vegetation from a million years ago.

"Children, pour some up here as well, on the grass." We do that, and the whole place smells like the bottom of a pond.

"All we need to do now is wait for the first light," says Uncle Alistair.

"Are you going into the water?" I ask Sorley.

"No need this time."

"Will you use your special watch?" Valentina asks Mairi, meaning the strange little radar that she wore on her wrist when we rescued the mermaids.

"Yes, there it is." Mairi extends her arm to show Valentina.

"Wow..." Valentina is in awe of Mairi.

"Why don't *you* do it?"

"Me? Seriously? Oh..."

"There, put it around your wrist. Press this button. And this one. Now stand as close to the water as you can, and put your arm up like that. When it starts beeping, it means that the zeuglodon is near."

I glance at Sorley. He has a brown briefcase with him. He opens it, and takes out what looks like... a gun!

"What's that?" exclaims Camilla, horrified.

"It's a tranquilliser. It only hurts for a second, just like a jag. It'll make him sleep until we get him to safety."

Poor zeuglodon. Drugged and tied up on a trolley. But I know it's necessary.

The sky is turning pink: dawn is slowly breaking.

We sit and wait.

And then, the sound of ripples...

We all freeze.

The radar at Valentina's wrist starts beeping, and Mairi jumps up quickly to switch off the sound.

The ripples turn into splashes. It's here!

In the soft light of dawn, I can make out his shape. He's lapping at the water, making satisfied gurgles. He hasn't seen us.

Following the feed, the zeuglodon lurches on land, propelling himself with his fins. He's even bigger than I imagined him – about the size of a small car. He has four fins, flat and diamond-shaped, and a long tail. His eyes are yellow, with a slit pupil like a snake's, and his skin is deep green.

Perfectly silent, like a cat, Sorley steps to the side of him. He's ready to shoot the tranquilliser, when the sea serpent – unexpectedly – rolls over, almost onto Sorley, who would be crushed under his weight.

Sorley barely manages to leap away and avoid being squashed, and his tranquilliser gun ends up right under the zeuglodon's belly.

At that moment, the zeuglodon sees us.

He raises his head, and then tips it to one side. His yellow eyes stare at us with no fear.

"Please move, please move, please move..." mutters Mairi under her breath, like a prayer. Camilla has her hands on her face, in trepidation.

The zeuglodon opens his toothless mouth, and looks up at the sky. A long, strident call comes out of him. Once, twice, he calls. The best way I can describe the sound is... Well,

"YEEEEEEEEEEEEEERK!"

We all hold our breath. What is he calling? What creature is about to appear from the waters?

Whatever it is, it heard the call, and it's answering. This one is not like a "YEEEEEEEEEEEEEERK", it's more like a "yeeeeeeey", said in a wee small voice.

A little green head emerges from the waves.

"A baby zeuglodon! It's a she, then," whispers Mairi.

"Now, that's a problem," murmurs Alistair. His words send a chill down my spine. Are those lovely creatures in danger? The zeuglodon and her baby?

The sea serpent propels herself back towards the shore to see to her puppy, and the tranquilliser gun lies there, free for the taking. Sorley jumps and grabs it.

"Mairi, Alistair!" he calls. "I can't shoot the puppy. The dose is too high, he might die..."

I hear Valentina gasp, and I feel quite ill myself.

The puppy has come on shore. He's as big as small dog, with the same yellow eyes as his mother. He starts lapping at the seaweed, making little gurgling noises.

"You need to shoot the mother. Then we'll take the puppy ourselves," whispers Mairi. "No other option."

"Yes. It's the only way," agrees Alistair.

And Sorley shoots.

The zeuglodon screams, a real scream of pain, and in a few seconds, she's out cold. The puppy is terrified; he's trying to scramble back into the water...

The five of us spring up, like one. Mairi is the first to get to him, and she holds him down with her body. The puppy is calling his mother, a "yeeeeeeeey" that would bring tears to your eyes. He's so distressed, flailing his little fins and trying to break free.

I think my heart is breaking.

Without thinking twice, I kneel beside him, and I start whispering. At first, it all comes out in English, "Your mum will wake up soon, you'll be fine, you'll be in Loch Glas together... no need to worry..." Then I realise that I'm saying words I shouldn't know. Words in the language of the sea, the same language I used with the mermaids. It flows easily, like I've done this all my life. Gurgly, swooshing sounds, full of "sh" and "gl", like the waves and the flowing waters.

Slowly, the puppy relaxes, he stops flailing his fins, he stops wailing. His *yey* is now low and thin, and a lot calmer. I'm *yeying* back, softly.

I look up, and I see that everyone is staring.

"It's like horse whispering," says Uncle Alistair. He seems... awed. Uncle Alistair, in awe of me? "It runs in the family. But this is taking it to a whole new level."

"Horse whispering?" asks Valentina.

"Something like that. I wonder does it work with all sea creatures..."

"I think so. It worked with the mermaids," remarks Valentina.

"What happened with the mermaids?"

"They... they spoke to me," I whisper, so as not to startle the puppy. "And I understood what they were saying. I talked to them in their own language. Not sure how..."

"It's sea-whispering," Sorley explains. "You can speak to sea creatures. It's very, very rare..." he's looking at me differently, as if only now can he truly See me.

"You're a sea-whisperer, Luca," says Uncle Alistair, and he's beaming with pride.

Like I belong to him.

Right now I'm a very happy sea-whisperer.

"Is Mummy zeuglodon ok?" asks Valentina.

"Don't worry, she's fine. And they'll be even better when we take them home," says Sorley reassuringly.

Valentina walks slowly towards the zeuglodon mother, and sits by her side. She puts a hand on her head, and strokes her gently.

"Careful..." I say, still holding the puppy.

"It's ok. She's out like a light," whispers Mairi, and joins Valentina, kneeling on the grass. Camilla rests her head on the sea serpent's great body, stroking her with immaterial hands.

The zeuglodon is something between a lizard, a dinosaur and, strangely, a big fish. I put my hand out, keeping the other around the puppy's back, and touch her skin. It's cold, dry, very rough. Her back rises and falls with her breathing.

"She's beautiful, isn't she?" murmurs Valentina.

"Yes. Are you taking her where the mermaids are?" I ask Sorley.

A look passes between Sorley and Uncle Alistair.

"Yes. And it's time for Valentina and the sea-whisperer to come and see where we live."

"Great!" says Valentina. I blush. I like being called that. Sea-whisperer, like this is what I was meant to be, all my life.

I'm dying to see this home of theirs, with all these incredible creatures, but... we must be back when we said we would, or Mum and Dad might not let us go with Uncle Alistair next time.

"We promised we'd be back by tomorrow..."

"We will be. Loch Glas is right across the water. We'll be there by lunchtime. And anyway, you need to come with the puppy. None of us could keep him calm like you do." I look down. The puppy has laid his head on my shoulder, breathing softly, just like a baby. A scaly baby. I pat his back gently. It's true, he needs me.

On our way to the van, the puppy in my arms, Mairi comes to my side.

"I knew you were a sea whisperer," she says.

"Did you?"

"I heard you talking to the mermaids. It's like I told you before, Luca. You're cool." And she walks on, leaving me looking at the dawn light shining on her hair.

With the zeuglodon mother asleep and safely tied up in the back, we set off in Sorley and Mairi's black truck. We leave our blue van parked by the loch. The puppy is on my lap the whole time.

"Do they not inspect trucks at the ferry?" I ask.

"They do spot checks, yes," answers Sorley, his eyes

on the road. The sky has turned grey, and there's a white mist rising from the hills.

"What if they find the zeuglodon? And Finlay?" The zeuglodon puppy is nuzzling my neck.

"Finlay?" laughs Valentina. "That's a good name for him!"

"We have our own boat, and nobody will ever inspect there, believe me," smiles Sorley.

"Lord McTire sees to that," says Uncle Alistair.

"Lord McTire?"

"My father," explains Sorley.

"Are you a lord too? And is Mairi a lady?" asks Valentina.

"I'm just me," Sorley smiles.

"He is the Honourable Sorley, and I'm a witch! Her Dark Highness Mairi!" whispers Mairi dramatically. Valentina, Camilla and I laugh. But I'm not sure she's entirely joking. Her grey eyes are very shiny.

Sure enough, when we reach the coast there's a boat for us. Only for us. She's called *Lady Margaret*, and she's sitting beside the ferry we take to go to Glasgow.

"Mr McTire and guests!" A woman with grey hair and a twinkle in her eyes greets us. She's wearing a yellow waterproof coat, and a woollen hat.

"Hi, Mum," smiles Sorley.

Mum? She's Lady McTire?

"Hi, everyone! Alistair, it's lovely to see you again."

"Margaret!" They hug.

"And you must be Alistair's niece and nephew. It's a pleasure. Ooooh, and look at this wee guy..." she strokes Finlay's head. Finlay gurgles. He likes it.

"Lady McTire..."

"Call me Margaret. All aboard now, Sorley will drive the truck inside, and then we're off."

The *Lady Margaret* is fantastic. It has a huge garage in the back for the black truck, but in the front it's just like a yacht. Margaret takes us to the cabin, while Camilla perches herself on the bow.

"Have a seat, everybody," offers Margaret, sitting at the controls.

She's actually the *captain*! Cool.

"Won't take long. Time to have lunch," she says.

"Hungry, anyone?" calls Mairi, putting her head into the cabin.

"Yes!" Valentina jumps up. We follow Mairi into a lovely carpeted room with two comfy sofas and a low table. Sorley and Mairi take out a hamper full of goodies: sandwiches, crisps and juice for everyone.

We sit, eating companionably. Finlay nuzzles at my hand. I whisper to him for a wee while, until he falls asleep. We can see Argyll in the distance, coming closer and closer.

When we reach the coast, we all pile up in the truck again, including Lady McTire. After a short drive, we get to an ancient mossy brick wall, and stop in front of a huge wrought-iron gate. On top of the gate, I recognise the coat of arms of the Royal Kingdom of Scotland with its two unicorns – we studied it in school last year. Beside it, there's another shield, with a dragon holding an elaborate C: it must be the McTire coat of arms.

Sorley presses a button beside the steering wheel, and the gate opens slowly.

"Welcome to Loch Glas," he says. We drive into the McTire estate, and into another world. Nothing, nothing in a million years could have ever prepared me for what I saw there.

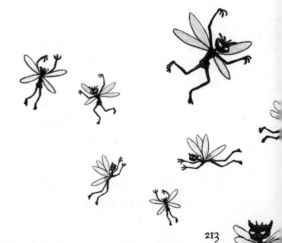

21. THE MOST BEAUTIFUL THING I'VE EVER SEEN

We make our way towards McTire House, driving the
truck through well kept fields. We spot deer grazing
on the grass, pheasants waddling around and a fox,
alert in the distance. Valentina and I are speechless at
the grandeur of it all.

McTire House is called a house, but it looks more
like a castle. It's a huge building of blonde sandstone
with an imposing entrance of stone steps and columns
at each side. Lord McTire is standing on top of the
steps, in front of the great wooden door.

He's tall – nearly as tall as Uncle Alistair – he has

grey hair and very blue piercing eyes, all creased at the sides like someone who smiles a lot. He's wearing a woollen jumper and a kilt woven in blue, green and white, with a sporran tied around his waist. He's also very muddy. There's mud all over him, actually, even his hair.

"Welcome back, everybody... Alistair... Oh! A puppy!" he gasps, as he sees Finlay. "Is he not asleep? How did you manage to get him here?"

"I didn't shoot him with the tranquilliser, wasn't sure of the dose..." says Sorley.

"You made the right call. Too risky. But how is he so calm?"

"Luca, here. He's a sea-whisperer, Dad."

Lord McTire stares at me.

"Are you? That's a rare talent, son. Not many have it, nowadays. Make good use of it." I nod. Lord McTire turns to Alistair. "You must be very proud of this nephew of yours."

"Oh, I am." He beams.

"So much to catch up on, Alistair. We'll chat later. We need to see to the zeuglodon, before he..."

"She!" Valentina and I say in unison.

"...before *she* wakes up and gets scared."

Sorley and Mairi open the back of the truck and slide the trolley down. The zeuglodon is still deeply asleep, thankfully.

"She's beautiful!" says Lord McTire.

"That's what I said," chirps Valentina, and Lord McTire gives her a smile.

"Come on," he says, and leads us to the back of the house... and that's the first surprise: McTire House is sitting right on Loch Glas. It's as if the loch is its back garden, with only a few yards between the building and the water. It's stunning.

Sorley, Mairi and Uncle Alistair lift the sea serpent and place her gently on the edge of the water.

"Look Finlay, there she is! Your mum!" cries Valentina.

"YEEEEEEEEEEEEEYYYYYYY" goes Finlay, and struggles to get free. I let him go, and he propels himself to his mother. He looks so happy. He curls himself against her, nuzzling her face.

"Are you going to wake her up?" I ask.

"No need," says Sorley. "She'll wake in…" he looks at his watch, "…I'd say no more than twenty minutes, and go straight into the water. They'll be safe here." He pats the zeuglodon's back.

"Well, welcome to Loch Glas!" says Lord McTire. "Camilla, it's good to see you again!" Camilla twirls. "So, Luca and Valentina! I've heard a lot about you from Mairi and Sorley."

We're both a bit awestruck by Lord McTire, even Valentina, who's not easily impressed.

"Are you following in your uncle's footsteps, children?"

"Hope not," says Alistair. It's a joke, but his face is serious. What does he mean? I'd love to follow in his footsteps. He gets so down on himself sometimes.

We make our way into McTire House. It's so grand, you could get lost in it. Lord McTire leads us to a sitting room with a tall ceiling and a huge fireplace, where Lady Margaret, wearing a beautiful cobalt-blue dress, is already waiting for us.

"Laura is bringing the tea. Come and sit down. What happened to you, Hamish? You're covered in mud! Don't tell me. It was the puppies again."

"Afraid so."

"Puppies? Can we see them?" asks Valentina. Sorley and Mairi look at each other.

"You certainly can!" They all laugh.

"What's funny about the puppies?"

"You'll see," says Mairi with a smile.

An old lady with a flowery apron comes in with a huge tray of scones, chocolate cake, shortbread and tablet, and a teapot with a stripy tea cosy. Then she goes, and comes back again with another tray, this time laden with crockery and cutlery.

"Thank you," says Margaret, and starts laying out the feast. I can see Valentina sitting on her hands, impatient to start.

"So how's Duncan? I haven't seen him since he was a wee boy..." asks Lord McTire.

"He's good. Writing."

"I hope things are better between you, these days..."

"Improving. He lets me take his children with me, so that's something. And I'm trying to sort out... what I need to sort out."

"I understand. Does Duncan know about the RWR? I mean, what the RWR really is?"

"No, he doesn't know."

"So what you're doing is a secret," says Margaret, looking me straight in the eye.

"Hopefully not forever. We want to tell them. Soon. As soon as we're sure they'll understand..." I say.

"As soon as I've made it up to him," intervenes Uncle Alistair, looking down into his cup.

"Of course they'll understand. You'll have to tell them everything, it's the only way to help them accept all this...If they don't have the Sight, they can't even begin to imagine what you can See..."

"Can you See, Margaret?" asks Valentina.

"No, darling. Our children found a way to show me, though."

She gets up, and takes a book from the library behind us. It's huge, and bound in leather.

Valentina cleans her hands – they're a bit jammy – and we open the book. It's full of drawings, some in black and white, some painted, some coloured in with crayons. The ones at the beginning of the book are clumsy and simple, clearly made by a small child, but the pictures get more and more beautiful, more and more skilled, as the artist grows up.

"Sorley has been drawing in this book since he was a wee boy, and he's still doing it now."

There is a portrait of the mermaids, painted in watercolour. Sorley is such a good artist. I'm speechless.

"And this is from his trip to the South Pole, three years ago..."

Oh my goodness. A polar bear. With a human face. A Yeti!

"I knew it!" cheers Valentina. "I have a magazine about Yetis. Nobody believes in them, but I do, and I was right!"

We keep turning the pages, marvelling at what we see. Some of the creatures are familiar, some I never knew existed: winged horses, glowing fish from the depth of the oceans, spirits and fairies and ghosts. Each has a name written carefully in black ink in the right-hand corner. I couldn't recognise half of them: Shony and Tangie, Luideag and Gruagachs, Fachan and Doonie and Crodh Mara... I hope I'm going to see them all, though some look pretty scary. Valentina is open-mouthed: I can see she's thinking the same thing.

"Right," says Lord McTire, breaking the spell. "If everybody has finished their tea, let's go and explore."

He leads the way down the stony steps.

"Loch Glas is a sanctuary for supernatural creatures," he explains. "We rescue them from all over Scotland and shelter them here. If you don't have the Sight, the place will just look full of exotic animal species and a few... interesting human beings. But if you can See... well, you'll be amazed. Valentina, you wanted to meet the puppies?"

"Yes please!"

"Let's go."

We walk around to the back of the house, right to the shore of Loch Glas. The zeuglodon and Finlay are not on there anymore. She must have woken and swum off with her little one.

"Good luck..." I say under my breath.

Lord McTire starts rummaging in his sporran, and takes out a sort of whistle, similar to the one that Alistair used to call the mermaids. He blows in it and, like the mermaid whistle, no sound comes out.

Valentina keeps looking left and right, impatiently.

Suddenly, I feel something nudging the back of my leg. A dog? I turn around. There's something sniffing me. A sort of... lizard, the size of a small dog. It's blue, and it's got wings.

"Oh, here are the puppies!" squeals Camilla.

There are two of them... three... five! And they're all sniffing us. Sorley and Mairi are greeting them affectionately. Valentina is enraptured.

"Dragons!" she cries out.

"That's right. Baby dragons," says Sorley, who has taken one in his arms.

They nuzzle us for a while, then they start flapping their wings, laboriously. They're plump little creatures, and their wings are only small. When they try to fly it's incredibly cute.

One by one, they manage to lift themselves off the ground, Camilla twirling in among them.

"They're still learning," explains Mairi.

They're all over us, flapping their wings as hard as they can, climbing on our heads, our shoulders. One perches on Valentina's head.

"Mind they don't bite you, their teeth are pretty sharp," Lord McTire admonishes us.

Oh.

"They're very good natured, though. Most of the time."

Just as well!

In a few minutes, we're covered in mud and dragon saliva. Now I know why Lord McTire was so dirty, when we arrived.

"Come on, now, before their mum arrives. She can be rather... protective."

Right.

A bit further along the shore Lord McTire rummages in his sporran and takes out two little fabric pouches hanging off strings.

"Tie these on. We're about to see the kelpie," he says cheerily, and strides forward.

"What?" exclaims Camilla. Can a ghost go pale? Because she has.

"Kelpie!" says Valentina, not interrupting her gait, quickly tying the little pouch around her neck.

"No, we aren't!" Camilla is clearly not moving another float further.

"What's wrong?"

"I can't stand kelpies. They drown children..." It comes back to me that Camilla drowned – that's how she died. She's shaking a little.

"Hey, sweetheart, come here!" Alistair opens his arms to the little ghost-girl, and at the same time, he stops in front of us. Camilla snuggles up against him.

"Whatever you do, Luca, Valentina, don't touch the kelpie," he whispers urgently, checking that the pouch string is safely around our necks. We nod.

He seems quite... anxious. That's not like him.

With Camilla floating very close to Uncle Alistair, we follow Lord McTire around a curve of the shore to find a figure sitting on a rock. As we get closer, I can tell it's a woman. She has long white hair that's dripping wet. Her eyes are as green as Libby McMillan's from Hag, but they have a glassy, sinister sheen. She looks a bit... crazy, really. I feel the hair at the back of my neck stand up, and take Valentina's hand to make sure she's safe.

"Hello, Lord McTire. Who have you brought to me?" the woman says. Her voice is deep, and a bit... gurgly. Like she has water, or mud, in her lungs.

"They're not for you, if that's what you mean. How are you, Morag?"

"Hungry," she says. Her hair is dripping, dripping, making a sinister noise as the water hits the stones. Like something you might hear in a black airless cave. I feel Camilla gasping softly beside me.

"Let's go..." she whispers.

"Nice to meet you, children," says the kelpie, and extends her hand.

"Don't touch her!" whispers Alistair. We keep our arms glued to our sides.

"Now, now, Morag. I thought we were over this. And anyway, they wouldn't taste nice," says Lord McTire, showing her the little pouches around our necks.

"Oh, but there are ways..."

A blood-curling wail rises from beside me. It's Camilla, her hair spread around her like a mane, her eyes black and hollow, her arms extended. She looks terrifying, all white floating rags and those empty eyes taking up most of her face.

The kelpie gurgles, a low fearsome noise, and slides into the loch. As she touches the water, her body seems to blur and melt. In a split second, she changes shape, and she's a white mare, her mane dripping like her hair did. She goes under without a noise, just a few silent ripples.

Valentina and I are holding onto each other. As soon as the water closes, we look back at Camilla, and she's a little girl again, pale and trembling in Alistair's arms, her black hair down on her shoulders.

"Sorry," she whispers.

"It's ok, sweetheart." Uncle Alistair strokes her hair, going right through her.

I realise I'm sweating.

"Come away, now," says Lord McTire, and leads us past the kelpie's stone. "Not the nicest of creatures, but we have her under control."

I doubt that, but I don't say anything.

Sorley strolls beside us.

"When I was a wee boy, my mum and dad always made sure we had our pouches around our necks, tied seven times, just to make sure."

"Why are we not supposed to touch her?" I ask.

"Her skin is adhesive. If you touch her, you'll stick to her skin, and she'll drag you under," Sorley answers calmly, like it's everyday stuff. Growing up on Loch Glas must have been pretty exciting. Camilla shudders in mid-air, and Valentina is very pale too. I squeeze her arm again.

"Look!" she cries out all of a sudden, pointing somewhere in the distance.

There's a white horse, galloping fast towards us. The kelpie is back! Valentina holds on to me. I'm rooted to the spot. The horse comes straight at us – I know she'll take us under the black waters of the loch!

"Snow!" Mairi waves to galloping animal.

I peer, trying to see better. The kelpie – is it the kelpie? – has something on her forehead. It's a… Yes, it's a horn! Her mane is so silky, it seems to shimmer.

"A unicorn!" smiles Valentina, and she relaxes. Just like the one on the coat of arms. Not a kelpie at all. Every vision, every myth seems to come true, here in Loch Glas.

"Would you like to ride him?" asks Mairi. "I'll take you."

Valentina nods. She's speechless with happiness.

Sorley helps her up, and they're off, Valentina's blonde and Mairi's red hair blowing behind them.

"So, is Loch Glas like you remember, Alistair?" Lord McTire takes his arm.

"Even more amazing, to be honest."

"You should see it at night. If you come out when it's dark..."

"Can we do that? Tonight?" asks Uncle Alistair.

"You and I, yes. But not Luca and Valentina. It's too dangerous. I'm sorry, son," says Lord McTire, and pats my shoulder.

"It's fine by me! I don't want to be anywhere near those stones at night."

"The kelpie wouldn't be the greatest danger, Luca, believe me."

I feel a chill going down my spine.

Heading back to the house, Uncle Alistair and I walk a little behind the others.

"*What was Lord McTire talking about?*" I whisper, making sure that Uncle Alistair can read my lips.

"Oh, this and that. Creatures, things, you know. The cù sìth, for example," says Uncle Alistair.

"Pardon?"

"The cù sìth hunts at night. It's a dog, white, with red eyes and ears."

"A dog doesn't sound very scary."

"It is if it's as big as a horse. And then there's the baobhan sìth."

"Another sìth? What is it?"

"You might call it a vampire."

"A vam... oh. Right." I swallow.

"Seriously, Luca, make sure that Valentina doesn't come out tonight," he says, looking straight into my eyes.

"I will." I swallow.

"Come on. I hope you'll see our pride and joy, unless she's being shy," calls Lord McTire. After the kelpie, and the stories of big cats and vampires, I'm a bit nervous about what this "pride and joy" might be.

Valentina and Mairi rejoin us. My sister is smiling, her cheeks red with the wind, her eyes shining.

"It was fantastic!"

I don't have time to ask more, because Lord McTire is taking out another whistle from his sporran, differently shaped from the one he used to call the little dragons. He blows in it, over and over again.

I look at Uncle Alistair. He's standing watching the water, his arms folded, smiling a little. He doesn't seem tense, so maybe this particular creature is not dangerous. Hopefully.

Tiny ripples start to appear on the water. Then, without further warning, a huge black shape raises its head about a hundred yards from where we stand. It has a long neck and a body like a black mound. It looks just like Nessie.

"Now, unlike our zeuglodon, *this* is a dinosaur," says Uncle Alistair, clearly delighted.

My heart is pounding. A real living breathing dinosaur....

"Can we get closer?" asks Valentina. Her eyes are shining.

"Sorry, she won't come to the shore, she's very shy. And we can't let you go in a boat on Loch Glas, it's too dangerous. She might capsize us by accident. And there are other creatures in there."

The dinosaur gazes about. She turns her head left, then right, slowly. It's like time has stopped. Like all centuries past have come together in one instant, here, now, on the shores of Loch Glas. Just for us.

Then she dives underwater, and disappears. Nobody speaks for a while, as the ripples break on the shore, one after the other.

That was the most beautiful thing I've ever seen in my life.

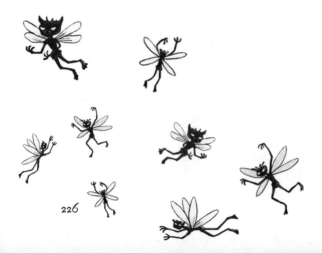

22. DARKNESS

You know when people say "I saw my whole life flash in front of me"?

Well, it really works like that.

As I was flying above the woods in the arms of a vampire, I saw myself as a wee boy, I saw my parents, and my home, and my school, I saw the beaches and the sea of Eilean, and the landscape I know as well as the back of my hand, I saw them right there, in front of my eyes, one scene after the other.

And I thought, "So this is what dying is like..."

I'll tell you how it happened.

At dinner we sit around a huge mahogany table in a room that's as big as my house. On the table there's a spread of lovely food. The McTires seem to like their meat: boar, pheasant, venison, and a few unidentified animals. I don't ask. I wonder what you could hunt, in the woods surrounding Loch Glas...

"Lord McTire, I was wondering. With all these dangerous creatures around here, are you not scared? Do they not attack you?"

Sorley laughs. "I'd say they wouldn't dare attack my father or me, or any of our family."

I'm dying to ask why, but it seems rude, so I decide against it.

"Why?" asks Valentina.

"Because we're more dangerous than them," says Lord McTire. His eyes are very clear, almost white.

"Am I at liberty to tell them?" asks Alistair.

"Of course. Tell them on the way back," answers Lord McTire with a smile. He has a toothy smile, I notice for the first time.

Valentina and I look at each other.

"Sorley, any chance that I could see the mermaids, before I go? And Finlay?"

"Of course. Tomorrow morning," he replies, and bites a big chunk off his roasted boar leg.

Our bedroom is huge, with two four-poster beds and a stone fireplace.

"Goodnight, children." Lady Margaret is tucking us in. She's brought us some chocolate milk and biscuits. I'm surprised it's not a steak, given the amount of meat they eat here.

"'Night, Margaret, and thank you."

"Oh, and children, if you hear noises out of your window, don't be alarmed, it happens all the time."

We nod.

The second she closes the door, I jump into Valentina's bed.

"What are you doing?"

"Valentina, whatever happens, don't go out of this room tonight."

"Why?"

"Uncle Alistair and Lord McTire are going to go out and look for... creatures. They said we can't go with them."

"Why?" she repeats. I can see she's disappointed.

"Why? Er, remember the kelpie?"

"Yes, but we have our pouches." She curls her hand around it.

"The pouches work against the kelpie, but Lord McTire said that there's worse than that out there. Big cats. And vampires!"

"Seriously?"

I nod frantically.

"Well, then, I'm getting dressed!"

"Valentina, no! Uncle Alistair told me to make sure you stay in." I'm praying she listens.

At that very moment, terrifying wild howling cuts through our talk.

A look between us, and then we both run to the window.

Uncle Alistair is outside, standing in a pool of moonshine. And beside him are two big dogs.

No, *not* dogs.

Two wolves.

The light of the moon is so strong, so white, that I can see the wolves' eyes. They're a bright clear piercing blue. Valentina and I look at each other again, and her face tells me what she's planning to do.

"Don't go." I whisper. My heart is beating so fast it's jumping out of my chest.

Valentina shakes her head. "We've got to. Uncle Alistair is in danger!"

And she bolts out of the room in her spotty pyjamas.

I have no choice but to follow, and we run out into the darkness. But the second we set foot on the grass, we both throw ourselves on the ground with our hands over our ears to shelter from an explosion of noise far worse even than the howling. A terrible sound, a sound so powerful that it hurts, has filled the air: three barks, each one louder than the one before, echo over the loch and the woods, and reverberate for a long, long time.

When the echo of the three great barks finally dies down, we get up and run towards Uncle Alistair and the wolves, with Valentina shouting, "Uncle Alistair!" at the top of her voice.

Uncle Alistair turns towards us, and so do the wolves. One is dark grey and enormous. The other one is smaller, leaner, with light grey fur.

They look at us for a few seconds with those crazy blue eyes... then they attack.

First, Valentina. She gets thrown on the ground with the light grey wolf's paws on her chest. Then it's my turn: the darker wolf pounces towards me and in an instant I'm on the ground too, waiting for the first bite...

The wolves' low growl is in my ears, and I keep thinking of my parents, of how devastated they'll be when they know we're dead.

I brace myself, but the bite doesn't come. The wolf's paws are heavy on my chest though, and I can't breathe. I feel like my ribcage is going to give way.

Soon I'll suffocate. Either that, or the wolf will bite my head off... I open my eyes in a panic.

But the wolf doesn't seem to be about to bite. It's not even looking at me: it's looking behind me. And growling. What's behind me? I can't turn to see, I'm stuck under the wolf's weight.

Suddenly, both wolves pounce. I take a big breath and scramble to my feet; I know I should turn around and find out what's there, but I can't help looking to Valentina instead – and I see that Uncle Alistair has her in his arms! Thank goodness, she's safe!

"Luca! Valentina! Run inside! Run, NOW!" he screams, pushing Valentina towards me.

I grab her hands, and we start towards the house. But between us and the door stand three growling beasts. The wolves, and what's the third one? I can barely make out its shape in the darkness; what's certain is that we can't reach the house. We have no choice but to stop, and pray that the beasts will be too busy with each other to notice us. They're staring at each other, growling low in the backs of their throats, baring teeth— is it another wolf, maybe? Suddenly, they're rolling on the ground, all three of them, one on top of the other. I can make out light grey fur, dark grey and one pelt of pure spotless white.

Now I know what's attacked us. It's not another wolf. It's the cù sìth.

The wolves are fighting it with all their might. I see a flash of red, and then suddenly the wolves take a step back – both of them at the same time. They stand in front of the cù sìth and growl, and look at it with eyes that command obedience, but they're not attacking anymore.

The cù sìth is huge, perfectly white, with red ears and bright red eyes. Its tail is so long it looks like a snake, and is made of three braided strands. It bows its head reluctantly and kneels on the ground, as in defeat. There's blood on one of its paws.

The cù sìth stays, immobile, for a few seconds and then, in perfect silence, with a single jump, it disappears into the woods.

Valentina and I are rooted to the spot, both panting in fear and awe, like we've been running miles.

Then something amazing happens.

One of the wolves, the darker one, turns its mighty head towards us solemnly, and speaks. A low growly voice, deeply frightening, and yet familiar... My heart stops. I know that voice.

"I told you to stay inside."

"Lord McTire..." whispers Valentina. She's shaking with fear and cold.

"I'm sorry, Hamish, I never thought they would..."

Uncle Alistair tries to defend us.

"We thought... we thought Uncle Alistair was in danger..." I manage to whisper. My throat is so dry, and my knees are giving way. Valentina and I hold onto each other for dear life. I struggle to formulate the thought: Lord McTire is a werewolf!

"Follow me. I'll take you inside," says the light grey wolf.

"And Sorley," murmurs Valentina, her eyes wide and white in the moonlight.

"That's right. It's me. Come on, children."

I can't believe what must be true. That's Sorley. And he's a werewolf too. Sorley's voice, Sorley's eyes... a wolf's body.

"Go with him. We'll speak tomorrow," says Alistair, with a face like thunder.

Sorley walks towards us on silent paws, and we can't help taking a step back.

"Don't be afraid. I won't hurt you. The cù sìth is gone, you're safe. But we must get to the house now."

Right then, something rips Valentina away from me, something strong, irresistible, like a whirlpool.

A face materialises beside me, floating in mid-air. It's white – chalky white – with two black sockets instead of its eyes, and its mouth is open in a silent scream.

The creature has Valentina under one arm. She's thrashing about, trying to get free, and she's screaming, screaming.

"LET HER GO!" I try to grab her back, hanging onto her hand with all my might.

"It's the baobhan sìth! LUCA, RUUUUUN!" shouts Uncle Alistair.

But how could I run? That thing has my sister!

And now it has me too. It slips its arm around my waist as I am trying to free Valentina, and it lifts us off the ground, one under each of its arms... Below, I see the wolves jumping, growling, circling angrily where we stood one minute ago, and Uncle Alistair, his hands in his hair, his face a mask of despair. All noises drift away as we fly into the night, up above the woods, into clouds of icy mists, towards certain death.

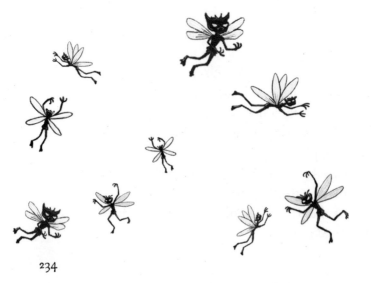

23. A NIGHT OF FEAR
AND MIRACLES

Alistair Grant's *Scottish Paranormal Database*

Entry Number 9: William Freshwater and the
baobhan sìth
Type: Fairy. Subtype: Vampire
Location: Unspecified, in the Highlands of Scotland
Date: 1801
Details: The first recorded sighting of a baobhan
sìth was in 1801, though many stories precede
it. An Englishman called William Freshwater was
travelling in the Highlands of Scotland with his
brother and two friends. A group of baobhan sìths
attacked them, and William took refuge beneath his
horse. His brother and friends were killed, while
William survived. He was told later by the locals
that baobhans hate iron; the horse he had hidden
under was wearing, of course, iron shoes. The
baobhan sìth is a vampire that drains the blood of
her victims using her sharp claw-like fingernails.
She can take the form of a beautiful woman in a
green dress, or reveal her true appearance: a
black-clad monster with chalky skin, empty sockets
instead of eyes, and deer hooves for feet.

We fly for a long time, or that's how it feels. Maybe
it's just a few minutes, but it's so cold and I'm so scared
that it seems like all night. Valentina has fainted; she's
lying limply under the baobhan's arm, her blonde hair
floating behind us.

Flying above the woods in the velvety night is
the loveliest dream and the most awful nightmare,

all mixed together. The moon is white, the sky is full of stars and the woods below are incredibly beautiful. Shame that I'm about to die, and I'll never see all this again. I see my whole life leading to this point, and my heart lurches for my parents, who have no idea how much danger we're in.

Suddenly, we head down at breathtaking speed. For a second I'm sure we'll crash on the trees – I close my eyes in terror, and I scream...

At the last instant, we land on a soft patch of grass. The baobhan is still holding us under her arms, and her grip is merciless. I try to break free, but I might as well not bother. She's too strong.

If I want to save our lives I've got to think of another way. Right now, I don't see any. Even if I could break free and run away – I'm a very fast runner – I couldn't leave Valentina there. And she can't run half as fast as me.

We both escape, or neither of us does.

The baobhan drags us towards a grassy mound with a black opening right in the middle. It looks like the entrance to a cave. A figure takes shape against its darkness... it's a woman, a woman with a long green dress and a beautiful face. And another one, and another one, all lovely and tall and wearing green dresses.

They all come out of the cave, and run towards us. The baobhan who kidnapped us throws us both on the ground. Valentina yelps – she's revived from her faint.

I scramble to my feet and then realise the chalky black-clad monster that has taken us has turned into a beautiful woman too, like the others. They're all breathtakingly, perfectly lovely, all with the same red hair, all wearing these long, long dresses...

I help Valentina stand up, and hold her tight. She's as white as the moon.

"*How are we going to get out of this?*" she whispers.

"I have no idea. Run?"

"They can fly! They'd catch us in a second!"

"Then let's hope Uncle Alistair finds us, or this is the last night of our lives," I whisper, shaking.

The women surround us, and they seem to be conferring in some weird language. It sounds a bit like the Gaelic we speak on Eilean, but it's not Gaelic. It's a melodious, singsong language that borrows something from the wind in the trees – it seems very ancient, like the language of the woods itself. If it weren't so horrifying, I would say it was beautiful.

One of the vampires moves towards us. I catch a flash of her foot, peeping out below the green dress: it's a hoof. A deer hoof. I shiver.

She raises a hand, and her long fingernails are sharp and curved like claws. She touches my face, then Valentina's. Her hand is as cold as ice, and her nails scrape my skin ever so slightly...

She's smiling. Thinking of dinner, no doubt. The other baobhans imitate her: they move towards us, touch our faces, our hair... They're all over us. I'm wondering if these are our last moments...

Then one of them says some kind of instruction in that melodious language, and they all get busy. They disappear into the woods, all except for one who's keeping guard. She's sitting right in front of us, looking at us longingly, like you'd look at a nice warm bag of chips on the way home from school.

Valentina and I hold onto each other. It's really cold, and we're in our pyjamas. We're both shivering, with cold and with fear.

"Can you call Camilla?"

"No, no...."

"Is it not working? Your telepathic thing."

"It's not that. I don't want to bring her here! What if they hurt her?"

"But she's a ghost..."

"So are they, in a way! What if they vanquish her, or something?"

"You're right. Better not risk it."

"We have to try something, Luca."

I nod. "We need to make a run for it. There's nothing else we can do."

She nods. "Ok. At my three. One, two, three... RUN!"

We jump up, and take a step. Just one step. No more.

Because all the baobhans are back, their arms full of kindling, standing in a row in front of us. Smiling at us, indulgently, as if we were naughty children trying to skip class.

"*That didn't work.*" I whisper. "What is all that wood for?"

"Luca, this is bad. They're going to light a fire!"

"Oh, no... They're going to cook us!"

"They're not going to cook us, Luca! They're getting ready to bleed us dry! I read it in one of Uncle Alistair's books. It's like a ceremony. They light a fire and do a

238

sort of dance and sing a special song and then they bleed their victims..."

I swallow. Where is Uncle Alistair? We need him to find us. We must try to delay the baobhans, to give him time. But what can he do, even if he gets here while we're still alive?

The baobhans make a little smouldering fire. They keep putting more wood on it and then some foul-smelling things that look like furs, or maybe little animals they hunted, and it grows bigger and bigger. It gets as big as a bonfire, its flames dancing red and yellow against the black, black sky.

"Luca, we have our pouches! Maybe that will work! It worked with the kelpie."

"Worth a try!" I take out the little pouch hanging from my neck, and thrust it up to the baobhans.

"Look! You don't want to drink our blood! We're poisonous! Look!"

The vampires stop throwing things on the fire for a second. They all turn towards me. And they laugh, a horrible barking laugh that sounds like a pack of hyenas, in contrast with the melodious voices they have when they speak.

I wince, and Valentina has her hands on her ears.

"That didn't work."

"UNCLE ALISTAAAAAAAAAIR! SORLEEEEEEEEY! MAAAAAAIRI! LORD MACTIIIIIIIIRE!" screams Valentina suddenly. I join her; we shout at the top of our voices.

The baobhans ignore us, as if we were background noise, some night bird, or the wind in the trees.

After a while, we stop. There's no point.

"Uncle Alistair will be in big trouble with Mum and Dad," I say to Valentina.

"How is he going to explain this one? Vampires killed your children?"

"Poor Mum and Dad..."

"And poor us!"

We huddle together. At least the fire is warming us, though the smell of those burning furs is horrendous.

When the fire is big enough, the baobhans decide that it's time for the party. A dinner party, probably, with our blood as the main course. They start singing an ancient, echoing, terrifying song, while circling the fire. Their red manes look on fire, and the light of the flames is reflected in their white faces.

Valentina bursts into tears, and I hold her in my arms. This is not like her – she's always fearless. There's nothing else I can do to comfort her. We huddle together on the grass.

One of the vampires breaks the circle, and comes towards us. She kneels in front of us, and raises a clawed hand to my neck.

I wince, then scream, as her nails break my skin and draw the first blood.

She screams too! A lot louder than me. She jumps back, recoiling in horror, and I see her lovely face turning, melting, until it's the chalky empty-eyed horror that kidnapped us. The other vampires all scream and transform from women into monsters. They lift off the ground to float in mid-air.

"What is it? *Why did they stop bleeding us?*" whispers Valentina.

"I have no idea!" I press my hand against my bloodied cheek.

The baobhans hiss and scream and float about, until they form some kind of circle over our heads, hovering, like birds of prey over a rabbit.

We wait for them to strike. They don't. They keep circling slowly, slowly, occasionally crying out to each other in their ancient language. It's like they want us, but something is repulsing them. What is it? What's keeping them at bay? It can't be our pouches – they had ignored mine completely when I'd thrust it at their faces.

"Let's try again. *Let's run.* We have nothing to lose." I whisper. "One, two, three... RUN!"

And they let us! We're getting away!

For a few yards. Then one of them comes down on me, and throws me to the ground. Her clawed hands are all over me, my face, my chest, my legs... Until they close around the velvet treasure bag hanging from my belt, the one with the troll's medallion and Mary's pearl in it. The baobhan pulls violently, and I hear the bag ripping... She's managed to yank it off.

It's too late. She has it.

But the bag has torn. It's flailing open, empty. Something's shining in the grass, just beside me... I scramble quickly, manage to close my hand around the pearl and the medallion, and push them both deep into my jeans pocket.

"WHAT ARE YOU GOING TO DO NOW? YOU UGLY MONSTER!"

Valentina is on her feet, and she's waving her little fist at them. She's herself again, at last! I know that what she's doing is crazy, but she's so brave.

"YOU AWFUL, SMELLY THING! JUST GO AWAY AND LEAVE US ALONE!"

I grab her hand tightly.

The baobhans are furious. They're circling, circling, whispering in their strange language. It must be either the pearl or the medallion, keeping them away. There's no other explanation. Otherwise, why would they have tried to take them from me?

Wait a minute. From *me*. I have them in my pocket. Valentina doesn't.

And then it hits me: I know what they'll do next, they'll try and separate us!

I hold Valentina tighter, with all my strength.

Right at that moment, the whole circle of them flies down at us, dragging us in two separate directions. I'll be protected by the treasure, but they'll kill my sister!

"LET ME GO! LET ME GO!" Valentina is screaming, but it's no use. We're wrenched apart. She's on the ground, and they cover her, like hungry crows...

And then, I hear howling, and again!

Two wolves, howling not far from us.

The baobhans hear it too. They float up and away from Valentina at once, and I can get to her. She has blood on her hands, but she's fine. I hold her tight.

The wood opens and the wolves arrive, pouncing into the clearing, eyes flashing, teeth bared. One of them is carrying Uncle Alistair on his back.

"Uncle Alistair!" I cry out. He runs to us and holds us tight.

"I thought I'd lost you! *I thought you were dead!*" he whispers.

"They didn't bleed us! It was the pearl, Mary's pearl! Or the medallion, or both!"

Uncle Alistair puts a hand on my mouth, to silence me.

Lord McTire is speaking, in the baobhans' language. I have no idea what he's saying, but it sounds menacing.

The vampires listen, hissing and whispering viciously. When Lord McTire is finally quiet, they fly swiftly away, and disappear into the fairy mound, dissolving into the darkness as if they were made of darkness too.

We're saved.

Sorley howls, a howl of victory.

Uncle Alistair takes my face in his hands. "It was the medallion. It's iron. Baobhans hate iron."

"And I hate baobhans," says Valentina fiercely. Uncle Alistair hugs us both, very tight and for a long time.

Lord McTire carries Valentina and me on his back, and Sorley carries Uncle Alistair. We travel silently among the trees, back from the horror, towards the safety of McTire house.

Not long later, we're in bed, exhausted like we've never been before.

"Luca..." says Valentina in a small voice.

"Yes?"

"If you had killed the troll, he wouldn't have given you the medallion. If he hadn't given you the medallion, we'd be dead."

It's true. I remember the moment I looked into the troll's pale, almost white eyes, and I saw such fear in them, and resignation. I just couldn't do it. I couldn't kill him.

And that act of mercy had saved my own life.

"*I know...*" I whisper in the darkness.

But there's no reply. Valentina is already asleep.

WINTER

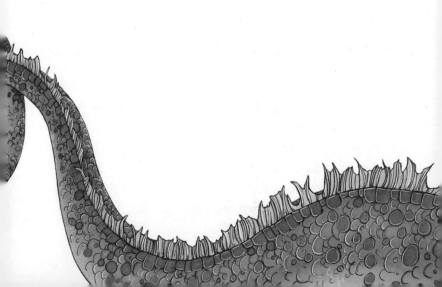

24. WHERE MY DAD FINDS OUT AND WE'RE IN TROUBLE

Alistair Grant's *Scottish Paranormal Database*

Entry Number 21: The haunted cliff
Type: Post-mortem manifestation
Location: Canisbay, Caithness
Date: The present
Details: A forlorn figure walks the cliff at Canisbay, occasionally sitting down to watch the sea. He disappears if anyone tries to make contact.

The next morning, at the McTire breakfast table, we're quiet. We're very much in the doghouse. Or in the wolfhouse, actually.

"I'm sorry, Uncle Alistair. When we saw the wolves..." I hesitate. Werewolves? Wolves? What do they prefer to be called? Lord McTire doesn't say anything, so I continue. "We thought you were in trouble. We thought you were being attacked."

"I know."

"It was incredibly foolish of you to come out..." says Lord McTire. We bow our heads. "...and brave. Both of you. The way you tried to save your uncle when you thought he was in danger..."

"The way you didn't run from the baobhan who had Valentina, you let her take you too..." intervenes

Sorley, looking at me.

"You're easily two of the bravest children I've ever met. This is for you."

Lord McTire stands up, walks around the dinner table – it goes on for miles, so it takes a good few minutes to circumnavigate it – and hands us a velvet case, one each.

We open them in silence. Inside, a dagger. A silver dagger, decorated with spirals and lovely intricate designs. The handle is carved in the shape of a wolf's head.

We're speechless. Even Valentina. I can feel Mairi's eyes on me. Lord McTire speaks to us solemnly.

"They've been in our family for generations. They were supposed to go to Sorley and Mairi, but we talked about it. They want you to have them."

"You're now part of the clan McTire, as well as Grant. That is, if you want to be," says Sorley.

"Do we have to be werewolves?" asks Valentina, matter-of-factly. I elbow her.

"It's not compulsory," laughs Sorley.

"You'll need these daggers. They're made of silver – a metal of great use against many creatures. Though we're not in the habit of harming anything, you might need to defend yourselves."

"Lord McTire, Sorley, Mairi..." I'm caught in the solemnity of the moment. "Thank you."

"Yes, thank you so much!" Valentina gets up and gives each of them a big hug, and then she hugs Margaret as well, who's looking on with shiny eyes.

Before we leave, the McTire family accompany us to

the loch shore. Lord McTire calls the mermaids with his special whistle and, after a wee while, they appear, swimming towards us. I kneel down, to get as close to them as possible.

I recognise the one who saved me from her eyes. She puts her blue-green arms out to me, and I hug her. I don't care about getting wet. I look into her black eyes, and she makes a deep singsong sound, like a whale.

"I'm so glad to see you too." My voice sounds just like hers.

She puts out her webbed hand, and I put mine against it, like we did on the glass when she was in the aquarium.

"See you again, soon," she whispers.

"Soon," I answer, and it sounds like water lapping on the shore.

They sing for me, a beautiful haunting goodbye song, and then they swim away, towards the heart of the loch. I watch the waters until they disappear. We're walking towards the black truck when I hear a lovely sweet sound coming from the loch.

It's a tiny tender *yeeeeeeey*. It's Finlay, saying goodbye.

I can still hear Finlay's small voice as I step into the truck. Right at that moment, Camilla materialises on the back seat between us.

"Hi! I'm back. Did I miss anything?"

"Camilla! Wait till I tell you what happened to us! We got kidnapped!" exclaims Valentina.

I let Valentina tell her about our terrible night, while Camilla aaahs and ooohs and floats upwards in excitement, while I drift away, lost in thought, reflecting on all that happened to us in Loch Glas.

The trees are golden and red and brown as we travel back to our van at Loch Brue, and then towards home. I have my rucksack in my lap, and I notice for the first time that it feels very light.

I rummage in it. No diary. Have I forgotten to bring it from Loch Glas? I can't have. I never took it out while I was there. Or at Loch Brue. I must have left it at home. A chill travels down my spine, a terrible doubt – but I push it to the back of my head. It'll be fine. I'm sure it's safe.

"About the McTire family..."

"One of the few wolf families left in Scotland," explains Uncle Alistair.

"There are others?"

"Yes. I know a couple."

"Have they always been like this... I mean, was Lord McTire the first, or..."

"Or. They've been wolves since forever. You see, thousands of years ago, Scotland had three clans, the Wolf, the Bear and the Cat. Many people could turn into their clan animal at will. This gift has nearly been lost through the generations, but some families still retain it..."

"Right... so are there werebears? And werecats?"

"They don't call themselves that, but yes, there are a few that can turn into bears and wildcats."

"I wish I was one," sighs Valentina.

"A werepoquito, Valentina?" I laugh.

"Very funny. And what about Mairi? Is she a werewolf too?"

"No, only the males in the family inherit the gene. She's quite remarkable, though, I can assure you. I think you'll find that out one day."

We drive on. It's beautiful here as autumn turns to winter, and my mind wanders, lost in a dream. I think of all that's ahead of us, all the adventures we'll have, the discoveries we'll make. One day I was a normal boy from a remote island nobody ever heard of, the next day I'm doing all this.

I feel brave, I feel strong. I feel like I'm doing what I should be doing.

Since Uncle Alistair appeared in our lives, we've freed the village of Hag from the stone fairies, and given baby Ella back to her people; we've saved Mr and Mrs Nicol from becoming troll food, and given the troll a new home; we've helped save the stranded mermaids; we've given Mary her ring back, and we're giving her a taste of life on land; and we saved the zeuglodon from becoming a science experiment, or ending up in some weird creature zoo. And, we've survived being attacked by a bunch of vampires.

Loch Glas is just the best place I've ever seen in my life. I'd like to go back there soon, and ask Sorley to tell me every single story of every creature they've rescued. I'll never forget the dinosaur's long neck rising from the water, its back like an ancient moss-covered hill... Like centuries past looking at me in the face, in a single magical moment.

I don't need anyone to know about what we do, about the RWR. I don't need the glory. It's enough to know that I'm doing something special, that I'm part of something necessary and unique.

And then, one day, maybe when I show him my diary, my dad will see that I'm just like him. He'll speak to me, ask me things about my life, and we'll chat for hours and do things together. I'll be his best friend. Better than boring old Reilly, who doesn't even exist.

Yes, it's all going to go the way I planned.

I look at my sister, her blonde hair falling on her face, immersed in the latest issue of *Reptiles of the Americas*. Then at Camilla, sitting between us, transparent and pretty in her white dress. And finally, at my uncle's profile as he drives, the straight nose, the determined blue eyes, the stripy blue and green scarf wrapped many times around his neck. We're a good team. I never, never want to be apart from them.

As we drive into Eilean, the brightly coloured houses seem to shine against the dark grey sky, and the sea is announcing a storm. It's good to hear the soft sound of the sea lapping against the shore, like a welcome home. We stop at Weird HQ to leave our bags and equipment, then walk on. Alistair is taking us home. We're chatting and laughing as we come through the alley at the side of our house and turn into the wee courtyard.

My mum is standing in front of the back door, her arms crossed, her lips pressed together. It looks like she's been crying. Something has happened.

Uncle Alistair stops in his tracks, frozen.

"You know," he says, in a blank voice.

"Yes."

"Listen, Isabella... I never meant..." His face is full of horror.

"What happened to you?" Mum shouts out suddenly, taking my face in her hands. The scratch from the baobhan's nails.

"It was... brambles..." I mutter.

"Oh, I don't even want to know!" Out of the corner of my eye, I see Valentina hiding her scratched hands behind her back.

"Isabella, I'm sorry..." Uncle Alistair takes a step towards us.

She raises a hand to stop him.

"I don't want to listen, Alistair. You put my children in danger. Terrible danger..." Her voice breaks. "Duncan explained to me what you used to do. It wasn't an accident, with your parents." She shakes her head in horror. "It wasn't an accident. It was an experiment."

"That's not true... It was meant to be a party trick... They asked me to... to... And I'm putting it right! I'm nearly there!" He puts his arms forward as if he's trying to reach out. Isabella takes a step back.

I realise I'm shaking.

I take a step towards Valentina. Our hands meet and we cling to each other.

"Duncan showed me the diary. Luca's diary."

"You weren't supposed to read that! Dad wasn't supposed to read that... Not yet!" I blurt out.

"Children, come inside and go upstairs. Your dad wants to see you. Alistair, just go." My mum interrupts me. "Duncan doesn't want you in our house and, to be honest, neither do I."

Alistair goes, back hunched, eyes downcast. Alone.

I feel something wet fall on my hands, on my forehead, on my cheeks. I look up, and there's a million little white flakes twirling in the darkening sky, falling and falling silently on us, and on the sea.

Valentina has been sent to bed. Camilla has gone to Alistair's house, because, she said, we're together and he's on his own again. I'm upstairs in my dad's study.

"I can't believe you deceived us like this. I can't believe you lied to us," my dad is saying.

"I'm sorry. I didn't want to lie to you. But if I told you, you would have made us stop..."

"Too right we would have, Luca!" booms my dad. His eyes are shining with a black, angry light.

Strangely, I'm not afraid. I'm angry too.

"What we do is important, Dad! I'm doing something valuable for the first time in my life, something that matters!"

"Everything you do is important to me," says my mum quietly.

"To you, yes. But not to Dad! He doesn't even speak to me!"

They both look at me, horrified. My dad's eyes are wide with upset.

"You're making stupid excuses now," he says in a small voice. My dad, a small voice?

"No, he isn't. He's right," says my mum. She looks steely, determined. "You don't speak to him, in fact. Or to Valentina. You barely speak to me, actually. All you do is... write."

My mum and dad fighting. This is not really happening. This is not supposed to happen.

"Isabella, this is not the moment..." starts my dad.

"It's never the moment, with you," I burst out angrily.

"Don't speak to your father like that!" retorts my mum, instinctively.

Phew. My mum and dad are allies again. Things are back to normal.

My dad turns his back at us. He's gazing out of the window. The day is turning into night, and the sea is getting angrier as the wind picks up. The snow keeps falling, falling.

"Luca." Dad takes a deep breath. He's not looking at me. I instinctively feel that what he's about to say hurts him deeply. "My parents... your grandparents... disappeared. They went, just like that..." The music. St Anne's Reel. It's starting again. "...Your Uncle Alistair did something thoughtless and stupid; he used them as guinea pigs for some crazy experiment of his, and they were *gone*. Forever. We don't know where. We'll never know."

The melody is twirling, full force inside my head, the fiddle and the piano, over and over again.

"He says that they asked him..." I protest feebly. I hate to see the pain etched in my father's face.

"They were dazzled by him, Luca! The prodigious boy, the boy with the Sight! The boy with powers! They would have done anything to allow him to shine! And he loved it!" My mum gets up and puts a hand on Dad's back, her head on his shoulder, her soft brown hair covering him like a shelter. Part of me want to go and cuddle them both, but I'm so angry, and the music is so loud...

"Uncle Alistair is trying to put it right!" I blurt out, above the din in my head. "Will you let me do this? Will you let me be part of the RWR?"

"Never. I won't let anything happen to you, Luca."

"You can't stop me!"

"What are you going to do, run away? You're only twelve!"

I'm about to say, "Yes, I will!" when I look into my mum's grey eyes.

I can't do this to her.

I bow my head. The music keeps playing, full blast, and my thoughts are all over the place.

"I'm going to my room."

"I'll bring you some dinner, *tesoro*..." My mum tries to stroke my hair, but I recoil. I'm leaving, too furious to speak. Dad is looking at the floor.

"Luca?"

I stop in the doorway.

"Your diary. You write very well," he says quietly.

25. MUSIC FROM LONG AGO

> **Alistair Grant's *Scottish Paranormal Database***
>
> **Entry Number 58:** Merry ghosts of Culzean Castle
> **Type:** Ghostly apparition
> **Location:** Culzean Castle
> **Date:** Christmas Eve, every year from 1818 to the present
> **Details:** Ghostly music can be heard in the grounds of Culzean Castle on Christmas Eve every year. Occasionally, dancers and musicians have also been spotted, making merry. (See Podcasts and Recordings, file number 34.)

A couple of days later, Mum comes into my room to have a chat.

"I know your diary is private, I know I shouldn't have read it, but I needed to see for myself what your dad told me." I hung my head. The last thing I wanted was to upset her. "The things you've seen, Luca... the things that you can See. It's amazing. I never knew about all this... about the Sight. Your father never told me about any of that."

"Mum, I can't pretend I don't have this gift. I can't just waste it."

"I know. I know." Our eyes meet. "I cannot tell you how proud I am of you." I nod. I don't trust myself to speak right now. "What you did was wrong, what your uncle did was wrong. Lying to us... putting you

258

in such danger... but... well, I want you to know that I understand why you did it. The call must have been impossible to ignore."

I couldn't believe what I was hearing. She understood!

"I couldn't stop. It was all too... amazing."

"I know. And I think your dad was wrong when he said he wanted you to forget about the Sight. You'll never be able to forget, or to ignore this gift... You shouldn't."

"You think I should use this gift I have? Then why did you agree with Dad?"

"Because you're too young. Too young, too vulnerable. You're just a wee boy..." she said, touching my face gently.

"I'm nearly thirteen!"

"When you're a man, you'll be free to make your own decisions."

"I want to make my decisions now!"

"Luca, listen. What your uncle does is extremely dangerous. And Valentina is even younger than you. You both must wait before you do what your Uncle Alistair does. But your dad thinks you have to give it up completely..." she looked determined, like she'd made up her mind about something, "...and I disagree."

"I could never give it up."

"I know. I'm just asking you to wait. Then you can make your own choices. Your dad will have to understand."

"Thank you, Mum." We smile at each other. Dad always says I'm a chip off my mum's block. Still, she's always surprising me.

What else. Things at school have been... ok. Boring, but ok. Gary is nicer than ever before. Well, not nice as such, more like *scared*. He avoids me, but when our paths cross, he's so sweet he's actually servile. I feel a bit sorry for him. Then again, it's easy for people to fall back into old ways. The other day, I saw him trying to torment a boy who recently moved from the mainland. Gary doesn't like newcomers. I went up to him and the new boy, and said hello. That was all.

It was enough. After that, Gary left the boy alone.

Valentina is doing ok too. She plays her fiddle, reads her crazy magazines, hangs out with Camilla, the usual. She is busy ignoring Adil, who has taken to stammering and tripping over his own feet every time he sees her. Embarrassing. She misses the RWR, I can tell. Terribly.

Valentina and I have been expecting to bump into Uncle Alistair, even though he's been banished from our house and we've been told we are absolutely not to go to RWR HQ. Eilean is a small place. We walk home extra-slow from school, looking around us, hoping to spot him in the bakery, or the bookshop, or the tiny supermarket on the corner. But we never do.

Then one afternoon he steps out of the post office, a package under each arm, both wrapped in brown paper and covered in stamps. We stop in our tracks.

He looks like he hasn't slept for days: his hair is sticking up, he's wearing a dirty shirt covered in green stains, and his eyes look swollen and small with exhaustion.

"Uncle Alistair!" calls Valentina. He turns towards us, giving us a haunted, regretful look – for a second, I'm sure he's about to stop and speak to us... but he doesn't. He strides on.

"Valentina, he looks terrible! We have to do something!"

"We need to go and see him," she says, resolutely.

"We're not allowed. We'll get into terrible trouble!" It feels like we do really need to talk to him, but the idea of my mum getting upset again...

We watch from afar as Uncle Alistair turns the corner – even from behind he doesn't look right. We owe this to him.

I'm about to chase after him, when I hear my name being called.

"Children! Luca! Valentina!"

It's Mum! She's waving from the other side of the road. The smile on her face tells us she hasn't seen Uncle Alistair. We change direction and she crosses to meet us.

"It's nearly four o'clock, Luca. You'll be late for shinty."

Valentina and I look at each other.

"Yes, Luca, come on. Let's go and get your strip, I'll come to shinty with you and see the practice," Valentina replies quickly.

I instantly know her plan. We'll go and get my strip, then run straight to Weird HQ. We're likely to get away with it: Mr MacDonald only contacts parents if players miss three practices in a row, and I can phone Adil and let him know I'm not going, so he won't come looking for me at the house.

The idea of defying Dad and Mum again makes me feel a bit ill. But Uncle Alistair needs us – things just seem terrible whenever I think of him.

"Good idea, Valentina!" I say brightly.

We walk home with Mum, run straight upstairs to get my strip and we're out again, each clutching a chocolate cookie she has insisted on giving us.

Standing by the road, I use Valentina's phone to leave a message for Adil saying I won't be at practice and I'll explain later.

"Sorted?" Valentina asks.

"Sorted."

And then I see Mary running towards us in her slippers, her hair flowing behind her, looking frightened.

That moment, I know we're too late.

"He's gone!" she says. "Disappeared! Something's gone wrong. I don't know what to do."

We grab her hands and rush back with her.

The floor of Uncle Alistair's laboratory is covered in shards of glass and flooded with a green, seaweed-smelling liquid. The ceiling light bulb has exploded, along with every single beaker, bottle and petri dish – everything in the room that could shatter has shattered. The big clock on the wall has stopped, its face split in two by one single crack. The curtains are flowing gently inwards – there's no glass left in the window. Uncle Alistair is nowhere to be seen.

We stand in the doorway, speechless. It's Mary who breaks the silence.

"I just heard a terrible noise, like an explosion. And Alistair was gone! His beans and sausages were in the microwave; I was expecting him to walk into the kitchen at any moment for them..." She's so distressed her eyes are full of tears, and her hands are shaking.

"What was he trying? What has he been working on?" I ask.

"I have no idea. Since you came back from Loch Glas he's spent day and night in his lab. He's been completely consumed by his work. He hasn't stopped for long enough to speak about it."

"Alistair!" A disembodied shocked voice resounds in the room, then a glowing blue hovering form takes shape. Her small, see-through hands are clasped on her mouth.

"Camilla!"

"Mary! What happened?"

"Alistair is gone," Mary says miserably, and Camilla flows into her arms, enfolding her into an incorporeal cuddle.

We're all sitting in the living room at Alistair's, trying to make sense of what's happened. He's definitely not here in the house – we looked everywhere. His clothes are all there, his suitcase is still tucked under the bed: he certainly disappeared in a hurry.

"We just saw him coming out of the post office. He looked awful. We were going to come straight here and check on him, but Mum saw us and we had to go home," Valentina explains.

"We thought something was wrong." I add. "We didn't see him for days."

"He was holed up in the lab. He came out for beans and sausages a couple of times a day, but that was it." Mary's black eyes are huge in her pale face. "I asked him what he was doing, but he said he'd show me when it worked..."

"Do you think he might have just gone off by himself, to get away from Eilean? From Dad?" I ask.

Mary shakes her head. "No. Something strange happened this afternoon. He came back from the post office – he always got these parcels, I don't know what was in them – and he went straight into the lab. I called him because his beans were ready, and he said he'd be out in a little while. Ten minutes later I heard a terrible noise, and... well, you saw what it was like in there."

"Wait a minute..." mutters Valentina, and springs out of the room. After a few seconds, she comes back clutching an alarm clock. "Look. This is Uncle Alistair's. It's stopped, like the clock in the lab."

Mary looks at her wrist. "My watch has stopped too," she says, tapping it gently.

"There's another clock in the kitchen – the oven one," says Camilla, and sticks her head through the wall between the living room and the kitchen. "Stopped too," she reports, her voice muffled by the bricks and plaster.

"Oh!" All of a sudden, the music in my head starts again. Usually it starts soft, barely audible and interrupted, a few notes here and there, and then gets louder and clearer when I concentrate on it. But this time is *so* loud, *so* clear – clearer than I've ever heard it before.

"Luca? Luca?" Valentina's voice seems to come from far away. "Are you ok?"

"Yes. Yes, sorry. I'm ok. It's the music in my head. It started again."

"Can you hear it now?"

"Yes. St Anne's Reel..."

"St Anne's Reel? I know that tune. I can play it. It was one of Granny's favourites Dad told me."

"Uncle Alistair said that too. You can't hear it now, can you?"

Valentina closes her eyes for a second, than shakes her head. "I can't." She sighs. "So did you talk to Uncle Alistair about it? The music, I mean."

"Yes. I told him a while ago. He seemed shocked, and all... intense, looking at me hard, and speaking like it was something very important."

"Oh. And what did he say?"

"Well... he told me to... umm, listen carefully, to concentrate on the music."

"What happens when you do?"

I pause and give my mind to it for a moment.

"It gets louder. It sort of starts taking over. There's a tingly sensation. And a strong... something... that I don't quite like. It's a feeling like just knowing that there's something dangerous near you."

"Something dangerous? And if it is, why would Uncle Alistair want you to concentrate on it?" Valentina is frowning like she's thinking hard. I am wondering whether she's trying to hear the music, when she says, "We know he was trying to put right losing Granny and Grandpa. That's what he was desperate about.

265

Luca, do you think he's vanished the same way they vanished?" I feel tight in my tummy. She's still all focused. "If he's stuck somehow, he'll need our help. Who else knows he's gone or what he does? Who else could rescue him? Who else has the Sight like we do?"

"But we don't know how to help," I say. "And he would never talk about what happened with our grandparents, so we don't know where to start." We are all quiet, sitting on the sofa.

I try to think along with Valentina.

"Remember when we saw a... a helmet thing, and a shield, and he was trying to hide them? Do you think they came from the place our grandparents are stuck?"

"What were his weird experiments about?" she asks, "And why have the clocks stopped?"

"He was always adding to the database." I'm desperate for something concrete rather than all this worrying and asking and confusion. I pull up a chair and sit at Uncle Alistair's computer. As I turn my mind to the screen and take it away from the music, it stops.

"I'll go and clean up the lab. You see what you can find..." says Mary, and disappears. We pile around the computer.

Our website, reallyweirdremovals.com, comes straight onto the screen. I click on the link to the *Paranormal Database*.

"Let me see... m-u-s-i-c." I type into the search box. An endless flow of information floods the screen.

Valentina gasps. "Too much! We'll never get through all this... Try 'ghostly music'."

"'Ghostly music'... let's see... Oh, an awful lot for this too... Right, let's get to work."

Half an hour later we've gone through pages and pages of sightings – well, hearings – but there's nothing we can use. Nothing seems significant.

"Maybe we're looking in the wrong place," says Camilla.

"What do you mean?" I turn my head – Camilla is floating right behind us. "Is there another website..."

"No websites. No computers." She shrugs. "Maybe the answer is here..." She touches my forehead gently. "And here..." Her hand points to my heart.

"Of course! Camilla is right!" exclaims Valentina.

"I don't know..." I hesitate. What am I supposed to do? Will I be able to do this? Without the *Paranormal Database*, without Uncle Alistair?

On my own?

"Give it a try anyway. Let's switch this thing off. Now, Luca... Please, see if you can stop worrying. Close your eyes. Concentrate. Listen..."

"Valentina, I don't..."

"Try. Come on, close your eyes."

"Ok. Ok." I do what she says. When she has her Bossy Voice on, no point trying to do otherwise. As soon as I close my eyes the music starts twirling again, as loudly as before.

"Can you hear it, Luca?"

I can't reply. I can't speak. Along with the music there is something new, something different.

Something I couldn't anticipate.

I don't only hear the music, I see it. I See the musicians, right in front of me.

They aren't ghostly at all. I can't see them clearly, but they look solid, not transparent like Camilla. The music is strong and present, and so are the people playing it. It doesn't feel like the memory of something gone – it's happening now.

Uncle Alistair's house, Valentina and Camilla have disappeared. All I can see now are the musicians – a piano player and a fiddle player, blurry, but here with me... And real. I feel a wrench, as if something is tugging me away from where I stand and towards the musicians – like a whirlpool pulling me in. The force is incredibly powerful, almost irresistible, so that I have to fold myself in two to avoid being dragged away. I open my eyes, gasping – the musicians disappear and the music stops at once.

"Luca! Are you ok?"

"I... I'm ok." I'm struggling to catch my breath. I realise that I'm not sitting at Uncle Alistair's computer anymore, I'm kneeling on the wooden floor with Valentina, Camilla and Mary beside me.

"What happened?" exclaims Mary. "I heard an awful noise! I thought you had gone too!"

"I'm here... I'm ok..." I pant. "I heard the music. And I Saw the musicians..."

"You *Saw* the musicians?" Valentina cries out.

"They were blurry, but right in front of me. And the funny thing was... they were in our living room."

"Our living room? As in... in our house?"

"Yes. I recognised the curtains, and the picture on the wall, you know Aunt Shuna's watercolour, the dandelions?"

"Weird."

"I know. Anyway, I Saw them, and then something pulled me towards them... I was going to fall in..."

"Fall in? What do you mean?" asks Camilla.

"I'm not sure. Something was dragging me towards them. Like a really strong wind... no, like a current. I had to open my eyes and pull back, or I think I would have ended up..."

"...one of them." Valentina finishes the sentence for me.

"Yes. I would have ended up not *here* anymore, but there with them." I shiver. "And who knows if there's a way back from there..."

"What if that's what happened to Uncle Alistair? What if he got dragged... somewhere else?"

My mind is racing. The Viking helmet... the broken clocks... the way I was pulled in... If I manage to put the pieces together the right way, the picture will be complete...

And suddenly a light bulb goes on in my head, and something makes sense.

"*Time!* It all has to do with *time*! The musicians... they're not ghosts, they're *in* another time. The stuff that Uncle Alistair was hiding – the helmet, the shield – that came from another time too. And that's why the clocks stopped when he disappeared. He was..."

"...time travelling!" Again, Valentina finishes the sentence for me.

"Exactly! He's not some*where* else... he's some *time* else! And if that... current thing pulled him in, he'll be stuck there. Like the stone fairies, remember? The way they were all sucked away... they disappeared, and they never came back." I hear Mary gasping softly. "But Uncle Alistair will come back. We'll get him back. I promise."

I hasten to reassure her. She nods, and my stomach knots up – will I be able to fulfil that promise?

I'm going to have to try.

"Luca, I think it's getting late. We're due home, or we'll be grounded. We don't want to have to explain where we've been since shinty practice finished," Valentina reminds me.

"Yes, ok. Mary, we'll be back tomorrow. I need to put 'time travelling' into the database. I'll see whether there's anything about time folds. That's what Uncle Alistair said he used when he got rid of the stone fairies."

"Tomorrow," says Valentina, and gives hugs to Mary and Camilla.

We run home, and we go through the motions: dinner, a bit of TV with Mum and Aunt Shuna, and then a sleepless night.

I see dawn breaking from my window, spreading light on the day I plan to step into a time fold. Who knows whether I'll be able to return.

The next day after school, Valentina, Camilla and I sit at Alistair's computer once again, consulting the *Paranormal Database*. Adil is covering for us – I said to Mum we might drop in at his house. We'll have to rely on him, even if he is the worst liar in the world.

Mary stands behind our chairs – she's very pale, her skin even whiter than usual. I bet that, like me, she hasn't slept a wink.

"I better log in." The database can be consulted without logging in, but then you can't use the forums, and we might need to. "Username... A-l-i-s-t-a-i-r G-r-a-n-t... password... R-W-R. There."

Suddenly, in a heartbeat, the webpage melts. It blurs and dissolves, its colours blending together in a slow-moving spiral.

"What's happening?"

"I have no idea!" I lift my hands off the keyboard.

The computer has gone crazy. The multicoloured spiral spins for a few seconds, and then a box appears:

INSERT PASSWORD	

"Insert password?" Valentina looks at me. "We just did. RWR..."

I shrug my shoulders, and type "R-W-R" in again.

PASSWORD INCORRECT	***

"What's that? Why?" asks Valentina. I shake my head. I have no idea.

"What could the password be?" Camilla twirls towards the ceiling, thinking hard.

"I'll try 'Alistair'." I type it in, but the same message comes up:

PASSWORD INCORRECT	********

"Alistairgrant?"

"Grant?"

"Grantalistair?"

"Loch Glas?"

"Troll?"

"Kelpie?"

"Sausage?"

"Beans?"

"No, no no no." I weave my fingers in my hair. "Not working!"

"Children." It's Mary's soft voice. I turn towards her. "Any ideas, Mary?"

"Try 'August.'"

We type in A-U-G-U-S-T.

PASSWORD CORRECT

"How did you know?" I ask her, amazed.

"Wait here." She goes down the hallway, and reappears a moment later holding a piece of paper. "Alistair told me a few days ago that he was leaving something under the red plant pot in the kitchen that might be useful in an emergency. I looked there last night and it was just a note that didn't make sense." I take the paper from her hand. It's a pencil drawing: sea waves, and a seal sticking out of them, with a black nose and whiskers. Over the seal, a speech balloon:

Tell the children: it's the month Mary came ashore.

"Uncle Alistair realised we might need to come looking for an explanation in the database..." I whisper. I'm astonished.

"But why did it not appear yesterday?" Valentina ponders.

"Because I hadn't logged in. Uncle Alistair made sure only we would have access... look!"

The *Paranormal Database* is back on the screen, but it's... different. It's another website entirely. A heading across the top says

TOP SECRET

and just below it, there's a disclaimer:

DANGER: For *Paranormal Association Net* ONLY.
Do not read unless you are part of the *Paranormal Association Net*. If this warning is ignored, we can hold no responsibility for possible injuries, death and/or temporary/irreversible madness.

"Wow!" whispers Valentina. "Did you read that?"

"Yes. Let me see. Search box. What shall we search for?"

"Try 'fold in time.'" Camilla suggests. I type the words in.

"This will take hours."

"I'll get you some juice and sandwiches," offers Mary.

Two hours later, we're still scrolling down, sifting through a sea of information. Valentina's eyes are crossing, Camilla is lying on the sofa, and I have a terrible headache. But we keep going.

"Wait... look at this... *Time folds can take the shape of time bubbles. Inside a time bubble, time is suspended. People stuck in a time bubble will repeat the same moment of action over and over again, like eating a meal, holding a conversation*"...

I think this is something for you to do, Luca. I think Uncle Alistair might be using the music to call you. To call you for help."

My heart skips a beat. I know that Valentina is right.

A wave of determination fills me.

Yes. This is my mission.

"Ok. I'm going to try," I say, more assuredly than I really feel. I stand up, run out of the room and out of the house, into Osprey Road, followed by Valentina and Camilla.

"Luca, wait!"

"I need to do this now!" I call, and run faster. I need to be home, in our living room, where the musicians stood when I saw them. I need to call the music again, and this time, I won't pull back.

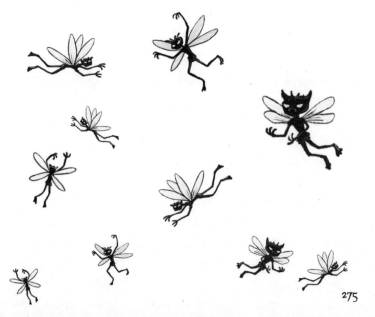

26. WHERE THINGS HAPPEN THAT ARE HARD TO BELIEVE

> **Alistair Grant's** *Scottish Paranormal Database*
>
> **Entry Number 25:** Aviation ghosts
> **Type:** Post-mortem manifestation/ time fold (disputed)
> **Location:** Glen Avich and surrounding areas, Aberdeenshire
> **Date:** 1919 - present
> **Details:** There have been a few reports of sightings of WW1 planes flying over Glen Avich, Kinnear and the surrounding areas. Disputes continue as to whether these are ghostly manifestations of pilots who fought in WW1, or a time fold causing the planes to cross over from their time to ours. This author is inclined to believe the second explanation.

Mum and Aunt Shuna aren't home. Dad is in his study, up in the attic, unaware of anything that goes on in the house. Perfect timing.

I stand with both hands on the piano, my eyes closed. The music is soft and low at first, and then it intensifies, as if someone was turning up the volume of an invisible stereo. I focus on it, with all my might – trying to zone out anything else.

Music in my head. In my heart. In my lungs. Running in my veins, mixed with my blood. Only music, nothing else exists...

Soon it's in full blow.

"I can hear it!" shouts Valentina over the din.

"Me too! You did it, Luca! You called the music here, into the present!" Camilla is tapping her feet. Valentina is looking at me expectantly, waiting for the next step.

I don't know what to do.

I don't know what to do!

Focus. Focus.

I close my eyes again, and I feel tingly all over, just like I felt that night in the wood when Uncle Alistair opened the time fold. An electric current is running through me – my thoughts are all jumbled up, but I still realise what's happening: time is opening up.

I'm going to fall into it! Get stuck there forever!

I panic – my heart is racing.

I can't do this. I can't!

I grit my teeth. I mustn't give in now. Uncle Alistair needs me.

Slowly, nearly against my will, I concentrate again, my eyes tightly shut... My head starts spinning and spinning, like the ceiling is falling on me and the floor is rising up. The electric current is now painful through my veins, through my muscles...

I hear Valentina and Camilla gasp.

Something has happened. I open my eyes slowly, trying to steady myself.

"Luca..." Valentina's voice sounds strangled, like she can barely speak.

I turn around, and there, in the middle of the room, are couples dancing. We're in it, and we're in our everyday living room, at the same time. There's people twirling all around us, but they're blurred, and I can barely make out their shapes.

And I see the musicians: there's a woman sitting at our piano. There's a fiddle player beside her. They're not blurred now; I can see them clearly, as clearly as I see Valentina.

They're smiling, they seem happy.

Happy in their bubble of time, forever playing the same tune. I look at their faces, and I realise I know them. I know who they are.

They're my grandparents. It's the night that photograph was taken, the one my mum keeps on the mantelpiece – the Grants of Eilean ceilidh band playing here, in our house, for my dad's graduation.

Valentina is frozen, staring at them.

Staring at *him*.

Another fiddler, standing on the other side of the piano. His bow is dancing, fast as a whip – he's playing like there's no tomorrow. Fast and loud. He straightens himself, and he's looking over to me, still playing. He's tall, he has a mane of blond-red hair, and a long, straight nose.

It's Uncle Alistair.

"Uncle Alistair!" I try and scream, but no sound comes out.

My head is spinning, the whole room is twirling, and the blurry figures are dancing all around me. I feel that if I try to take a step, I'll fall. I can hardly make out up from down, left from right. I'm rooted to the spot.

And then I realise that the scene is beginning to fade. The music is getting softer, the dancing figures more blurred. Uncle Alistair and my grandparents are beginning to look less defined... They're going!

I've got to do this. I've got to.

It's like when you're in a nightmare, you try and run, but your legs refuse to move. I lift my arms up, trying to reach my grandparents and Uncle Alistair. The music is fading, and so are they... I take a small step, and another, and another... until my hand rests on Alistair's shoulder. He looks me straight in the face. His eyes are full of relief. His fiddle falls on the floor as he grabs my grandmother's jumper. She looks at him, surprised, and mouths: "What are you doing?"

He signals for her to reach for my grandfather.

With a huge effort, I manage to turn around and, keeping a hand on Alistair's shoulder, I can grab Valentina's arm. She covers my hand with hers, keeping me anchored.

We're all linked in now, joined in a chain of five: my grandparents and Alistair in the time bubble, Valentina in the present, and me, between two worlds. I'm holding onto Uncle Alistair with all my might, but the force pulling them away is as strong as the tide. I close my eyes in the effort of not letting them go... If only I can manage to hang on until the current stops... It's so strong, so strong...

My fingers are losing their grip... I'm losing them...

In an instant, just as we are about to slip apart completely, the current stops.

Everything is still.

I fall on the floor, panting.

My grandparents are looking at us, wide-eyed, astonished. The bubble has burst! Time is flowing again. *I put it right.* Alistair's terrible mistake, all those years ago, I put it right!

"Who are you?" says Granny.

"I KNEW YOU'D MAKE IT!" booms Uncle Alistair.

Their voices come to me from far, far away...

"You're back..." I manage to whisper, before a swarm of little lights appear in front of my eyes, like multicoloured stars, and then it's all dark.

"We didn't know." Someone is saying, "We thought it was... well, we thought everything was normal. We were just playing away. It felt like a few minutes... Then Alistair turned up, telling us to play very loud."

"You didn't notice you were stuck in time?" Valentina's voice.

"No. We had no idea. How many years did you say have passed?"

"Fifteen," says Uncle Alistair.

"Fifteen years... I just can't believe it. All the things that must have happened during this time..." This must be Papa speaking.

"Oh, William!" says Granny, holding his hand. "We've missed fifteen years of our children's lives!"

"We're here now, Beth. We're back."

"I can't get my head around it... Fifteen years playing

the same tune... and we're not a day older. Oh, he's waking!"

I open my eyes. My grandparents, Uncle Alistair, Valentina and Camilla are crowding around me. Valentina is holding my hand.

"I did it..."

"Yes!" smiles Valentina. Uncle Alistair hugs me tight.

"And you're here again!" I hug him back.

"Thank goodness it worked, Luca. I knew I could depend on you!" Uncle Alistair is beaming at me.

"So this is what you were doing! When you kept saying you were trying to put it right... to make it up to Dad..."

"Yes. I was looking for my mum and dad. I just didn't know where to find them. The places I've been... some nicer than others, believe me!"

"I knew it! We worked it out – that you were time travelling! All those things you turned up with... the Viking helmet, and those furs..."

"And the slime! What was the slime, Uncle Alistair?"

"Dinosaur vomit. But let's not talk about that."

"And the parcels you got in the post? What were they?"

"Stuff for my survival kit. I needed a new one. You know, a rope, a mosquito net, paracetamol, a couple of cans of beans, a compass, clean socks, my Doctor Who comic in case I got bored. A little centurion guy stole the lot. They're small, those Romans, but quick fingered, I'm telling you!" Granny and Papa are looking at us with eyes as big as saucers. "By the way, how long was I away for? Stuck in time, I mean."

"Three years," says Valentina.

"Three... OH YOU." He laughs his booming laugh. "Seriously, how long?"

"It was two days," I say.

"Wow. It felt like a few minutes. Time to play a reel... But I also knew I was stuck, and I might not ever stop playing."

"How did you find Granny and Papa in the end?"

"It was you who gave me the idea. Whistling that tune. I thought, well, what I have to do is *listen*. Open a time fold, focus, and see where it takes me. When I finally listened hard enough, the time fold I opened took me there, to the ceilidh in this house fifteen years ago."

"And then you were stuck too!" Camilla chips in. All along, she's been hanging onto Uncle Alistair's arm. She can't let him go, as though she's worried he'll disappear again.

"Yes, but I knew that Luca was listening too. I was confident that he'd bring us back!"

"Were you? Were you confident I would?"

"Well, let's say I hoped so. Actually, I was scared out of my head."

"Oh."

"Still, you did it! I wanted to explain everything before I went. Give you the right instructions in case I got stuck in time somewhere. But it was all so sudden. I was terribly upset after Duncan and Isabella found out about the RWR... I just started opening time fold after time fold, looking for Mum and Dad, and I always made it back. Until I suddenly opened the right one at last. I had known it might happen abruptly. I left a clue for you when I was adding to the database a few days ago – the note I told Mary about – so if I wasn't there to explain things there would be a way you might find out. Thank goodness I did that. Because when I stepped into the fold... something weird happened. I got stuck. It was a time bubble. Time bubbles can't be opened from the inside, you see. It has to be someone from the outside, opening it and pulling its prisoners out."

"Who's Mary? Alistair, do you have something to tell us?" says Granny, her eyes twinkling.

"Beth, I think we have more pressing questions, here. Like, who are these children. Are they yours, Alistair?" asks Papa.

"Alistair is our uncle, and Duncan our dad. Isabella is our mum," explains Valentina.

"Ooooh! Duncan and Isabella's children! I always knew he was serious with that Italian girl, did I not tell you, William? A lovely girl she was, if a bit eccentric..."

"I'm not sure *she's* the eccentric one, Mum..." smiles Uncle Alistair.

"Well, a great cook anyway. And what lovely children you are!" exclaims Granny happily. "And you, Alistair? What did you do all this time?"

Uncle Alistair opens his mouth to answer. I can see he's flustered.

"He went away to England. Dad was angry with him." I tell them.

"Angry? Why?"

"Because he *did* it. He opened the fold in time that trapped you, by mistake."

"He did it? He was the one who trapped us in time? We asked him to do a trick..."

Some trick, I say to myself.

"How did you do it?"

"I... I just opened a fold. It was supposed to be simple. And then the fold turned into a time bubble, and there was no going back. I couldn't get you back." He winces, remembering the pain and upset.

Opening a fold in time can be so dangerous. Still, he did it again, that night in the woods at Hag, when he sent the stone fairies to another time. With us an inch away from it. I shiver.

"Poor you, must have felt terrible about it!"

Uncle Alistair looks away.

"He's always been a special boy." Papa explains to us. "He Sees things, you know, things that nobody else can see... My mother was like that... your great-grandmother... But not me..."

"I can See too, and so can Luca!" says Valentina.

"Good for you, pet! I'm so proud of you both! I wish I'd never missed a day with you..."

"We can catch up now, Granny!" Valentina snuggles up to her.

"Can we see Duncan now? We need to explain..."

"He's upstairs writing, Papa." He's in for a surprise... I wonder how he'll react.

"He's writing? He always dreamt of having a book published!"

"He did it, Granny. He's had many books published. He's very famous," I say, proudly.

"That's wonderful!"

We all wander into the hallway, Granny and Papa looking around, whispering about how the house has changed... I'm still quite dizzy, and Uncle Alistair has an arm around my shoulders. Valentina is skipping happily.

We stand at the bottom of the attic stairs for a moment, looking at each other.

"Who's going to explain everything to Dad?" Valentina asks, cheerily.

"I'll go."

This is up to me. I take a deep breath, and make my way to his door. I'm very nervous.

"Dad?"

"Mmmmmm."

"Dad, there's someone here to see you."

"Luca, I'm writing."

"I know, but you've got visitors."

"Who?"

"Come and see."

"Is your mum not in?"

He drives me mad!

"No, Dad. And these visitors are for *you*. Come downstairs. Please."

Reluctantly, he abandons his computer, and walks down.

And he sees them, standing at the bottom of the stairs with their noses up. Granny and Papa.

"Hello, Duncan. Well, we thought we only saw you a little while ago at the ceilidh, but apparently it's been fifteen years," says Papa, in a trembling voice. Granny is crying.

And my Dad is out cold, on the landing.

He can't keep his hands off them. He keeps touching their back, their shoulders, their hands, as if to make sure they're here. I stir sugary tea for everyone, for the shock.

"It's time you make peace, you two," says Granny, her eyes going from one son to the other, fondly.

"He promised he wouldn't do anything dangerous. But he started involving the children in his crazy stuff... I was so scared they'd get hurt, or disappear, like you..." Dad rubs his brow. Poor him. Uncle Alistair looks exhausted, blue shadows under his eyes. Will Dad not give him a break now?

"But we're here, aren't we? Alistair and Luca got us back."

"I know, but..."

"*MAMMA MIA!*" A scream resounds in the living room.

My mum is back. She doesn't pass out, just throws herself into my grandparents' arms.

"I thought you were dead!" she manages to say. "Where have you been?"

"Stuck in time," Granny says.

"What?"

"Long story."

"*Santo cielo!*" Mum exclaims, and a few other Italian expressions. She always does that when she's very happy, or very upset. I think that right now she's a mixture of both.

"Mum! Dad!" Now it's my Aunt Shuna's turn to throw herself into their arms and cry.

"You told me they were dead!" says Mum, looking at my dad.

"I thought they were never coming back..." he replies, feebly.

"I knew it! I knew it'd be all right, one day!" says Aunt Shuna, sobbing. "But what happened?"

"We got them back. Luca and I," says Uncle Alistair.

"Something strange is always happening, with you... but this..." Shuna has tears streaming down her face. "I can't believe this! Duncan, Alistair brought them back!"

"And Luca. They did, yes."

We all wait, in silence.

And then Dad stands up, walks over to Uncle Alistair, and holds him very tight, for a long time.

"But what did happen, exactly? How did you make it back?" my mum asks my grandparents, drying her eyes. Everyone is crying. Everyone, even Camilla, whose sniffling has an echo.

Everybody starts speaking at the same time again.

"Guys! GUYS!" says Valentina. Everybody quietens down. "Luca will explain." They all look at me.

"Oh. Well. Yes. Uncle Alistair opened a fold in time to look for Granny and Papa, there was an accident, it turned into a time bubble and he was stuck in it with them. He didn't know how to sort it..." and I tell them everything, about Uncle Alistair playing loudly, about how I heard the music and how we worked out what might have happened and opened the bubble.

"Isn't he a hero!" chirps Camilla.

"He *is* a hero, Camilla," says Dad.

Uncle Alistair, Valentina, Camilla and I look at him.

My dad can hear Camilla. He can see her.

My dad has the Sight.

27. WE'RE A FAMILY AGAIN

Alistair Grant's _Scottish Paranormal Database_

Welcome to the _Scottish Paranormal Database_,
commissioned by the Scottish Executive. I thank
them warmly for this opportunity, and for the
chance to meet my esteemed colleagues Finbar
Kinsella and Peter Hamilton-Smith, authors of
the Irish and English _Paranormal Databases_
respectively. This is the product of many years of
research, travel and wide consultation: here you'll
find a complete catalogue of paranormal phenomena
in Scotland and the seas around it. I hope you'll
enjoy reading and using it as much as I've enjoyed
compiling it. Remember: this database is always
growing, so if you have any sightings, visit
ReallyWeirdRemovals.com, fill in the sightings form
and let me know what you saw!

Special thanks to Luca, Valentina, William, Beth,
Shuna, Duncan, and Isabella Grant.
And, of course, to Mary.

"You can see Camilla?" cries out Valentina.

"You have the Sight?" Alistair and my grandparents say in unison.

"Duncan? Is Camilla here?" asks my mum, looking around frantically. She's read about her in my diary, but of course she can't see her.

Aunt Shuna is gawping.

My dad looks like a rabbit caught in headlights. Everyone is quiet for a split second.

And then:

"You can see me, too!" shouts Camilla delightedly, twirling towards the ceiling like she does when she's happy.

"Duncan, I want an explanation. Now," says my mum, in her deadly serious voice.

Dad looks from her to us, from Alistair to our grandparents.

And then he bolts upstairs, followed by my mum.

A moment of silence.

"Another cup of tea?" asks Shuna in a shrill voice, and busies herself with the teapot. Her hands are shaking.

"He never told us..." whispers Granny.

"All along, he could See... He could do all that *you* could do!" Aunt Shuna is gulping down sugary tea.

"I sort of suspected it..." says Uncle Alistair.

"Why did he hide it?" asks Valentina.

"You'll have to ask him," answers Papa. "Mind you, your father was always a shy boy... Not like Alistair. Alistair was the life and soul of the party, chatting non-stop, cracking jokes, entertaining everyone. Your dad was always in his room, writing..."

We all stop talking at once. My dad has reappeared, followed by my mum, who's as pale as her amber skin can get.

He stands in front of us. We all look at him, expectantly. He takes a deep breath.

"I always had the Sight. But I was frightened of it. The things I saw... They weren't always good."

I nod, remembering the baobhan sìth.

"I thought that if I didn't talk about it, it'd go away. Alistair was always the centre of attention anyway. It was easy to be invisible."

My dad, the invisible child?

I always felt *I* was the invisible child. Invisible to him.

"I've even kept it from Isabella. I thought she'd be horrified..." my mum shakes her head vehemently, "...and I never wished this curse on my children."

"It's not a curse!" I shout out. "It's a gift!"

"It means everything to us, Daddy." Valentina's eyes are blazing.

"So I'm the only one in the family who didn't inherit the Sight," says Shuna sadly.

"Just be thankful!" Dad cries out.

"No way! I wish I had it! I agree with Luca and Valentina, it's a gift."

"Shuna, this *gift* you talk about stuck our parents in a time loop for fifteen years!"

"And it *saved* them as well! Luca saved them!"

"Duncan," says my mum quietly, and everybody looks at her. "Our children are special. They can do things most people can't even dream of. This is your fear, not theirs. And I won't let you pass it on. They're happy, and proud to have the Sight. And I'm happy I married into this wonderful family..."

"Crazy as well," says Shuna cheerily.

"Yes, that too," smiles my mum.

"Well, you've always been the eccentric type, my dear," says Granny.

My mum ignores her. "I wish I could see what you

all See," she adds passionately, looking from my dad, to me, to Valentina.

"I can show you, Mum. I'll write down all that happens, just like I've been doing, so that you'll know."

"Please do that, Luca," she says. "Your dad and I will be so happy to read about your adventures. Won't we?"

My dad nods. "Had I accepted the Sight, had I explored it, instead of denying it, I could have got you back earlier," he says wistfully.

"Duncan, that was yesterday," says Papa, in a choked voice. "This is today. We're here, and all the secrets are out."

Valentina coughs, like she's clearing her voice. We all look at her.

"*Nearly* all the secrets..."

"What, now?" says my mum, in mock exasperation.

"Last week... I sort of... sort of melted some of your jewellery. Sooner or later you were going to find out."

"YOU WHAT?" Uh-oh. Someone's in trouble. I remember seeing Valentina sneaking into my parents' bedroom with a jewellery box. She was probably putting it back.

"To make silver bullets. In case there's werewolves around."

"That's why there was a smell of smoke in the kitchen that day! Now, that beats the seaweed all over the garden." Mum covers her eyes with her hand.

"Sorry. I didn't really think it through."

"Werewolves?" laughs Papa. "There's no such thing as werewolves!"

We all look at him.

"Is there?" he murmurs.

Dad, Alistair, Valentina, Camilla and I nod.

"There is. Right. Oh well. What do you know?" He beams at us.

EPILOGUE

We're all in the living room, the fire's dancing and crackling and hissing, and the rain is tapping on our windows. Uncle Alistair is sitting between my dad and Mary, occasionally glancing at them like he can't believe his luck. Valentina is perched on the armrest beside my dad, her head on his shoulder. My grandparents survey the scene – they can't have enough of looking at us, like they still can't quite believe we exist. My mum and Aunt Shuna are still and peaceful, as ever. And Camilla is revelling in the fact that someone else, someone unexpected, can see her. It's perfect.

Completely perfect. Because my dad is with us, not upstairs with Reilly.

I'm reading my diary out, and Dad is helping me with my writing. On the cover, I've glued a picture drawn by Sorley McTire – a boy, a girl, a tall man, a little ghost, and our blue van. With us are the zeuglodon mum, Finlay and a few stone fairies. It's such a brilliant picture; I can't get enough of it.

"So, where were we? Read this bit for me, Luca," Dad says, his face all serious, like this really matters to him – like my writing is *important*. Out of the corner of my eye, I can see my mum looking at us, smiling in her serene way.

"When he's near enough to smell the pickled onions, he stops in his tracks, just a few inches away from my face. I can smell him, too: a mouldy revolting stench..."

"What's the smell like?" my dad interrupts. "Describe it for me."

"Well, it's mouldy, revolting and... and it's like it comes from the depth of a bog."

"Yes! Perfect." He glows with pride. My mum and Aunt Shuna exchange a look. I'm so happy, I could burst. I write it in and go on:

"...I can smell him too: a mouldy revolting stench that seems to come from the depth of a bog. The troll scrunches up his face again and makes the same gagging noises, then he howls in anger. It's my moment..."

Dad is listening intently, a frown on his face, his eyes shining – yes, *this* is my moment – our moment. And this is also just the beginning.

There are many more stories to be told, many more adventures to be had. And to be written, by my dad and I.

Do YOU need help from the Really Weird Removals Team?

Email sos@reallyweirdremovals.com with your name, town and details of your creature.

We're experienced in removing
- Stone Fairies
- Merpeople
- Trolls
- Vampires
- and much, much more

You can also visit our website
www.reallyweirdremovals.com
for fun, competitions and to
read more about our adventures!

MONEY BACK GUARANTEE.*

*Special Offer
3 Removals for
the Price of 2
when you quote
"RWR-Book"*

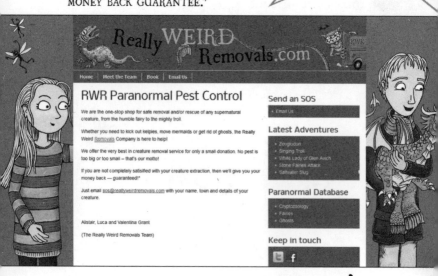

Really WEIRD Removals.com

Home | Meet the Team | Book | Email Us

RWR Paranormal Pest Control

We are the one-stop shop for safe removal and/or rescue of any supernatural creature, from the humble fairy to the mighty troll.

Whether you need to kick out kelpies, move mermaids or get rid of ghosts, the Really Weird Removals Company is here to help!

We offer the very best in creature removal service for only a small donation. No pest is too big or too small – that's our motto!

If you are not completely satisfied with your creature extraction, then we'll give you your money back — guaranteed!*

Just email sos@reallyweirdremovals.com with your name, town and details of your creature.

Alistair, Luca and Valentina Grant

(The Really Weird Removals Team)

Send an SOS
- Email Us

Latest Adventures
- Zeuglodon
- Singing Troll
- White Lady of Glen Avich
- Stone Fairies Attack
- Saltwater Slug

Paranormal Database
- Cryptozoology
- Fairies
- Ghosts

Keep in touch

EMAIL US TODAY!

*If you are not completely satisfied we will refund you in full.
Money back guarantee only applies if no member of the RWR team has been eaten during the investigation